ISLAND SKETCHBOOK

FRANK LEDWELL

Island Sketchbook
Frank Ledwell

Illustrated by
Danny Ledwell

The Acorn Press
Charlottetown
2004

Island Sketchbook
Text © 2004 by Frank Ledwell
Illustrations © 2004 by Danny Ledwell
ISBN 1-894838-09-2

Editing: Jane Ledwell
Manuscript Preparation: Christine Gordon
Cover Illustration and Design: Danny Ledwell and Patrick Ledwell
Design: Matthew MacKay
Printing: Transcontinental Prince Edward Island

The Acorn Press gratefully acknowledges the support of The Canada
Council for the Arts' Emerging Publisher Program; and the Prince
Edward Island Department of Community and Cultural Affairs' Cultural
Development Program.

National Library of Canada Cataloguing in Publication

Ledwell, Frank J., 1930
         Island sketchbook / Frank Ledwell.

ISBN 1-894838-09-2

         I. Title.

PS8573.E3469I85 2004   C813.54   C2004-900631-2

The Acorn Press
PO Box 22024
Charlottetown, Prince Edward Island
Canada C1A 9J2

www.acornpresscanada.com

For all Islanders at home and away

Contents

Preface

Prince Edward Islanders, like many non-urbanites everywhere, love storytelling. It has been a long tradition with them, and especially with those old enough to remember telling tales around the warmth of the kitchen range or the potbellied stove of the country store, or in barbershops, or in sewing circles, or at the Women's Institute meetings. I grew up in such a world.

As a boy, I read, enjoyed, and stored away in my memory Stephen Leacock's *Sunshine Sketches of a Little Town*. Even as a youngster, I wondered at Leacock's transporting his creativity from downtown Montreal's McGill University where he taught economics — often referred to as the "dismal science" — to rural Ontario as the more appropriate ground for storytelling. My aspiration, as time went on, was someday to do something similar for our Island, though without Leacock's satirical intent. *Island Sketchbook* is a fulfilment of that dream.

A novelist whom I admired greatly once told me, "Writers don't create characters. They remember them." That is certainly true of this collection. Although some of the stories are purely fictional, such as "The Secret" and "Holding the Farm," they have their real-life models. Others, while mainly fictional, are based upon actual characters and events, such as "Ashes to Ashes" and "Aubin and Jennie." The majority of the stories, however, are accurate sketches of real living (or dead) Islanders, such as "Sir Roderick MacDonald," "The White Hope," "The Old-Timer Talks about the Country Store," the retrospective series about St. Dunstan's University, and many more.

Like Huck Finn, most storytellers are not beyond telling "stretchers." Facts are never permitted to get in the way of a good story. This collection, in the end, also respects that tradition, without apology. You can never be sure of what you'll run into around the bend in the road.

Frank

Frank Ledwell

Cover Story

66"The Island has six more shades of green than Ireland." That's a claim I've always made to summer visitors to PEI. They have accepted me at my word, but it wasn't until my wife, Carolyn, and I made a recent trip to the Emerald Isle that I was able to confirm the theory. It's true that Ireland is a lovely green place, but it also has lots of rocks, brown spaces, and barren landscapes. Our Island, now, is green all over, excepting the red soil.

The varieties of green across the Island range from the woodlands to the grasses, the clover, the potato fields, the unripened grain fields, the golf courses, and the lawns and gardens. And when the soil is broken by spring and fall ploughing, its iron oxide yields a gashing red. Ireland, without the harsh winters of our Island experiences, has bountiful flowers and shrubbery, but it is rare to see the splendour of a sea of grass waving in the onshore wind, and you'd be hardpressed these days to find a potato field or a vegetable garden while touring around the country. So much for that; the case is closed.

It is notable that the Island's first settlers, the Mi'kmaq, without sophisticated surveying and mapping equipment, could visualize the shape of the Island, seeing it as a cradle on the waves and naming it Epekwit'k (or "Abegweit," in English). Their name remains much more pictorially appropriate than the monarchist appellation, Prince Edward Island. As well, the Mi'kmaq spiritual tradition, which extends to the present day, has a more resonant explanation of the Island's grand hues of green and red. According to Mi'kmaq legends, the great culture hero, Glooscap, at the bidding of the Great Spirit, came down with his hand and painted the Island in the variety of colours we now experience.

Further to the First Nations traditions, the Icelandic historian, Gisli Sigurdsson, speculates that the Vikings explored the Island around the year 1000 A.D., describing it as "well wooded and with low hills." And later, in 1534, Jacques Cartier, stopping off here, declared it "the fairest land 'tis possible to see." So, despite the encroaching tarnish of the natural environment, the handiwork of Glooscap, and the observations of the Vikings and of Cartier remain a legacy to be cherished by our Island to this day. Our responsibility to that tradition is to keep pristine our Island's red and green, a provident home for us and a welcoming retreat for visitors who come to enjoy our verdant landscape.

The Storyteller

"I mind the time...." That's the way old John Joe MacKenzie always began. It didn't matter if he had a crowd around the kitchen stove or if there was just a small boy or girl to listen to him.

Tall and gaunt, John Joe had a weathered face and a prominent nose, and, although he was ninety-two years on his last birthday, he still had his teeth and he didn't wear glasses — except for reading the *Evening Patriot*, and then with glasses he got at the "Five and Ten" for half a dollar.

It was a story in the daily paper about three fishermen being swamped off East Point in a sudden squall resulting in their drowning that set off his storytelling. "'Two poor fellas and a Newfoundlander,' was how the people up east described the tragedy," he reported without comment.

"I mind the time when dozens of ships wrecked off the North Side here. They'd get blowed onto the shoals and the waves would tear them apart. Most of them was carrying lumber to the other side, good lumber too, the best of Island lumber. It all would come ashore, and lots of houses along the coast got built from that lumber windfall. One of them ships wrecked just below us here. Sure, my own house was built with lumber from her.

"Oh, yes, there was loss of life, too. We went down with dories and rope once and saved a lot of them. I mind one poor fella who washed ashore a few days later — bloated. We buried him up behind the dunes there. The marker cross is long gone now, probably buried by the sand drifts."

The only way to stop John Joe to take a breather — once he got going — was to fetch a match for him to light his pipe. Once lit, the pipe occupied his full attention for a short while. He smoked it in vigorous pops, the smoke circling around him until he waved his hand to disperse it. Everyone waited in silence for him to recommence his "I mind the time .... "

"Sometimes at night when the wind is up and the combers are roarin' in on the shore, we can hear footsteps and moans in the attic. The spirits of them lost sailors are still in that lumber we drug home from the shipwrecks to build this house."

"So you believe in ghosts?" a small voice asked. He didn't need to. Everybody else there knew John Joe believed, and just about everyone else there did, too, except for Tom Lewis.

Tom said, "When I was twelve year old, I was at the Mac-Cormacks' an' they were tellin' ghost stories all night. It was pitch dark when I was comin' home across the fields, an' I could hear these footsteps followin' me. Every time I stopped, them footsteps stopped, too. An' when I started up again, so did they. Well sir, I was sure it was a ghost an' I was a goner, so I picked up a fence post an' turned to face me fate. As it turned out, it was Angus MacCormack's pet pig. I never believed in ghosts after that. An' here I am fifty years old."

"Be that as it may, Tom," said John Joe, "but you yourself mind the time when you and I were walking home from the Bay one evenin' just at dusk, and we saw this rough box on a wood-sleigh turn in at Joe Duncan's gate. And, sure enough, Joe died the next day."

"That's a forerunner," protested Tom. "I never said I didn't believe in forerunners. I just said I didn't believe in ghosts."

"Janey, would you be so kind as to set a pot of tea, and get out some scones like a good girl?" said John Joe to his grand-daughter who had just come downstairs. She had heard her grampa's stories so often that tonight she absented herself.

"How many scones, Grampa?"

"Just one each for everybody else. Two for me." He turned back to the company.

"I mind the time that poor Howard Hayden drowned. He used to cross the ice from Cable Head West to Morell in the wintertime to go to the store there. We called him 'the ugliest man in the world.' He had a little shack down the road there about half a mile from the school. He was dead before most of you were born. He had a face a yard long, deep-set eyes and bushy eyebrows, and the look of a bloodhound. Well sir, this day he was coming back from acrost the ice in a big blizzard. He couldn't see his hand in front of him. He fell into a spring hole and wasn't never seen again 'til the followin' spring when the ice started to go out. The funny thing is that, every winter since, someone puts a stake into that spring hole to warn people. I'm sure it's old Howard's ghost does it. Leastwise, nobody else around here takes credit for it."

"It's still there every year. I see it on my way to the school," said a young girl who was there.

"Ah yes, every year for forty years. It's there all winter and goes out with the spring run-off," said John Joe.

John Joe got up, walked to the kitchen range, raised the lifter, and tapped the ashes from his pipe. He took out his pouch of Picobac, refilled his pipe, selected a match from the warming oven, lit his pipe, and resumed his seat in the rocking chair beside the stove. Rocking always lulled him into another reverie.

"I mind the time when Joe Hughie and Mamie died within a week of each other. They didn't have a will; nearly everybody didn't have one then. But what people had said they wanted was taken as their word — be damned the will. Joe and Mamie had no bairns or close relatives, but Joe Hughie said his soul wouldn't rest unless Josie Dan Ronald and his family took over the place after he and Mamie went to the other side. Well sir, Josie and the missus had a place of their own, so Joe Hughie and Mamie's place was empty for a coupla years 'til this family from acrost came to work in the lumber woods up in Ashton, and they moved into the place.

"That's when the trouble began. Joe Hughie's felt hat was hung on a nail in the kitchen. The next mornin' after they moved in, the hat was on the pillow between the man and his missus. Then all hell broke loose. The rocking chair rocked all by itself, the lifters came poppin' off the stove, and the dishes rattled in the cupboard. They lasted two days there and then took off like a bunch of scared rabbits."

"Yes, Grampa," said John Joe's granddaughter, Mary Ann, to confirm her grampa's story, "and I heard that a crowd of young people went there one night a few summers ago and tried to stay the night, and their lanterns blew out by themselves and the doors banged until they took off, too. They said Joe Hughie and Mamie didn't want them there for sure. They wanted me to come with them, but I wouldn't dare — nohow."

"Ain't it the truth?" said Mary Ann's boyfriend, Alex. "As

you know, my momma died when I was eight years old. After that I got to be a sleepwalker, and one night I walked down to the Cape, and just as I got to the edge, she put her hand on my shoulder and woke me up. I seen her clear as day, just like she was alive. Honest t' God, if I'da fell off that cliff, it woulda been the end of me."

"If you are ready now, I can serve you all a cup of tea and a scone with lots of homemade butter," said Janey, hustling in from the pantry.

Everyone ate quietly, some having to saucer their tea, it was so hot. Tom Lewis — not John Joe, who had his teeth intact — had to dip his scone into his tea to soften it for his toothless gums. When lunch was over, it was a sign for people to go home.

"Before you go, I have one last story for you," said John Joe, sitting upright in his rocking chair. "I don't like tellin' this one myself. It always scares me in the tellin'. After the war, when the lads came home, some of them were pretty unsettled. This night they got together at the Bay for a poker game, and they all got pretty full. One fella — I won't tell y' his name — was winnin' everything and the air was blue with cursin' and swearin'. The other fellas wanted to quit; they were tired of losin'. This fella says, 'I'd play with the devil himself, if he was here.' Just then a stranger came in out of the winter storm and offered to play him. This fella who'd done all the winnin' dealt out two hands, but he dropped one of his cards on the floor. When he reached down to pick it up, he saw the guest had cloven feet. Well sir, y' never saw a bunch of lads clear outa a place so fast. I'm told that before he left, the devil burnt a print of his hand on the table top. Them fellas never played poker again."

It was now past ten o'clock, and it was a moonless night when everyone fetched their coats and got their coats on, ready to leave. John Joe's parting shot to them was: "My pet pig is in the barn. So, if you think you're being followed, it's not him. If I was you, I'd run like hell!"

The Old-Timer Talks about the Country Store

When you get around to talking about the country store, times have changed most about money, as far as I can see. Back in the Hungry Thirties people would go to the store with a handful of change and do all their shopping with that: some sugar, coffee or tea, and something in the line of hardware. Sugar was four cents a pound. Anyway, a lot of doing business with stores was by bartering. You'd get eight cents' worth of groceries for a dozen of eggs. Or the store might barter for blueberries or perhaps for grain, if it operated a feed mill on the side.

The people who worked in the store back then weren't paid a salary, but were paid off in goods at the end of the week. Russel Clark was that kind of a store owner, and he was pretty careful with the dollar. Larry Gallant, a witty Acadian, worked for him and had a large family. One Saturday evening, in the Hungry Thirties, Larry was called into the office, and Mr. Clark said to him, "Larry, you are taking home too many groceries," and told him he'd have to cut back. "What'll I cut back on, d'bread or d'molasses?" said Larry.

A fella died out in Dromore and his neighbour, Mick McGuirk, went to Mr. Clark to buy a coffin and rough box. In those days, general stores in the country sold them. Mr. Clark said, "I can't sell it for him, Mick; his family owes me too much on credit already." To which Mick said, "Well then, Mr. Clark, if you won't give us a casket to bury him in, what would you take for a hun'red pounds of rock salt?"

Maybe they should've buried that fella in Dromore like the people in Uigg wanted to do once. An old gal, quite a tartar in the community, died in mid-winter. The volunteer gravediggers were having a gawdawful time getting through the heavy ground frost to dig her grave. One of them said, "Sure, we should sharpen her like an old stake and drive her into the ground."

Country stores always carried a line of dry goods, too, and most often the clerks were women. This presented a real problem to the men shoppers and how they could explain their long-john underwear needs to a woman clerk. Often, they would just blurt out, "Give us a look at your drawers," and both they and the clerk would be embarrassed for the rest of the transaction. The women shoppers were not beyond buttering up a clerk to get a little extra for their money. Nancy Dominic from up the North Side would say, "Give me five cents worth of candy …for a sick boy up there." And then she'd nudge the clerk with her elbow and add, "And a few cloves." Chewing cloves was a common relief for toothaches, obviously the result of the candy. Nancy wasn't fooling anyone. The candy was for herself.

The country store was also a place to hear the latest gossip and to meet the neighbours. It was at its best in the wintertime, and around the store's potbellied stove where there were usually a few chairs for the customers to sit around and spend an hour or two. Once, in Kinkora, a man rushed in and reported that a woman, his neighbour, had just had a miscarriage. Right off, one of those around the store said, "My God, if it's on the go, we'll all have it."

Hard liquor wasn't easy to come by, with the Prohibition still in force, so two of the more popular and accessible spirits were pure vanilla and pure lemon. Country stores stocked both, but stored them in the office safe for security. When my brother, Bill, and I were small boys, we went to Pratt's store in St. Peter's on an errand for our mother. The store clerk, Stanley Kearn, a crotchety older man, was the only clerk in the store. Suddenly, Vince Sutherland, a local fisherman with a big thirst on, came charging into the store. "Have ya got any *laa-mon*?" he ordered of Stanley Kearn. "No, I haven't got any *laa-mon*," said Kearn sarcastically. Whereupon, Vince grabbed him by the throat and tilted him back over the slant-back candy counter and said to my bother and me, two very scared boys of six and four, "Will I hit the slut? Will I hit him?" Vince got his lemon, and we escaped with our lives.

Winter hours were often whiled away by sittin' around the country store stove, as I was saying before. I heard tell about this chap up west, name of Joe Laporte, who owned the village store. The customers had the chairs filled around the stove, some of the men chewing twist tobacco and spitting into the

provided receptacle. One fella says to Joe Laporte, "Hey Joe, I bet ya ten dollars dere's four doors in your store." Well, Joe owned the store, and he knew how many doors it had, so he said, "I hate takin' yer ten dollars, but I bet ya." The fella then said: "D'front door; dat's one door. D'back door; dat's two doors. You, Joe Laporte; that's anudder door." And then pointing to the receptacle, he said, "'N dat cuspidor, dat's four doors." "Well, I'll be damned," said Joe, forking over the ten dollars.

A week later, with a different crowd in the store, Joe seized the chance to get his ten dollars back. "I bet ya ten dollars dere's four doors in dis store," he said, and a knowing customer takes him on. So Joe starts: "D'front door; dat's one door. D'back door; dat's two doors. Me, Joe Laporte; dat's t'ree doors." Then he stopped and scratched his head and, after a long pause, said, "'N dat damn spittoon just cost me ten dollars."

Bachelor Brothers

Henry McGlinchy looked done for. He'd been bedridden at home for eight months, surviving on weak tea and soda biscuits. His eyes were sunk into his head like two chunks of anthracite coal, jet black with an eerie blue aura. There was never a question of a diagnosis. The neighbours would nod gravely when his name came up: "Bladder trouble, y'know," they'd say. Some people called it "black water," a disease they were all too familiar with in horses.

Dr. Gus MacDonald from up in Souris dropped by now and then in his calls around the district, and finally hinted that Henry should go to the Souris hospital. "He'll get better care there," he suggested to Andy, Henry's brother, who had lived all these years with Henry in the old farmhouse on the Curtis Road. Neither had ever married. They were asked only once why they never married, and they answered in unison: "Didn't see any need to." That closed the book on the issue. No one ever asked them again.

But to Dr. Gus's advice to take Henry to the hospital and thus to separate them for the first time in their lives, Andy had to draw a lot of circles in the barnyard sand with his foot before finally raising his head and answering, "Well now, I don't know. Henry and me, we get along, y'know; and I have time to look after him now. I have a bit of a problem getting him down onto the chamber pot twice a day, but we get along, y'know."

It's true, Andy did have lots of time. The only stock they had was an over-the-hill nag with a sulky for getting to the store in Selkirk for supplies; one cow, gone dry two years back; a pet pig; three hens; and a rooster. The animals resided in a draughty lean-to shed, the larger hip-roofed barn having long since entered the process of being reclaimed by nature. The house hadn't been whitewashed since the year the *Turret Bell* went down in a storm off the North Side.

Andy was tall and gaunt. A neighbour said if he took a drink of tomato juice he could pass for a thermometer. When he went to the store for the monthly supplies he stuck to the same list: a pound of tea, some sugar, matches, kerosene oil, soda biscuits for Henry, some flour and cream of tartar for biscuits for himself. Andy's bib overalls, his only and ever-present attire, highlighted his spindly shape. People hanging around the store called him "no-arse Andy."

Henry and Andy didn't otherwise get around much. They made one annual pilgrimage to church on Trinity Sunday, the last day to make their Easter Duty. They did it to stave off the threat of eternal damnation. Neither did they see much of their neighbours, except for now since Henry got so sick. People now dropped by with a plate of squares or a pie or a crock of beans. Andy never had it so good.

"Too bad poor Henry can't stomach a bite of it," he'd say ruefully, feeling sad for his brother's meagre fare of soda biscuits and weak tea.

Once a well-meaning neighbour thought Henry might profit from some spiritual consolation. The neighbour was a member of the Come to Jesus church in Forest Hill. He entered Henry's sick room with the salutation: "I've come to bring you knowledge of the new God." And Henry, despite his weakened condition, raised himself up on his elbows, looked the poor fellow square in the face, and said, "And where in Christ did the old one go?" That ended his conversion.

Two weeks later, Dr. Gus had a neighbour of Henry's in to his office for treatment and the doctor inquired as to how Henry was doing. The neighbour said, "Y'know doctor, about all that's left of him is the gearshift."

"Well, I must get out there to see him tomorrow," said Dr. Gus, "But don't tell them I'm coming." Henry would have to be eased into the idea of going to Souris and then quietly persuaded. Dr. Gus knew all too well how queer some people in the remote areas were about the idea of going to the hospital.

Dr. Gus got his way. Henry came along with him to Souris. But he didn't last long there. He was dead in three days. The neighbours had their say to that, too: "Wouldn't y'know? They took poor Henry in there and because he hadn't washed in years, they gave him a bath. That's what brought on the pneumonia. Little wonder!"

So they brought Henry home from Souris for waking and burial. The young lads on the road had occasionally had their fun with the two brothers, especially at Hallowe'en. But Andy would load up the old ten-gauge with rock salt and fire a couple of volleys in their general direction, and that would be the end of it.

At wakes in the community it was customary for neighbours to come in and keep an all-night vigil of the body along with the bereaved. And so, they offered to do the same for Andy. But Andy said, "Well, y'know Henry and me were alone together all of our lives so tonight I'd just as leave stay with him by meself."

The young lads saw this as an opportunity to play one last trick on the brothers. Henry's casket was right beside the parlour window. So, while Andy was out in the yard bidding the neighbours good night, two boys sneaked in and tied a nearly invisible cord around the corpse's head and ran the cord up and over the window frame to the outside. Later, while Andy kept vigil by his brother in the dim kerosene lamp light, a couple of boys sneaked the cat into the room, and the others on the outside gradually began pulling on the cord, raising the remains from the casket. To their surprise, Andy wasn't the least bit startled. He rested his hand on Henry's corpse and said: "Never you mind now, Henry, I'll put the cat out."

And he did just that.

Binder Twine

Not having grown up on a farm, my first encounter with binder twine was in grade school. Three brothers from a poverty-stricken family used it as a belt to hold up their pants. The pants were invariably two sizes too big for them, with binder twine through the loopholes, tied up in the middle, to bring the outsized waists together. Their mother must have tied them up before they left for school because, after they'd visited the outhouse, the knots would have lengths of cord dangling to their knees.

On one occasion, the teacher's favourite leather strap went missing. About a week later, the eldest brother arrived at school sporting a leather belt hooked at the middle by a homemade contraption. His brothers remained hitched with the binder twine.

Everyone waited in silent anticipation for the teacher to make accusations about the missing strap, but she refrained from bringing the matter up. For this we all admired her restraint, attributing it to sympathy for the boys' poverty. She simply went on about her business and, within a week, had a new strap on her desk. There it sat unused for several weeks, as she seemed to have lost her heart about using it.

In fact, during the interim, the two young brothers had arrived with leather belts, hooked up as crudely as their older brother's. When I asked them how they got their belts, they said that their father had found a discarded set of horse reins and made all three belts from them. "It took him quite a while to make three belts," they said, but they never had to use binder twine again. While they wore the twine belts, we called them "the three stooks of grain," but we dropped the nicknames when they got the new belts. The teacher's strap never went missing again.

School Days, School Days

My father recalled that, when he was in school early in the twentieth century, his teacher was an elderly man. The teacher sat at the front of the room, his feet up on the desk, invariably smoking his pipe. A student coming to him to seek an answer to a problem was dismissed, "Go to your seat. Can't you see I'm smokin'?" Father told me he went to school until he knew more than his teachers, and then he quit, which was too bad because, in later years, he always regretted not going to study medicine.

A minority of students prevailed in spite of poor teaching in those early days in the rural schools, and went on to achieve a higher education. They did a year or two at Prince of Wales College in Charlottetown — the equivalent of Grade Eleven for a second-class teacher license and Twelve for a first-class one, respectively — or took four years of college and apprenticed with a lawyer, or entered the clergy, or went to medical school. The teachers trained at Prince of Wales went back to the rural communities to teach. The majority of these were women; whatever their gender, they improved the level of education in every community.

Still and all, up to the 1950s students took a provincial examination in Grade Eight, called the "School Leaving Exam." And so, many considered that quite enough education and moved on to other endeavours. Those remaining in school went on to Grade Ten and another provincial "Entrance Exam," which qualified them to go to Prince of Wales College or St. Dunstan's.

Some kids never did make it to Grade Eight. The problem was that they either didn't like school or weren't good at it, or their parents — many of them illiterate — didn't make it an obligation for them. Two brothers were talking at breakfast, one in first and the other in second grade, both with a speech impediment. The older one says, "Erit, is 'oo goin' t'school t'day?" The younger one says, "No." The older one says, "Well, if 'oo's, I'm dan sure I'm not." Neither ever made it beyond fourth grade.

Despite having to teach ten grades with upwards of thirty-five students, teachers' pay was scant compensation for the work involved. They were in the school an hour before opening, and at least an hour after the students left for the day. Planning was both a necessity and a secret to their success. The range of blackboards across the front of the room and often along the side walls had to be filled with exercises and assignments to keep other classes occupied while the teacher gave her full attention to the class at hand. For pay, male teachers with a first-class license received $900 annually, women $650, and, with a second-class license, males were paid $600 annually and women $500. Each school district provided a teacher's supplement of between $100 and $200. Room and board in a home in the district was $3 a week. One generous teacher promised her students a dollar for perfect attendance in October. All thirty-five had perfect attendance, costing her her entire month's salary. "I didn't do that ever again," she said.

A dollar meant a good deal more to some children than it did to the teacher, especially in the Hungry Thirties. Makeover clothes and poor footwear were more common than not. A retired teacher recalls a bright young boy coming to school on a cold winter's day, binder twine holding up his much-too-big pants, his bare feet in a pair of cast-off rubber boots, and wearing a thin buttonless jacket. It was a Friday, storytime day. After hearing several stories the teacher said, "Jimmy, do you have a story for us?"

"Yes, teacher, I have. When my mother told me to go upstairs to bed last night, I stepped between the boards and came through the ceiling. I landed on the stove and burnt my goddamn ass."

That ended the storytelling for that Friday.

Having a good knitter at home meant warmth and comfort for many children on winter days. A little girl in Grade Two was removing her boots on arrival at school and the teacher said to her, "My, what beautiful home-knit socks you have." She glowed, "Thank you, teacher. My grandma made it." Pulling off her other boot, she added, "She made one for this foot, too."

In earlier times, slates were used instead of scribblers. Remember the song, "I wrote on my slate, 'I love you Joe, when we was a couple of kids'?" Slates had the advantage of being cheap and reusable, but they also had hygienic disadvantages. Boys would spit on them to erase them with their shirt or sweater sleeves. More often than not, they would also clear their noses on those same sleeves.

Many of the teachers were no older than their Grade Ten students, so discipline could sometimes be a problem. One seventeen-year-old beginning teacher was thought to be too immature to teach, but was the only one the school trustees could hire. She recalls that the three male trustees came in a body to observe the first day's proceedings. They sat ominously in the rear, and lessons got under way. After an hour, they decided that everything was under control, so they got up and left.

School inspectors also took special care in monitoring young teachers. When a student, looking out the window, would blurt, "The inspector is coming!", it was hard to say who was the more nervous, the students or the teacher. Although inspectors were humane and helpful, they carried a certain strict authoritarian air about them, and, if they had a sense of humour, they kept it to themselves when visiting a classroom. Their amusement came after departing. An inspector recalled visiting Kelly's Cross school where the students still had their Irish brogue. Questioning them on geography, he asked, "What's a lake?" A youngster, putting up his hand, offered, "A 'LAKE' is a hole in an old tea kettle."

The school was usually placed in one corner of the schoolyard, leaving room for a large playground for games at recess. The only other building on the lot was the outhouse, with its sections for girls and for boys. The schoolhouse was of simple gable-roofed architecture, most often painted white, not the red of the fabled Little Red Schoolhouse. Inside the entry were two rooms, one for the coal bin and the woodbox, and the other a cloakroom, which also had the stand for the bucket of water. Students either had to carry water from a neighbouring home or from a nearby brook. Older students got a break from the tedium of the classroom by alternating in pairs to fetch water. Sometimes they made an hour out of the chore. The centre of the schoolroom itself was the location of the potbellied stove, which, when it got piping hot caused the students adjacent to it to swelter, while those by the windows remained chilled to the bone. The desks with their fold-down seats were fixed to the floor so they couldn't be moved closer to the stove. That's how it was in wintertime. Children had to walk to school, some of them more than two miles. In winter, many came by horse and box sled, and it was not uncommon for them to turn the horse around, hitch up his reins, and send him back home by himself.

The school year went from mid-August to the end of June with two weeks off in the fall, called "Potato Digging Holidays," which, given the labour involved, were anything but holidays. In good weather in fall and spring, everyone, including the young teacher, got lots of exercise in the schoolyard playing tag, softball, bull in the ring, lee over the schoolhouse, tug o' war, and, in the spring, stick in the mud. Otherwise they did physical training (PT) in the schoolroom beside their desks, doing knee bends, arms firm, standing, walking, and the like. Each spring a provincially appointed retired military man, Mr. Erlim, came to examine them on their proficiency at PT. At our school, we welcomed him with this song:

"How do you do, Mr. Erlim? How are you?
It's so nice to see you here
With your pleasant smile and cheer.
How do you do, Mr. Erlim? How are you?"

Most students looked forward to Friday afternoons with anticipation. Besides the storytelling time mentioned earlier, they had a Junior Red Cross meeting, the Red Cross printed code giving solid healthful advice, such as, "If you cough or sneeze or sniff, be quiet, my boy, use a handkerchief." That was followed by place name identification contests. The Hershey Bar company supplied the maps, and, by the process of elimination, the winner was the last one able to point out the location on the map. Sometimes, too, teacher had trouble pronouncing the place, as one teacher would call, "Salt-Sti-Marie" or "Braddle-bane" or "Q-bec City." Alternate to the map contest was the spelling match, again the last one to stand being declared the winner.

Mentioning the spelling match brings to mind a final story. These were the days years before Adult Education or Community Schools, when Syl MacInnis, a rural teacher, decided to do something about the illiterate men in his community. He had them come to night school. After a couple of weeks of teaching them letter recognition, he moved on to spelling. Two huge brothers, Lem and George Russell, occupied a front seat, so he began with them. "Lem," he said, "spell 'cat.'" Lem thought for a bit and said, "Can't com'er Syl. You try'er George." George couldn't spell the word either, but he had brought a creamer of home brew, and everyone got loaded on it, including Syl the teacher. Thus ended the first experiment in Adult Education on PEI.

School Christmas Concert

In the days of the one-room schoolhouse, every rural school on PEI had an annual Christmas concert. It was the most exciting time of the whole year. For two weeks before the concert, the students practised their songs, carols, recitations, and dialogues, all under the watchful eye of their teacher. It was going to be a matter of pride for her to have a successful concert. On the last day before the performance, there were no classes. Instead, all the students helped trim the tree and set up a curtain of borrowed sheets at the front of the room between the performers and the expected audience.

The children made chains of coloured paper, and strings of popcorn and cranberries to garland the tree. They unpacked a box of shiny ornaments and hung up those that weren't already broken. Drawings of Santa Claus, reindeer, angels, and crib scenes, all crayon-coloured and cut out, decorated the windows and walls of the one-room schoolhouse. In the afternoon, the women of the village came to help out, and packed bags of fudge for sale during the concert.

In 1943, the St. Peter's schoolhouse was crowded by six o'clock, a half-hour before the concert was to begin. Since the community still had no electrical power, the room was lit by kerosene lamps placed in brackets at intervals along the side walls. The big potbellied, cast-iron Enterprise stove in the middle of the room was piping hot. Two parents squeezed into every free desk; dozens of others stood around the sides of the room. Most of the students were huddled behind the curtain, awaiting their turn to perform. Babies were hushed. To start the evening off, everyone sang "Silent Night, Holy Night," led by Lomah Anderson, whose voice was too high for the men present to join in, but was just about right for the women and the child sopranos. Then the minister got up and asked a blessing for all.

The curtain parted and out came the Grade Ones and Twos, each one with a gilded letter to spell "Merry Christmas." The Grade Twos were the "Merries," and the Grade Ones, the "Christmases. The "Merries" did well with a small speech for each letter: "*M* is for Mary, Baby Jesus' mom, *E* is for evening, the eve of His birth, *R* is for the rustic stable he was born in, the next *R* is for the retinue of shepherds and animals that were present at His birth" — Sally MacKinnon had this letter and didn't quite know what a "retinue" was, so had a hard time pronouncing it, boldly calling out "RAY-tin-noo!" — "and Y is for Yuletide, which we celebrate each year." Proud of their accomplishments, the Grade Twos shifted from foot to foot, excited that they had done so well. The Grade Ones had some trouble getting lined up for their C-H-R-I-S-T-M-A-S. The *H* got after the *R*, and the *M* went to the end of the line, so the teacher had to come out from behind the curtain to get them back into order. What she failed to notice was that one *S* was backwards and that little Jerome Wilson had his *M* upside-down, so "Christmas" appeared as "Christwaz."

The "Christmases" started off well: Susan got through *C* for cheerful, and Johnny got *H* for happy, but when it came time for Billy MacEwen to show his *R* for radiant, all he could say was "R ...R ...R is for ...I forget," and he started to squirm, and the people in the front rows noticed a trickle of wetness tracking down the front of his pants. The rest of the Grade Ones were so thrown off by Billy's stammer that they all rushed back behind the curtain, leaving the "Merries" to bow to the audience.

After such an inauspicious beginning, the teacher thought it best to change the order of the program. She was confident that Andrew McCarthy, the smartest kid in the school, wouldn't mess up "'Twas the Night Before Christmas," and he didn't let her down. He stood up boldly and, with his hands in the pockets of his britches, recited the whole fifty-six lines without a hitch. He did have to slow down a bit to get the eight reindeers' names straight, but otherwise he rolled right through it.

The Grade Fives were on next and sang, a bit off-key, but nonetheless vigorously, the song "Hark the Herald Angels Sing." They sang "harold" rather than "herald," because Harold Lewis was a farmer in the community, and they were more familiar with this rendition of the word.

Jock Sutherland, one of the school trustees, feeling the need to be noticed, got up and put three more sticks of hardwood into the potbellied stove, even though the fire was already so hot the stovepipe had a red glow. People struggled out of their heavy coats. Then two very bashful Grade Three girls sang "Sleep Holy Babe" and several mothers were heard to whisper, "Aren't they just sweet?"

Suddenly, a commotion arose at the back of the room. Some of the older boys from the village, thinking themselves above going to such things as Christmas concerts, were trying to climb up on the roof of the school with a bunch of potato bags, with the apparent intention of plugging the chimney and smoking everyone out. Stern fathers sitting at the back heard the noise, went out to investigate, and caught them in the act, thus saving the day.

When everything settled back down, Frankie MacLaren, a Grade Six boy, got up and sang "Mountain Dew": "They call it that good old mountain dew, and them that refuse it are few. I will shut up my mug if you fill up my jug with that good old mountain dew." Even though it wasn't entirely appropriate for the occasion, and the teacher was uncomfortable with it, Frankie had performed the same song in the past two Christmas concerts, and, as before, he got a good round of applause.

Then came the highlight of the evening for the children. After a lot of stomping and shuffling in the porch, the village Santa Claus came bounding into the schoolroom. He was dressed in an oversized beaver coat and an ear-lugged fur cap covering most of his head and face. His cheeks were rouged from his wife's makeup kit, and he had a not-too-believable cotton-batting white whisker. He toted a big bag of presents to distribute. There were books: *The Hilltop Boys* for the lads, *The Campfire Girls* for the lassies, from their teacher; pencil boxes and crayons for all the children, provided by the Women's Institute. For the teacher, a frilly blouse the children had chipped in for, which Mrs. MacCormack, a good shopper, had purchased on their behalf, wrapped in white tissue paper, and done up with a large red bow.

At last, Santa called the teacher and all the children from behind the curtain, had them join hands with him, and then led everyone in the singing of "We Wish You a Merry Christmas! We Wish You a Merry Christmas! We Wish You a Merry Christmas! And a Happy New Year!" He sang with a deep bass voice, making it hard for the young voices and the women to get down there, but the men in the audience were happy to give it a rousing volume.

People leaving the school, going out into the dark December night, were saying, "Wasn't it a grand concert? Even better than last year's!"

Ashes to Ashes

In 1946, Jonathan Fleming worked as a mud hog in the construction of a new pier to berth the *Abegweit*. She was the sleek ice-breaker — the biggest one in the world — to replace the smaller and aged *Prince Edward Island* to carry trains, trucks, cars, and passengers from Port Borden to Cape Tormentine. Jonathan's role in the construction was as a "hard-hat driver," outfitted in a heavy brass helmet with a glass window to peer through, a diving suit, and breathing hoses. So equipped, he cleared away the muck and silt to make secure footings for the pier walls. It was rough work, but just the kind of challenge Jonathan welcomed. Besides, the pay, including danger pay, was better than anything else he could get on the Island. And, when the new *Abby* slipped into her moorings for the first time that August, Jonathan was there to greet her.

"God, she's some nice," he kept repeating with the pride of being a part of the accomplishment. It goes without saying that he was aboard for her first crossing to Cape Tormentine.

After that summer, Jonathan had gone on to be a policeman in Winnipeg, eventually becoming an Inspector and chief investigator of violent crimes. A big, gangly, easygoing man, he was a natural for getting along with the many ethnic groups in that city. But his heart was always back on the Island, and his summer on the Borden pier remained the highlight of his life. It was not a surprise that, upon retirement, he and his wife Mary Jane bought a rambling century home in Victoria-by-the-Sea, a mere stone's throw from Borden, where he gardened, fly-fished, and revelled in the sight of the *Abby*'s daily comings and goings across the Northumberland Strait.

When the provincial referendum was called to determine Islanders' wishes about a Fixed Link to the mainland, Jonathan campaigned against it, and was heartbroken when the majority — however small — favoured the proposal. He told his wife, "They may build it, but you'll never find me crossing on that hanged Fixed Link." He didn't have to worry about it. The fabrication yards in Borden had barely assembled their steel and concrete when Jonathan, becoming ill, was diagnosed with lung cancer and told that he had six months to live.

Before he died, Jonathan told Mary Jane that he had one wish above all: "Would you keep my cremated remains until the last crossing of the *Abby*, and scatter them from her bridge into the middle of the Strait?"

"I'll do that, and I'll take it as a sacred trust," Mary Jane promised. Jonathan died, and, true to his wishes, Mary Jane stored his remains in a wooden box in the upper shelf of the guest room closet.

A few months after Jonathan's death, Mary Jane felt the need to "re-enter the human race," as she put it. She was an excellent cook, and she had this big five-bedroom house. Besides, the hundreds of people working on the Link construction were casting about for places to stay. What better way to appeal to her own natural warmth and need for company than to open a B and B?

She didn't have to wait long. The day she put out her shingle, the yard office called to ask if she could take five young men that very day. They arrived that evening after dining at the "Red Rooster," and were happy with the lodgings she showed them, a bedroom for each — she set up a daybed in the den for herself.

That first night, a young pipe-fitter named Charles from Tatamagouche was assigned to the guest room. Although the bed was, as Mary Jane told him before retiring, "The most comfortable bed in the house," Charles got very little sleep. Kept awake by an annoying buzzing sound, he thought at first it was a harvest fly. But when he turned on the light, he could not see the insect.

"Did the sound come from the closet?" Mary Jane asked him at breakfast.

"No, it was buzzing around my head," said Charles.

"Even with the light on?"

"Yeah, even with the light on."

"Well, maybe we'll have you trade rooms with one of the other men. Would that be all right?"

"Suits me," said Charles.

Mary Jane laid a breakfast table that would make any workman happy. She gave them Red River cereal with honey and cream, bacon and eggs, fresh-baked bread, apple pie, and well-brewed tea. Then all five went off to work, Charles bleary-eyed but the rest none the worse for wear.

As she sat in later to toast and tea with her neighbour, Faye, Faye wondered about that buzzing sound that kept Charles awake. "Could it possibly be coming out of the closet?" she asked. Mary Jane couldn't imagine what she meant, until she considered the box with Jonathan's ashes. She had a brief recall of studying *Antigone* in Grade Twelve and Antigone's defying the king's orders and burying her brother so they could be friends in their afterlife — even if doing so meant a sentence of death to her.

"I really should have buried Jonathan right away," she thought, "that's the way things are done. Maybe that's what Jonathan is buzzing about."

She was sure the buzzing was his restless spirit. Otherwise, he was back to his old ways of being an investigator, testing the motives of these young Link workers. "Maybe he suspects Charles of some misdemeanour. Who'd know?" she said. Whatever the case, he'd asked to make the *Abby*'s last run, and she wasn't about to deny her husband's final request.

Mary Jane's intuitions about the origin of the buzzing were well-founded. On subsequent nights, many more eerie phenomena happened and intensified. No longer restricted to the guest room, the other bedroom doors started slamming. Kitchen cups began rattling, rocking chairs rocking, and on the third night the bathroom mirror shattered. Mary Jane was forced to ask the Fixed Link workers to find other lodgings.

After they left, the house was at peace again. Now certain it was Jonathan's spirit run amok, she went to the closet and addressed his ashes, "So, Jonathan, you're still campaigning against the Link. You can't let it go, can you? But did you have to take it out on those young men? They're just trying to make a living. They're innocent. I didn't realize you could be so vengeful." She got no response from the box that day, nor any day thereafter. She took in other guests, but was careful not to accept anyone with any association with the Link. None of the guests ever registered a complaint about being disturbed by nocturnal noises.

Finally, the day arrived for the *Abegweit*'s swan song. It was a celebratory event with bands, singers, dancers, and a host of guests. And there was Mary Jane Fleming in the midst of them, the box in an oversized handbag, and looking sombre and purposeful, not feeling the least in tune with the goings-on. When the ferry neared the midpoint of the Strait, she made her way to the bridge and brought out the box from her out-sized purse. She opened the lid and began the process of fulfilling Jonathan's last wish. But just as she began, a stiff breeze came up and blew the ashes back at her, scattering them across the deck, catching them in the riggings, in the portals, and in every nook and cranny they could find. Mary Jane thought it quite appropriate. From the lower deck below came the sounds of a large group singing an impromptu *Auld Lang Syne*.

Moncton Left, and Other Directions

You don't have to go back too many years to when the Island had mostly dirt roads and few road signs. These conditions were only a small inconvenience to resident Islanders. Everyone knew how to get from here to there. Roads remained unploughed in wintertime and were a quagmire of mud in spring. No matter, those with automobiles put them away for those months. A horse and sleigh in winter and a horse and truck wagon in spring were the respective means of conveyance then. And, if you were close enough to a station, trains could get you to centres along the way — unless snowdrifts were so high even the trains with their huge front-end ploughs couldn't buck them.

The fact of the matter was that Islanders were stay-at-homers anyway. Visiting two maiden aunts in Elmira one summer, we heard Aunt Sarah complain that she never got to go anywhere. Her sister, Aunt Annabella, chided her, "You did get to go. Sure, weren't you in town once?" This was true. Relatives took Aunt Sarah to Charlottetown one warm sunny day in the 1930s. Her most memorable experience there was seeing the War Memorial outside the Provincial Building. Sarah was moved by the sight of the three soldiers going forward on the monument. Studying it carefully, she observed about one soldier, "Isn't he t'in? Look at his t'umb." Aside from that single trip, neither she nor Annabella ever got to town again.

Although isolated, people weren't entirely unaware of the world out there. Many Islanders went off to "the Boston States," and the Island was amply represented in the two World Wars. Going to Boston they considered going far away, but going to war in Europe was a distance that ran well beyond their imagination, made all the more mysterious by such incomprehensible place names as Passchendaele and Ypres ("Passiondale" and "Eepers," they called them). A young sailor from the Cardigan Road wrote home, and, in order to maintain military secrecy, his envelope was marked "sans origin." No one on the road knew where that was, so they went to the best-educated person in the community, a Jimmy Steele. After examining the envelope, he said, "As far as

I know it must be someplace in South America." That satisfied his inquirers. "Wouldn't that beat all? Our Clarence in South America?"

Islanders returning from away had no difficulty with the absence of road signs to bring them home, but that was not the case with first-time summer visitors. Their only access was to stop along the way and ask directions from a local. Stopping at St. Peter's, visitors asked John MacLean how to get to Cardigan. "Well now," he said, "you go up this road over there, and you go out a ways to the 'sharp hill,' then you go on a bit to 'the seven-mile tree' and you're halfway there. You go on quite a piece after that, and at the end of it you take an ugly turn. Go down that road and you'll see Cardigan. If you see a church steeple, you'll know you're there. If you don't, you won't know where the hell you are."

Another visitor, wanting to get to the North Shore, stopped a fellow in Tracadie and asked, "Could you tell me how to get to Dalvay?" "Sure now," said the native. "You go down this road and turn left." Then, scratching his head, he said, "Begor, if I was goin' to Dalvay, I wouldn't start from here at all."

Although getting from one place to another was not baffling to native Islanders, such was not the case when they went "to the other side" or "away." Going to the other side meant anywhere in New Brunswick or Nova Scotia where they had at least some road signs. The story is told about a couple from Mont Carmel where French was the common language. Driving towards Moncton, their point of destination, they came across a sign reading "Moncton left," so they turned around and came home. And Jack MacLeod from the North Side went to visit his uncle in Boston. Not having his uncle's address — never even thinking he so much as needed one, there being no such thing on the North Side — Jack walked up and down Boylston Street asking, "D'y'know Angus MacLeod? He's an uncle of me own. Cou'd y'tell me where he lives?"

Getting directions on the Island, despite well-marked roads and directional signs, can still be a startler. Three years ago, we motored to Bedeque to visit a quilters' co-op, not knowing exactly where it was located. We came upon three little girls in Bedeque and stopped to get their help. "Do you know how to get to the place where the women make the quilts?" we asked hopefully. "Yes, we do," they said in unison. "It's out on the other road, just next to the place where the fella hung himself."

Long Live Patronage

When I was coming up for my first vote, I told my father at the supper table that I was going to vote Liberal in the upcoming election — to see what his reaction would be. "If you do, you'd better put something light on your feet the next morning," he warned. The household was Conservative. Rabidly. To break the family tradition was nothing short of heresy. Two loyalties back then were paramount, religion and politics, and it was difficult to say which one held ascendancy over the other. People would inquire of someone, "Is he a Baptist?" The answer: "No, he's a Liberal," as if one had anything to do with the other. Still, knowing one's politics was sometimes more recognizable than identifying one's religion.

When it came to election day, the turnout was always huge, running in the range of 90 per cent, another indication of the importance placed upon it by the *vox populi*. The wonder of it all was how, when people were so bound by party loyalty, there could be a change in government — the assumption being that the Liberals would always vote Liberal, and the Conservatives, Conservative. Yet, governments did change.

The answers were found in the swinging power of patronage, jobs, disenchantment, and rum. Joey Smallwood, Newfoundland's first premier, knew the value of patronage from his PEI roots, and godfathered the doling out of Federal Family Allowance, Unemployment Insurance, and Old Age Security cheques to the outports, thereby insuring his long stay in power. Not to be outdone by such a ploy, the Island's own blustery "Great West Wind," Robert Campbell, MLA, hand-delivered such cheques to the residents of his riding with the mild hint that he was the source of such goodies, securing their gratitude at the polls for an equally lengthy tenure. These two examples of patronage carried the art to its highest level, placing its proponents somewhere on the scale between Mafia dons and sellers of indulgences.

On another scale, the return of jobs for votes was rampant in every riding. On the morning after being elected in Second Kings, Leo Rossiter loaded his vehicle with party loyalists, went to a job site on the highway, and replaced the workers there with his own crew — in one fell swoop. One of the sweetest jobs in the district was the appointment to Road Master, whose powers extended to which roads got service and which lanes were graded or paved, as well as to the hiring and supervision of workers, in consultation with the MLA. Poll chairmen usually got the position, and they always knew who voted for whom at the polls.

When it came to road work, the trick was to make the jobs last long enough for the workers to qualify for the pogey. A local businessman in St. Peter's watched in amazement at how slowly the crew was working on a job on St. Peter's bridge. On his way home for lunch, he stopped by the Road Master, Johnny Bernard O'Hanley, and said, "Look here, Johnny, if these fellas keep working so fast, they're gonna work themselves out of a job." Johnny Bernard took his pipe from his mouth and said, "Ain't that just what I was tellin' them."

Another road crew, a group of twenty, by some mystery or subterfuge lost all their shovels. The Road Master put in a call to the Department of Highways for twenty replacement shovels. The answer came back: "We are out of shovels. Tell the men to lean on one another." And if a driveway didn't get a new culvert as promised, or if there weren't enough jobs to go around to the party faithful, the result was disenchantment and a vote switch the next time around.

In the final analysis, when it came to a close election, rum was considered the determining vote. Poll captains were kept busy doling out pints of Demerara Rum to prospective voters on the eve of elections and throughout election day. And if they ran out, as they often did, the promise of a pint would sometimes be persuasive enough. The sweetening of the pot didn't always work, however. Some voters took the pint, but voted as they pleased anyway. Little Paul, a cripple, had to do his ballot on the floor. He had imbibed his whole teddy and, when it came to marking his ballot, he missed it entirely and marked his X on the floor. When a first-time voter asked Harry Cox for a pint to vote for him, he replied, "Why give you a pint when I can get a vote from the fisherman on the North Side for a single drink?"

In fact, he probably didn't even need to give them anything. Most of them were in hock to him for their boats and fishing equipment.

On occasion, political candidates promised a small monetary donation for a vote. Joe MacKinnon from the Seven Mile Tree was promised five dollars by a federal candidate for his vote. Anticipating it, he borrowed five from my father. Five dollars was a lot of cash during the Depression. The candidate was elected but welched on his payment, and it wasn't until years later that Joe could repay my father. His payment was a hundred-pound bag of carrots.

Like Joe MacKinnon, all farmers on the Island had an abiding interest in politics, and they would gather at the least excuse to discuss the upcoming election. A story I shared with the late Hon. J. Angus MacLean, and which he included in his memoirs, bears retelling here. A gathering of farmers were talking politics in the corner of Manderson's field. Along came a campaigner and, seeing the men, got out of his car and came towards them. There was a manure spreader beside the men. The candidate hopped aboard the spreader and declared, "Gentlemen, this is the first chance I've ever had to speak from a Conservative platform." Quick as a flash, Manderson shouted, "Well start her up, Mac. She never had a bigger load on her than she has now."

Further to campaigning and the dexterity and equivocation on the Island, in the nineteenth century, when communications from community to community were rarer, politicians could play to the patriotic and religious loyalties of one and do a complete turnaround for another. Such a candidate was Mr. Sullivan of King's County. Poet Tom Lewis recorded his method in verse:

> Along the roads of Forest Hill
> He sang an Orange lay,
> And on the banks of Morell
> He danced St. Patrick's Day.

It worked; Sullivan never lost an election.

The Legend of Lester O'Donnell

Nowadays, lawyers are polished and sophisticated and are generally thought to be colourless. Occasionally, too, they can be the butt of jokes, such as: Question: What would you call fifty lawyers at the bottom of the ocean? Answer: a good start.

Such was not the case with lawyer Lester P. O'Donnell. Idiosyncratic and eccentric, he created his own legend in his own way and his own time.

When money-strapped college students from St. Dunstan's or PWC, or people like them in similar circumstances, ran into a spot of trouble with the law, Lester would be there to defend them the next morning before the magistrate. He had a habit of talking fast and of repeating himself. For pay, he'd say to the defendant: "Wha'd'y'got? Wha'd'y'got? What'd'y'got? A pack of cigarettes? An old watch? A pocket knife? Anything?" And for that he'd defend them before the bench.

And he could make up the most creative and outlandish cases for the defense. "Yer honour, the defendant is the only son of a widowed mother," he'd say, and then add, "The sole supporter of a family of six." The judges were not naive enough to believe him all the time, but they admired his imagination so much that he got most of his cases off with a reprimand.

And, of course, as a lawyer for the defense, he was not above countering one deception with another. A notorious moonshiner from Dundee was arrested after the investigating policemen came to his house in the wintertime, at 10 o'clock at night, dressed in hockey uniforms. After purchasing the spirits from him, they put the finger on him. The accused was a tall, thin, emaciated scarecrow of a man.

Some time after O'Donnell got him off, the man was in the lawyer's office to pay his bill, and one of O'Donnell's friends came in. "Come here a minute. Come here a minute. Come here a minute. I want you to meet someone," he ordered his friend. After the introductions he said to the moonshiner, "What was it we told the court you had? TB was it? TB? TB?" "No," said the fellow. "Leukemia." "That's right," said Lester, "Leukemia. Now, for God's sake go home and don't ever get caught again."

O'Donnell's one ambition in his career was to be a judge. He was a Liberal in politics all his life, and he courted the favour of the party — a good way of making it to the bench. Once an opening came up and he applied, but he didn't get the appointment. His main claim to fame in his letter of application was that he had won the prize for Catechism in Rollo Bay Church when he was young. That didn't win him the judgeship, but he never seemed to be embittered or daunted by being passed over, unless you put that kind of interpretation on this incident I now recall.

The Liberal convention that nominated Alex B. Campbell leader and eventual premier was held in the large Confederation Centre Theatre in Charlottetown. The outgoing leader, Alex Matheson, all six-foot-eight-inches of him, rose to speak on the occasion, and said, in a loud, stentorian voice that his predecessor, Conservative Premier Walter Shaw, was the biggest crook ever to sit in the Premier's office in PEI. Lester O'Donnell, braced with a generous belly full of rum, and hanging over a rail at the rear, shouted: "Second biggest! Second biggest! Second biggest! You were the biggest!"

It was one of the more embarrassing moments in Island politics, and no one could shut him up.

O'Donnell's law offices were on Richmond Street in the central core of Charlottetown. On his daily crossings of the square to the courthouse to search out a deed, he would often be stopped by one of the many tourists inquiring about the surrounding buildings. Brusque and impatient to get going, he'd point to the PEI Legislature and say, "There's Legislation," and to the Courthouse and say, "There's litigation"; and to the Queen Square School — or where it used to be — and say, "There's education." Then he'd sweep his arm in an arc to St. Paul's Anglican Church, Trinity United, and St. Dunstan's Basilica, and say, "And there's *salvation*!" and he'd stomp off, leaving them confused and befuddled.

Stormstayed

The whole family came home to Kinkora for Sunday dinner, leastwise all those who had remained on the Island, working in town, or teaching up west, and sometimes a couple who worked across and came over on the ferry. Often as not each brought along a friend or two, or a beau. This Sunday was St. Paddy's Day, so they came early enough to join their parents at church.

"Too bad it didn't happen on a weekday." Poppa sat up from the kitchen couch, his favourite roost after a hard week's work in the potato warehouse. "Then we could break our fast both on Sunday and St. Paddy's Day. Lent's long enough as it is without a couple a' breaks."

Maureen, the eldest daughter and a stickler for detail, snorted, "Forty days and forty nights, Poppa. That's how Jesus fasted. He didn't take breaks for Sundays and St. Patrick's Day. Least of all, that's what the nuns told us down at the convent."

Momma, who always fasted religiously (taking her skimpy meal on a saucer, not even sitting in at the table with the six who were still at home), intervened, "St. Patrick is our patron saint, and I'm sure Jesus wouldn't have put his day in the middle of Lent without letting us celebrate his day."

While the rest of us smiled, gloating, Maureen blushed and went to the pantry to peel the vegetables for dinner. She could never stand in the way of her mother's wisdom.

"Maureen's such a gommie," whispered Mary Ellen, the youngest, after she left the kitchen.

"Shush!" warned her Momma. "They say up west that she is a great teacher. That counts for a lot." Mary Ellen knew better than to brook her Momma. She'd got a shingle across her knuckles once. Enough.

The kitchen was large enough to handle the whole crowd of them. The table seated twelve with chairs around three sides and a long bench at the back for small bodies. Besides Poppa's couch, there were three comfortable lounging chairs, and a Ke-mac oil-and-wood-burning range kept everyone toasty warm. Those without seats either circled the kitchen or sat in the adjacent den, converted from a bedroom since the older ones went away.

The smell of rib roast wafting from the oven created an appetizing atmosphere. "Make sure you don't overdo it." Advice from Michael who had studied in the States where he said, "The roast was always rare and juicy." Momma had heretofore roasted her beef until it was dark and crusty on the outside and dry and well-done inside.

"The same goes for the vegetables," he said. "you overdo the turnips and boil all the sweetness out of them."

It was now three o'clock in the afternoon, and it had been snowing lightly but steadily since they got home from Mass in the morning. No one seemed too concerned about it. Those home for the weekend talked about people they saw at Church, asking why old Mr. McCabe had to use a cane now. "He was always so tall and straight there in the front pew. And, my, how his wife, Annie, has aged since we last saw her. Only last summer." "And did you look at old Janie Mullen? Her slip hanging down a half a foot and a dirty old bandana on her head. We always knew her for a clart." "And that O'Brien guy, looking weirder than ever. Does he still put his dishes on the rack behind his house so the rain can wash them for him?"

No one had noticed that it was now snowing heavily and that the wind had picked up so that the snow was lashing across the farmyard almost parallel to the ground. Since trees and hedgerows had been removed in the territory to make more room for growing potatoes, there was nothing to break the drifts coming from miles to the north. "That's the pure St. Paddy's Day storm coming as faithful as Christmas Day. I've never seen it not happen," said Poppa getting up to look out the window. While he was at it, he picked up a cushion and threw it at the black-and-white cat sleeping on the windowsill. He enjoyed scaring the cat.

"You never tease animals in the barn," said Momma, "so why the poor cat?" she didn't expect an answer. She had asked the same question dozens of times before. So she moved on to another question: "Did any of you get the probs? Sure, if you knew a storm was coming you probably would not have come this weekend."

"Who needs the probs for St. Paddy's Day?" said Poppa.

"We always know there'll be a snowstorm on St. Paddy's Day. Whatever, the more it snows the better. Poor man's fertilizer."

"As long as there's not a freshnet right after and there's erosion from the fields," Michael took pride in remembering the word, "freshnet," which his father had used with him since he was a young lad on the farm.

"If this keeps up, we'll be sure to be stormstayed. At least, Patricia and I and Liam and Bridie will never make it to the other side this night," offered son-in-law Tom.

"We have lots of room. We can put everybody up as long as you don't mind cold bedrooms upstairs," said Momma, showing not the least of worry over the situation. Secretly she was excited about the prospect of having the house full on a storm night.

"What everybody needs is a quick one," said Poppa, making a move toward the cellar door. When the children were small, the only spirits used in the house were for fevers, but now Poppa kept a bottle of Scotch whisky for special occasions. And, although he was Irish, Poppa had a love of Robbie Burns's poetry, especially "Tam O'Shanter." Coming back from the cellar he had a teddy of whisky in each hand and was reciting, "Inspiring bold John Barleycorn! / What dangers thou canst make us scorn!"

Always generous and heavy in the hand, he poured a glassful for everyone of age. After everyone was finished, he said, "A bird can't fly on one wing," and refilled their glasses. By then, all were in high spirits, totally ignoring the storm outside.

"Enough of your foostering around," said Momma. "Dinner is ready. Girls set the table. Poppa, you'd better let Michael carve the roast." Although it was Sunday and St. Patrick's, Momma's conscience was still squeamish, so she'd limited herself to a small serving of Scotch. Poppa, meanwhile, was in full gale, reciting Burns.

Dinner was worth the waiting. The beef was, yes, tender and juicy. Accompanying it were heaps of mashed potatoes, turnips, and carrots — lots of gravy — a typical Island dinner. Mary Ellen declined the turnips, "I hate them." "Don't be such a groik," said Maureen. "Try a small serving." Mary Ellen scrunched up her nose.

Poppa had to give a speech. He always did on such occasions, especially when he was bolstered. "Home is home, be it ever so humble.... Society is built on the strength of the family and the home." Everybody knew the speech. It was the same as on many previous occasions. Yet, they loved him for it and expected it. He went on at great length.

Momma said, "Let's all clear away the table and have a kitchen dance. It's too cold in the parlour for it, so we have it right here in the kitchen."

"We've got no one to play the piano in the parlour anyhow," said Poppa, "since Kate had to take herself off and join the nuns. I wish she was here."

"Someone will just have to jig," said Momma.

"I'm a great jigger," offered Tom, "and Liam can help me by playing the spoons."

They started off with "The Irish Washerwoman," a good fast piece and everyone danced a quadrille. Even the youngest jumped around like a bunch of leprechauns. It went so well that they did the same tune four times. Then Michael and Maureen, both of them with lovely voices, sang "Danny Boy," Poppa and Momma's very favourite song, bringing tears to their eyes. After that, everyone joined in a circle and sang "When Irish Eyes are Smiling" and "Galway Bay." By then it was well on to eleven o'clock.

"What about tomorrow? How're we going to get back to where we came from?" asked Maureen. "We'll not get out of the yard with our cars."

"I'll be up early and get the mare into the woodsleigh and break a road to the train station. Then I'll come back and take you all down there," said Poppa. "There's always a thaw after St. Paddy's Day, so you can come back for your cars next Sunday."

"And I'll set a big pot of porridge tonight, so you'll have something on your stomachs before you go," said Momma.

In the dark of their own bedroom later that night, Poppa nudged Momma, "That was the best St. Paddy's Day we ever had in this old house."

"'Twas," said Momma, "now get to sleep so you can get up early in the morning to break the road."

The Scriss

Jock MacKenzie was the last of the inshore fishermen to fish lobsters from a dory. Small and wiry, he handled the oars with unusual dexterity, but it was a wonder to other fishermen how he could handle the trap line without a gunnel to haul the traps onto, not to mention a trap hauler. He hauled them by hand, across the dory's narrow bow, one at a time, emptying his catch and dumping each trap over the side before bringing up the next one. He fished off Cable Head on the North Shore of the Island. Launching the dory for the day's work, and hauling it back up the beach or slip logs, was far easier for him than for those using motorized, larger fishing boats.

"I jest pulls 'er up on the shore and ropes 'er to the rocks." Joe was proud of working without being beholden to anyone. Motorboats needed two men.

Matilda, his wife, had also grown up by the shore. She was a big woman, standing a head over Jock. As if salt-air-cured, she had rusty red hair and freckles the size of dimes. She handled the business, bringing the daily catch in the horse and wagon to the lobster factory up at Sutherland's Landing, and stretching the few dollars they got there to maintain a household of six. Porridge was their staple. Cooked the night before and heated in the double boiler, there was enough of it for Jock who ate and was at the shore before dawn, and for the children before they went off to the one-room school in Cable Head.

Jock and Matilda were Catholics of the old school. They had large pictures of the Sacred Heart and of Our Lady of Perpetual Help on the kitchen walls, and they never missed going to church "of a Sunday," as they called it. Once when a neighbour died and someone in the village asked Jock, "What did he die of?" Jock said, "He died of a Tuesday."

Jock and Matilda and the children of the age would go to confession once a month and, being of the old school, would keep a silence from then until after Communion on Sunday morning lest in opening their mouths they would "say a sin." And any other Sunday they wanted to receive they would have to confess first. Jock, like most fishermen, had a salty tongue.

At confession he would say, "Bless me father. I said bastard sixty times, and son of a bitch forty-five, and Jesus Christ, a hundred, and Goddamn it ...oh, Goddamn it, Father, I don't know how many times." Other than that he had nothing more to tell. Matilda would confess, "I said yes when I shooda said no, and no when I shooda said yes, twelve times." And the children would have sins such as, "I farted once and fighted twice." They always had the boat blessed before fishing opened on May 1 of each year, and Jock blessed himself each day before heading out to ten fathoms.

When Jock travelled by himself on land, he always went by bicycle. He drove it with the same vigour as he used rowing his dory, only this time his legs pumping up and down in an unbroken rhythm. He drove weekly to the village for groceries, a trip of three miles one way, and on occasion he biked all the way to Charlottetown and back, a return trip of seventy miles. He never blessed himself when he drove his bike, but the air would be blue when he broke a chain.

People in the village would say, "You must be pretty lucky to get all the way to town and back without a breakdown or an accident." Jock would answer, "I got great faith and a good wife and lots of fish and potatoes and porridge. That keeps me legs pumpin'."

"And that must be what keeps you safe when you're out there in the dory in the Gulf all by yourself?" they'd say.

"Oh, I doesn't take any chances with that. I got a horseshoe nailed to the stern, an' I allus walk around the dory three times 'fore launchin' her fer good luck. An' I allus bless meself. An' I never goes out in the Gulf on Friday the thirteenth."

It's true, Jock and Matilda were firm believers in bad luck and good luck omens. They'd be especially careful for the rest of the day if a black cat crossed their path, and they wouldn't think of walking under a ladder. If either happened, they'd be sure to shake salt over their left shoulder to remove "the scriss."

Once when Matilda brought the children to the village, they met a man whose face had been severely burned in a gasoline fire. His face was all scar tissue, and parts of his nose and ears were missing. The children called him "The Broken Ear," and after seeing him he caused them nightmares for weeks. Matilda didn't help matters. When they misbehaved she'd say, "Yus better take care or the Broken Ear'l git ye." That would send them howling upstairs.

Matilda's favourite story for her children was about the little boy who wouldn't say his prayers, the most ominous part of it being when his parents went to check on him: "And when they turned the kivers back, he wasn't there at all!" Then she'd repeat the last line for effect: "The goblins'll git ya if y'don't watch out." Little wonder they were so afraid of "The Broken Ear." Jock, for his part, wasn't as afraid of goblins and ghosts as Matilda. He told his children that when he was younger, he got cured of his fears. He had been at a neighbour's house a mile away from home one night, and they were telling ghost stories. He and a friend decided to end the night with a detour through an abandoned house reputed to be haunted. When they heard a ghostly noise that sounded like a baby crying, his friend ran off, but Jock investigated, only to discover two tomcats fighting near the base of the house. From that day on, he said, "I was never afraid of ghosts."

"Still 'n all, everyone on the road believes in them, 'n you yerself wouldn't shave in front of a broke mirrah," Matilda would say to Jock. "'N y' don't chide me when I takes a slug of holy water when the lightnin's gittin' heavy."

"Well now, that's a different story," Jock'd say. "The broke mirrah is bad luck, 'n the holy water is religion."

"Sure, yer own fahther believed in ghosts, 'n it was all right with him," Matilda'd counter.

Jock's father, Angus, not only believed in ghosts, but he also had special powers. He was called the Diviner. Everyone in the area called upon him to find new wells. He'd take a forked branch of witch hazel in his hands, and when he came to where there was water, he couldn't hold it from pointing downwards. His arms would be vibrating like a threshing machine shaker. That was not all. Once a young woman in the village got a steel filing in her eye and was in great discomfort. A visitor from Cable Head said, "No problem. Angus can get it out for you." "Take me to him," the woman said. "Oh, you don't have to go. He can do it without you. He puts a half a glass of water on the dining room table. Then he goes outside the house and goes 'round and 'round it three times, saying some kind of formula. And when he comes back in the house, the filing should be in the glass." The woman asked the visitor to go to Angus on her behalf, and when the filing didn't make the three-mile jump from her eye to the glass, Angus simply said, "She didn't have the faith. If she woulda had the faith, it woulda been right there in that there glass." Next day, the village doctor removed the filing with relative ease.

When the war came, Jock was one of the first to enlist in the Canadian navy. He took along a rabbit's paw, "Jus' to be on the safe side," and Matilda gave him a prayer book to keep in his shirt pocket, "Jus' in case y' gets shot there. It'll stop the bullet." Jock's frigate was one of the first to be torpedoed in the North Atlantic, and all hands were lost. When the station agent came to deliver the telegram to Matilda, he found her already grieving. "Oh, I seen it all in a dream las' night," was all she could say to the agent. "First time my Jock ever had bad luck, and it had to go 'n take him from us."

Aubin and Jennie

Aubin Lapierre was a good fisherman out of North Rustico. He'd learned the trade from his father, as his father had from his. Aubin fished lobster each year during May and June, the season for the North Shore. When lobstering was over, he trawled for cod and hake, and, later in the summer, hand-lined mackerel. He had left school in the sixth grade. All he knew was fishing. All he ever wanted to know was fishing.

"I'm d' best fisherman in d' Crick," he'd say with pride to anyone who watched him unload his catch at the pier. Nobody doubted that he was.

Come Saturday night, Aubin always headed for the Legion. After a few beers with the boys, he mounted the stage to play with the band for the dance. He played the traps. He was an energetic drummer, beating out a fast time in accompaniment with Pierre, the fiddler, and Yvonne, the pianist. His hands were large and nimble, and, the longer the night went, the louder and faster he played on the traps, the sweat pouring off his unshaven whiskers. "I'm as good on the traps as in settin' the lobster traps. I'm d' bes' drummer in d' Crick,'" he'd boast, and nobody doubted that he was.

When he played, he especially excited the single girls at the dance. They swung and gyrated on the dance floor to the beat of the drums, and squealed with delight at the final crashing crescendos. Jennie Doiron, the daughter of Gélas, the storekeeper, and Anita, was one of these adoring fans. She'd share with her friends, "He's d' best drummer, yes, an' he's the handsomest guy in d' whole Crick, too." Nobody disagreed with her. They all thought he'd be quite a catch, but because Jennie herself was a knockout, and the daughter of a storekeeper to boot, and therefore a cut above the rest of them, they were not about to try to compete with her.

Despite his bravado when he was with his buddies, Aubin was bashful when it came to girls. Oh, he loved their response to his drumming antics, but that was a group thing. When it came down to one on one, he didn't know what to say or do. Pierre, the fiddler, looking over the crowd from the stage would say, "Look at dat Jennie. She's taken a likin' to ya. She t'inks you're the cat's meow." Aubin would blush, and now and then steal a peek at her to see if anyone else was making a move on her. No question about it, he had designs on Jennie.

Jennie worked the fishing season in the cannery, but, come the end of it, she had to get work. Having a cheerful personality, she had no trouble getting on as a waitress at the Old Spain restaurant in Charlottetown. She did well as a waitress. Older customers loved her charming ways and her efficiency. They tipped her well for her service. She soon had enough money to go to Moore and MacLeod's store and buy a couple of fancy fall outfits. When she came home for a weekend dressed in her new style, with costume jewellery to match, Aubin saw her at Sunday Mass with her parents and thought, "She's gone 'way too high for me. I'll never be able to reel 'er in now. I may as well go lookin' for other fish in d' pond. Even if I am the best fisherman in the Crick, I won't be able to catch this Jennie now."

"Well, what d'y' 'spect?" Pierre queried him in a quiet moment in the fishing shanty. "Y' never even put out a baited line for her. How d'y' 'spect to get her on an empty hook?" Aubin thought long and hard about this, but said nothing.

Meanwhile, Jennie went back to town to her job. The Old Spain was a favourite haunt for the college crowd. They came in droves at night and munched on their French fries and sipped on their cokes. They were high-spirited and noisy, but Mr. Bell, the owner, tolerated them because they supplemented his profits made on mealtime patrons. But they didn't tip. Jennie could put up with that, but she had trouble putting up with their sass and lip. They were relentless in teasing her about being from "the Crick," and about her accent.

"Did you bring those French fries from 'da Crick'? They're so soggy you must have caught them in the ocean. Did you catch them in a lobster trap?"

"Where d'yuz t'ink I got 'em? At Prince of Wales College?" she'd come back at them.

"Wha' d'y't'ink, Jennie? Wha' d' y' t'ink? I t'ink I'd like to take y' for a tumble in the clover. Wha' d'y'say, Jennie?"

"D'on'y clover youse guys know of is d' Clover Farm store

up at the corner. Yez wouldn' know real clover if y' seen it."

She could only hold her own so long. The odds were stacked against her. Within a month of such nights, she packed her bags and went home. Her parting shot to her harassers at the Old Spain was, "Yez may try to take d' Crick outa me, but yez can't keep me from goin' back. I'm goin' home. Yez'll have to pick on someone else for a change."

Back home, she helped around the store with her father, Gélas, stacking shelves and waiting on customers. Since it was now November and the fishery was closed down for the winter, Aubin had lots of time on his hands to make daily calls to the store, sometimes on the flimsiest of excuses, such as pulling out his pocket watch and asking, "D'yez have d' right time? Me watch seems to be runnin' slow." To this Jennie responded, "Any time is d' right time for me, Aubin," Aubin blushed, but he was stumped for a comeback. "What I really want is a pouch o' Ogdens and a pack of wrappers," was all he could muster.

Pierre, Aubin's confidant, finally decided that he had to do something for his friend. So he went to their parish priest and explained the whole situation. "I've got an idea," said Fr. Ayers. "It's getting close to Christmas, and we always have a couple go around the parish to collect gifts and groceries to give to the needy. What do you think if I asked Aubin and Jennie to do it for me this year?"

"Dat's a bang-up idea, Fodder," said Pierre. "I'll keep mum about it. I'll leave it up t' you. T'anks, Fodder."

Fr. Ayers had the pair to his house and made the proposal to them. They both agreed to do it. "Christmas is pretty busy at d'store, but I could do it evenin's, if dat's okay with you, Aubin," Jennie hesitated. "Sure," said Aubin.

On December 2, they decided to start their first calls up the Cavendish Road, a few miles from the village. It was a blustery night, but Aubin had confidence in his Fargo truck. "She's been in a few worse den dis," he assured Jennie. By the time they had made three calls to homes in Cavendish, the weather had begun to close in. A strong nor'easter was driving heavy snow across their paths, and, as often happens near the Gulf shore, a sudden snow squall came up. "Damn, I wish't I'd remembered to put blocks in d'back of the box t'keep 'er from slewin','" Aubin said. Now it was time for Jennie to be silent.

The words were no sooner out of his mouth when the truck went into a spin and came to a crashing halt against a roadside abutment. The impact drove Jennie's head into the dashboard, knocking her out cold. "O, mon Dieu, wha' did I do now," Aubin said aloud. He reached over and cradled Jennie in his arms. "My poor Jennie, I mighta killed ya," he moaned. He began to pray. (He had learned his prayers in French, the last vestige of the language in the community.) "Sainte Marie, pleine de grace, le Seigneur est avec vous ...." All the time, he was caressing Jennie's hair. Then his emotions for her burst their floodgates. "I love you, Jennie, more den anything else in d' world, better den my boat an' my traps an' anybody in d' whole Crick. I love ya. I love ya. I love ya. An' here d'on'y way I can say it is when yer out cold."

What he didn't know was that Jennie had come to while he was holding her. When, at last, he seemed to be running out of things to say, she spoke. "An' I love ya, too, Aubin Lapierre. I allus did and I allus will. It's just taken us so long t'say so." She planted a big kiss on his lips, and he returned it, kissing her lips, her eyes, her hair, and her nose.

He got out to check any damage to the truck, and discovered only a small depression in the front bumper. Getting back inside, he said, "Dis old Fargo's got a great heavy bumper. She didn't get hit 's hard as ye did, Jennie. I'll have her back on d' road 's quick as a cat's tail."

The squall, as squalls do, passed as quickly as it had come. The driving was still heavy, but manageable, getting them home without further incident. Only now, Jennie sat close to Aubin with her arm around him, and they had no difficulty sharing their affection for each other.

The next day, Aubin shared his story with his friend, Pierre. Finishing off, he said, "I'm d' best luckiest guy in d' Crick, an' I got d' storm God sent t' make it happen."

"Ya," said Pierre, "an' Fodder Ayers is d' best damn matchmaker in d' Crick, too." And he let it go at that.

The Rest of the Story

William Harris came down for summers to Bay Fortune on the Island and found the compelling story of Johnny Belinda. Belinda, the deaf-mute daughter of Miller "Black" MacDonald, became Harris's heroine in a tragical story of exploitation, abuse, and rape. The story became a Broadway play, later an Academy Award-winning Hollywood movie (starring Jane Wyman, Ronald Reagan's first wife), and finally a musical on Confederation Centre's main stage, an extraordinary expedition for a ragamuffin girl who spent her days carting bags of grist from the mill, and being referred to by all, including her father, as "the dummy." Her story remains well-known. But what of the child born out of her being so brutally raped?

In real life that son was Bill Dingwell of Dingwell's Mills. If one could draw parallels between Dingwell's Mills and the Moor country of the Brontës, then one's imagination would not have to stretch to see Heathcliff in Bill Dingwell. Dark-complected, wild-eyed, and bushy-haired, he struck apprehension, if not terror, into the hearts of villagers when he came to do business there. He'd have driven his horse and sulky at breakneck speed for the full ten miles, unsparing with the whip. His horse would be frothing at the mouth and steaming with sweat. Bill, his hair askew from the wind, his eyes darting, would alight, do his business quickly, with as few words as necessary, and get back on his sulky and charge home.

People's suspicions of him were confirmed when, during a particularly cold snap one winter, his wife burned to death in her bed. Bill was immediately suspected of murder, but eventually he was cleared on the assumption that his act was compulsive and simply in bad judgement: "a queer act by a queer man," as the coroner's jury said. His wife was unwell and cold in her bed. Hot water bottles being a rare commodity at the time, it was common practice to heat flatirons or bricks on the stove top, wrap them in towels, and place them under the covers at the foot of the bed. They worked well. Bill, however, went too far; he got the irons so hot that they set fire to the bed, torching his wife.

Despite being exonerated by the coroner's jury, Bill remained suspect in the eyes of the community. That drove him deeper into reclusiveness and little was seen of him thereafter. People reported hearing his horse going at a rapid trot on the road late at night, but nobody ever saw him in the daytime. "What can you expect from a bastard child?" they'd say.

Being illegitimate in a small Island community was an unforgiving condition. Carry Flynn was such a person. Everyone else in the village knew her to be a "misbegotten child," and most were pretty sure who the father was. Carry herself didn't know her story until it came time for her Confirmation. To qualify, she had to present a Baptismal Certificate. Baptismal records of the time entered the illegitimate child's mother's name with the addendum, "father unknown." Thus Carry Flynn discovered that the couple parenting her were her actual grandparents, and her sister Maggie — seventeen years her senior — was her actual mother. She seemed to be the last to know, but that explained why her peers shied away from her, and grownups appeared to whisper about her when she went by. Although she was just ten years old, Carry was strong-headed, so she now said to anybody who looked askance at her, "Yes, my sister had me, if you really want to know."

She early developed a striking resemblance to Angus MacLeod, the suspected father. She had his deep blue eyes, red hair, and high cheekbones, and, as people would say, "Right down to his flat mouth." Angus MacLeod had long since left the community and gone off to work in the lumber mills in Rumford, Maine, so Carry had never seen him. But, once she declared herself her sister Maggie's daughter, she became fair game for the taunts of her schoolmates. They would tease her at recess in school: "When your ma and Angus were doin' their lovin', you were the one they put in the oven!"

Maggie was unable to take the jibes and putdowns, so she packed up and went off to be a domestic servant in Boston. When Carry was in her twenties, her grandparents died, leaving her enough to buy a small place for herself. Which she did. It was a cottage well back from the road where she could have the privacy she craved. Thereafter, she saw very few people. She didn't go to church, and she ordered her groceries and household needs by telephone and had them delivered. She did walk the long lane to the mailbox every day. She didn't subscribe to a newspaper, but she got mail "from away," as the postmistress reported to the inquisitive.

If they pursued their inquisitiveness far enough to wonder how she survived financially, they might have connected it to her letters from away. In fact, she got money regularly from her mother in Boston, but also from a letter postmarked Rumford, Maine. Their contributions were always in cash, saving her from having to go to the bank, and they were generous for the times. She got the occasional big parcel as well.

Carry Flynn spent the next forty-five years of her life in seclusion. She fed the birds and squirrels in her backyard, who, along with her cats, shared her exile. Her single contact with the community was George Coffin, the general merchant, who made biweekly deliveries to her house. A large, generous-hearted man, George eventually earned Carry's confidence and rarely spoke of her to others. Once, he mentioned her cats because he was so intrigued by the names she had given them: Mut and Toots and Tiddleyoots and Pickenunes and Dot and Lucy.

Two years into the Second World War, a battery-powered radio came to her through the mail. Already in her mid-seventies, and having spent so long as a recluse, she was getting pretty senile. The radio brought visitors to her house. When she heard on the news that Churchill, Roosevelt, and Stalin were coming together, she went to work to welcome them. When George Coffin delivered her grocery order, he found the table set for four. "They're coming. I have to be ready for them," she said.

"But Carry, they're going to Yalta. That's not here," said George.

"Well, Hitler and Mussolini were here last week," she said, "and I had a nice lunch for them."

Carry Flynn never heard of Bill Dingwell, nor him of her, but both in their own ways were fodder for much speculation behind closed doors and scuttle-butting in the community.

They had that much in common. Further to that, in their exile, each preserves an individuality — and even an integrity — beyond the community's judgement.

The Secret

Jack MacSwain loved his daughters, the whole lot of them, all six. He and Elsie tried to have a boy, and they wished the fifth and sixth would be one. But it wasn't in the cards, so, after six, Elsie got her tubes tied and that was it. "I'm happy if you are," Elsie said.

"Well, look at what we got? Six lovely daughters," Jack said. He loved watching them grow up, just eight years separating the lot of them. "You used to just have to look at me, and I'd be in the family way again," Elsie often said.

"And look at George and Clare, not a chick or a child between them," George waved at his brother's wedding picture on the living room shelf.

"We've got a lot to be thankful for," said Elsie. None of the girls were home at this time of day. The older ones were out working and the two youngest were still in school. Elizabeth had seasonal work in the lobster cannery at Red Head. She was the oldest. Marilyn — she was born the year Monroe died — had a job at the local Co-op store. Sally was with a house-cleaning company in Charlottetown, and Lilly, the bright one, was waitressing at Gentleman Jim's and going to the Vocational School at night. Everyone came home for weekends. They were tied to the home place in Strathcona; they wouldn't think of not coming home. Twyla and Anne, being still in high school, were already there.

The truth was, they were needed in the small Presbyterian Church there on weekends. Evalina MacEwan had been pumping on the old organ for years, her corned toes tramping gingerly on the pedals, and generally striking the wrong key, squeaks and squawks permeating the high arches of the church. The MacSwain girls had sweet voices and stayed on key, overriding the others in the choir whose voices had long since gone to pasture.

"We need your girls here, Jack," the Reverend MacCallum always said after services. "I'm afraid, if we left Evalina and the older members of the choir to take over, even our most loyal folks would quit coming. Just you imagine their guilt if your girls stayed away." He'd give Jack's hand an unctuous and grateful squeeze.

When the daughters all got home together, they congregated around the kitchen table with their mother. They were great yakkers, everyone talking at once. Or else they were upstairs, doing things with their hair and discussing the latest tints and styles. Jack, meanwhile, took up his favourite chair in front of the television, his sock feet up on a hassock, either waiting for the Saturday night Hockey Night in Canada, or watching it when it did come on. But he was careful to keep the volume low enough so he could overhear the chitchat.

"The cannery is a good place to work, Mom, but look what it does to my hands." Elizabeth held out her reddened, cracked hands for her mother to examine.

"Rawleigh's Salve is what you need, dear. The best thing in the world for those hands. Put it on three times a day," Elsie advised.

"We carry it at the Co-op," said Marilyn. "I'll bring some for you next weekend."

Jack hadn't noticed his daughter's hands, but he was somehow reminded of putting balm on his milk cows to keep their teats soft. He had a good herd of Jerseys, and their cream, sold to the butter factory in Bridgetown, kept a steady cheque coming into the house. Keeping his cows in top shape, hard work, and his Presbyterian religion were his main preoccupations.

"I wear rubber gloves in my housecleaning work, the cleansers are so caustic," offered Sally, showing off her well-manicured hands.

The topic shifted before long to boyfriends and prospects. "There's a school dance next Friday," Twyla and Anne said in unison. "Can we go, Mom? Do you think Dad will let us go? The MacDonald twins, you know them Mom; they really want us to go."

"They're really nice guys, Mom," said Twyla. "Nice-lookin' too, and they don't drink or anything like that."

"We weren't allowed to go when we were your age," said Elizabeth in her eldest-sister role. "So why should you think you can go? Have the rules changed around here?"

Jack's ears perked up. He wasn't interested in the intermission on TV anyway, so he stepped into the conversation. "Not on your life. Not until you're in Grade Twelve, me ladies," he said with finality.

"Oh, Dad, get with the program," said Lilly. "There's no threat in their going. Everybody in Grade Ten and Eleven goes. All their friends...."

"We're not their friends. We're the MacSwains and we have MacSwain principles," Jack was raising his voice. A sure sign that the storm clouds of his Scottish ire were gathering. He wasn't about to be brooked by one of his daughters, not even by his wife, for that matter. "That's final. They're not to go." He returned to the second period of the game. His pride in his daughters had its limits.

"Mom, you just sat there and didn't say anything," Lilly confronted her Mother, in whispered disappointment. "Why didn't you support me? You know Dad's just being a stubborn old Scotsman. It'd be good for Twyla and Anne to get the socializing that was denied us."

"You know your father and how inflexible he can be about some things," whispered Elsie. "He always thought you girls should get out of school and into work as soon as possible. The only concession he's made is for you to go to the Vocational College, Lilly."

"Yes, but I'm earning my own way to do that, and I've gained my independence, so I have a right to speak out." Lilly raised her voice loud enough for her father to hear; at least she hoped he'd hear.

Elizabeth and Marilyn, although now in their early twenties, had had few dates and were beginning to worry about their prospects. Sally, in her work, had been caught in a house where the husband was home alone and he made a move on her. "I gave him a good shot of Windex in the eyes. It wasn't pepper spray, but it did the trick." She demonstrated how he covered his eyes, ran to the bathroom, running square into the doorjamb on his way. "He didn't have me back," she said, relieved. "But don't tell Dad; he'd probably have me out of housecleaning next week."

"Or he might go in there and collar that fella. Nobody's going to touch his daughters and get away with it." Elsie knew how protective Jack was when it came to his girls.

Lilly had said very little after asking her father to loosen up with the two youngest daughters. She had news for the rest of the family, but she wasn't sure whether the time to break it was now. She had been dating a classmate at the college, who also happened to work beside her in her part-time job at Gentleman Jim's restaurant. The chemistry between them had been instantaneous, and they had been together several hours a day for a year now. Just last week he had asked her to marry him, and she accepted the diamond. But instead of wearing it on her finger in coming home, she wore it on a gold chain around her neck, making sure it was not exposed. Her boyfriend was a tall, handsome, intelligent young man with — as his teachers assured him — a brilliant future in drafting. In this, he was a good match for Lilly, who showed equal promise. But his name, Michael O'Connor, was a dead giveaway that he was Catholic — not Presbyterian.

Lilly and Michael were hoping to have a spring wedding — it was now November. They had already signed up for a Marriage Preparation course in Charlottetown, and she had already gone to a weekday Mass with Michael, after which they spoke to his pastor about their plans. He told them that, because it would be a marriage of mixed religion, Lilly would have to take a battery of instructions and would have to sign a document agreeing to have their children brought up in the Catholic religion, and that Michael, for his part, would have to strive to have her convert to his religion. Then there was the question of getting a dispensation from the Bishop to permit the marriage to take place.

Lilly and Michael, being very much in love, saw these as only small obstacles to their union. But, Lilly knew in her heart of hearts that the real obstacles would come at home. The only Catholics in close proximity to Strathcona were in Little Pond, but there was virtually no communication between them and the Presbyterians of Strathcona. So, the prospect of announcing her plans at home gave her the shivers. She decided that, if there was one sympathetic ear in the family, it would most likely be her mother. So, she wracked her brain for a way to keep her mother up while everyone else retired.

"Remember that great Chocolate Wonder Cake you made last year, Mom? Could you and I make it tonight to have for dessert tomorrow? I'd love you to show me how to make it," said Lilly.

"I'll have to make sure I have enough cocoa," her mother went to the cupboard. "Yes, I have. The rest of you trot off to bed, and we'll fill your dreams with chocolate cake."

Jack came stretching to the kitchen and said, "I guess I'll go up, too. Milking time comes around pretty early."

Elsie and Lilly got all the rattling mixing bowls, spoons, pans, and ingredients out on the counter so as not to bother those who had retired. Then they set to work, Elsie instructing her about the procedure: what to begin with and what to add to the mixture, each in a predetermined order to assure the best results. The cake now in a greased tube pan, they had forty minutes to wait until it was fully baked. Elsie had already set down a pot of tea for the wait.

"Mom, I have something to show you," Lilly removed her necklace to reveal the diamond ring.

"My God, it's beautiful. Where did you find it? Did you pick it up on the street? Have you advertised for the owner?" Elsie looked at her own modest ring which Jack had given her twenty-five years ago, obviously making comparisons, in awe of the expense of Lilly's find.

"No, Mom, it's mine. I just got engaged this week," Lilly let it blurt out abruptly.

"But we didn't even know you have a boyfriend. This is so sudden. Why didn't you tell us? Or, is this one of those act-on-an-impulse kinds of things? That's not like you, Lilly." Elsie was searching for a context for her astonishment.

"I didn't tell you or the rest of them that I had a boyfriend, because Michael — that's his name — is Catholic, and we're such Presbyterians. I thought it would cause such trouble in the house that I wouldn't be able to stand it. Besides, I wanted to be sure of my love for Michael before raising red flags at home,"

Lilly confided. "We're already making plans for a spring wedding. I know the other girls will not be a problem about my marrying a Catholic, but I'm worried about you and Dad.... Especially Dad." She fidgeted with her ring on the table, hoping her mother might provide her apprehension some kind of relief.

"You're not pregnant or anything? You know how easy it was for me to get pregnant."

"Oh God, no."

"And you love this young man, Michael what's-his-name?"

"Michael O'Connor. He studies and works with me. Yes, I do love him. We've been going out for nearly a year."

"And do you know you have to make certain promises when you marry a Catholic? And that's something we Presbyterians object to strongly."

"Yes, that's what worries me so much about you, and especially Dad. I can just hear him: 'Imagine me, a Presbyterian, having a Catholic grandchild. There was never a Catholic in the whole MacSwain clan. Never!' That's what he'll say."

"But you know your father loves you and how he's always been proud of how well you did in school. Besides, you are more like him than the rest of the girls." Elsie looked into her teacup rather than looking at her daughter.

"Yes, and just as stubborn," Lilly added. Then Elsie drew a deep breath and was silent for what seemed a long time. "Lilly, I have something to tell you, too, something that no one else in the family knows, but something you should now know."

"Are you sure you should tell me whatever it is?" said Lilly, not wanting to put her mother in an embarrassing position.

"Oh yes, I should, and I'm going to," Elsie seemed more assertive than Lilly thought her to be.

Her mother spread her fingers on the table and began.

"When your father was a young man, he used to go with his friends to the Saturday night barn dances in Rollo Bay. People came to them from all over. They were great times with Cliff Peters and his orchestra. I wasn't allowed to go. I was old enough, but my parents thought they'd distract my mind at

Sunday services.

"Your father met a girl there from Little Pond, a good Scottish girl, but a Catholic. They fell in love, and, like you, they planned to marry. His parents were unaware of their relationship, but when Jack came home and announced he was going to marry this girl, the fat was on the fire.

"His father wanted to put him out of the house right away, but his mother intervened. But his father assured him that if he married her, he would not leave him the farm, and he would disown him entirely. Your father was always a loyal son, so he was shattered by the finality of his decision.

"I was from here, as you know, and I was eligible. So two years later he began to come calling at our house, and parents on both sides were never happier. I loved your father, but I was sure his heart was still with that girl from Little Pond. I guess you could say our marriage was a marriage of convenience.

"Oh, how hard I worked at making him love me, but I wasn't successful until you children started to come along. He was so fond of you all that it must have reflected back on me. And as you grew up, the fonder he became of me. Our past twenty years, after a pretty uncomfortable first five, have been very happy.

"So now, dear, your announcement will take him back thirty years, and I'm sure he won't make the same mistake his own father made." Elsie reached across the table and took both of Lilly's hands in hers.

"But what about you, Mom?" Elsie said.

"I've spent half my life adjusting. I'm sure another adjustment won't break me."

Names

Up east where I come from — as I suppose happened up west as well, and in the Acadian communities, where if you were not a Gallant you were an Arsenault — up east, if you said John MacDonald or Joe MacInnis or Mary MacCormack you could be referring to as many as a dozen people of the same name.

And so, to identify who you were talking about on the North Side, you would have to go back as many as six generations of begats. That was so in the case of Kenneth MacDonald who was known locally as Kenny John Dan Jim Angus Allan the Butcher. Kenny's genealogy was something of a record.

In Monticello there was another man who used to "sell a drop" during the Prohibition. He'd be out in the morning — early — raking away the tire marks of his patrons from the dirt road, like a hen scratching, so the police wouldn't know he had done business the night before. He was known as James Andrew Jim Ban, the Man with the Hen-skin Shoes.

A sampling of other names was Joe the Crusher, who ran a travelling threshing machine; Reggie Alex the Soldier, who ran a rum-running trade between Souris and St. Pierre et Miquelon; Angus Dan the Boxer, who boxed; and Jimmy Joe Peter the Codfish Eater, a fisherman.

The most common name of all, I think, was Joseph MacInnis, and so to distinguish one from the other they were given names such as Joe Railroad, who worked for the CNR; Joe Ford, who was as strong as a Ford truck; Joe Johnny George; Joe the Hill, who lived up the Sharp Hill; Big Joe and Little Joe; and Joe the Post, who ran the post office in Souris. All were Joseph MacInnis.

The last Joe, Joe the Post, was famous for his free-spirited, mythic cow who rambled untethered around the town, nibbling at people's lawns and gardens, and who was purported to be the town's only imbiber of spirits during the Prohibition. She inspired a folk song:

> In the town of Souris, of which you all know,
> Best known for its farming and fishing also,
> Was the wonder of wonders, I'll tell you right now,
> For the name she went under was Joe the Post's cow.

She was round as an apple, as slick as a mouse,
Tho' you never found her around her own house;
She'd switch in the air, and she'd give a low mow,
"I'll make my own livin'," said Joe the Post's cow.

One day, Mick the Brewer he came into town
With whisky and moonshine to sell all around.
The whisky all went, but no one knew how,
For the only one drinkin' was Joe the Post's cow.

Gasoline Bob

Gasoline Bob and his wife, Margaret, lived by the roadside in the small community of Marie, just east of Morell. They had a modest V-roofed home and a much larger hip-roofed barn where they kept their percheron horses. Their massive male percheron, whom they called Charlie, stood at stud for visiting mares in heat. He was 18 hands tall and weighed close to a ton. Margaret, big-boned and strong, was what was known in the area as a "barn woman." The term was more descriptive than derogatory. She ran the farm, more familiar in bib-overalls than in print dresses. She handled the stud horse when visiting mares came, lining them up in the homemade chute for Charlie and helping Charlie mount them. "C'mon now Charlie. Take your time now. Don't you get too excited," she'd say.

Bob ran the road machine. Each day he hand-pumped gas from a barrel into the big machine for the day's work. Invariably he got gas on his clothes. His coveralls reeked of gas, and that's how he got the name Gasoline Bob. He was tall and skinny in contrast to Margaret. He was excitable and nervous; Margaret was as calm as a percheron mare. He left early in the morning to scrape and smooth the side roads within thirty miles of their home. The main road to Souris running past their house had been paved since the postwar economic boom. Springtime, when the red mud made huge ruts in the back roads was his busiest time. In early winter, when snows on Island roads were light, he lowered his maintainer blade to remove snow on them. But, as the snows accumulated into the dead of winter, the roads were left unploughed. The machine couldn't handle the heavy drifts.

Bob and Margaret had the only phone in the community, made necessary for communication from Gasoline Bob to the Department of Highways in Charlottetown. Sometimes he'd call and say, "Big 'sheen, she broke down." That was his way of calling for help.

Having the only phone, he was also the only conduit for information to the community. It was a role his nervous nature did not relish. On one occasion, in winter when the roads were blocked, he got a message that Mrs. James had died in the hospital, and would he bring the message to her husband in on the Church Road? He ran the four miles to the house, bucking the deep snow to get there. Breathless, he pounded on the door, and when the husband came, Bob blurted, "Guess who's dead?" "Who?" asked the husband. "Your wife," said Bob.

Despite having a job as a road maintenance man, Bob was known on occasion to be light-fingered. He and Margaret lived next door to the Marie United Church. One spring, the elders decided that the church needed painting, and so purchased several gallons of cream-coloured paint and ivory trim to do the job. The paint was stored in the church, ready for use. But somebody stole the paint. Bob and Margaret were members of the church and expressed the same concerns about the theft as the rest of the congregation. That fall, lo and behold, Bob and Margaret's house and barn had a new coat of cream-coloured paint and ivory trim. The elders naturally accused Bob of pilfering the church's paint. That's when Bob and Margaret converted to the Evangelical Church on the Millburn Road. Their first night in the fundamentalist church, Bob stood up to testify. He said, "The Lord are my shepherd. He are Margaret's too, he are." That would settle the Marie United Churchers and their accusations.

Bob got pretty serious about his new religion. He and Margaret went twice weekly to prayer meetings. He believed literally that faith could move mountains. He was especially impressed to learn that Jesus displayed his faith by walking on water. Bob thought, after several weeks, that his own faith was strong enough to give it a try himself.

On a sunny spring morning he went to Webster's Pond and sawmill. He tied a slab of wood on the sole of each of his work boots with binder twine and began his Christlike trek across the pond. He sank like a stone into the deep water, and, because of his awkward pontoons, had to be rescued. His rescuers, not of his faith, admonished him severely.

After that, Gasoline Bob stuck to the safety of what he knew, his road machine. And Margaret to her percherons. They still attended the Evangelical Church, but only rarely.

Daniel MacEachern Remembers
Georgie Partridge

Although they had wealthy relatives who came to visit in summers, Georgie and Watson Partridge lived in a modest home on a small lot in St. Peter's Bay — just four doors away from my own home, where I lived with my parents, Lester and Melita MacEachern. Our house, along with everyone else's, stretched along the right-hand side of the road going through the village. Before them was the highway, the railroad tracks, the breastwork, and then the Bay, each in close proximity to each other.

Watson was a First World War veteran on a total disability pension. He showed no signs of having a war injury; he wasn't legless like Colin MacBeth, nor severely gassed like raspy-voiced Emery MacNeill. Thin and delicate-looking, he probably suffered permanently from shell shock — at least that was the speculation.

Georgie, on the other hand, showed much more vigour. She walked with an assured step and carried herself erect. This, even though she was older than he; Watson, slower of step, was younger than Poppa, whom I had to run beside to keep up with on the road. Georgie walked everywhere and every day. Rain, snow, wind, or sleet didn't deter her. In summers she walked daily to their vegetable garden on the Minister's manse property, their own property being too small for anything but flowers. And, on Sunday, she walked to church. Her daily walks took her past our house. Most often she walked alone, unless Watson was not off fly-fishing, or hunting with Frank Jay.

Even though I was still very young, I had this inquisitive streak, and my attention had been drawn to Georgie's daily meanderings. She seemed friendly enough, but private and reserved. Her hair was white and fine like the fluff on a dandelion, and her skin was the colour of milk. On sunny days she wore a flowery cotton dress, on cold days, a tweed coat buttoned up to her chin, and on rainy days a rig that looked like a sou'wester.

Everyone in the village knew that she had been a Power's model in New York before she was married. That, to my young imagination, was a matter of great interest. I knew next to nothing what being a Power's model meant, however impressive that might have been. Nor did I know much about New York, except that's where the Rangers played out of. In our house, we were hockey fanatics — Montreal Canadiens fans, not New York Rangers, but we did listen in occasionally on Sunday nights on our old battery-powered radio to get Frank Ryan's biassed play-by-play of their games — until the dry-cell batteries would lose their power.

Why would anyone who has lived in New York come to live in St. Peter's Bay, I wondered. They had no relatives here, where just about everyone was related, one way or another, to everyone else. "Why don't you ask her?" my momma said when I raised the question with her. I had said a shy "Hello, Mrs. Partridge" to her often, and she smiled her own "Hello" back to me, but it never before went beyond that greeting.

I told my momma, "Some sassy kids say 'Missus Partridge is a rare bird,' and they call her husband 'watchin' Partridge' because he's always walking behind her going down the road. But they never say it to their faces."

Momma warned me, "Now you pay her the respect that's due her. After all, she is a refined lady, having been a Power's model and all."

The very next day she was coming along to her garden, and I sidled in beside her asking if I could walk along with her. "Sure, Daniel," she smiled. "So what would you like to talk about?"

"When I was in Grade One in school, the Hindenburg came right over our school on its way from New York to Germany. We all went outdoors to watch it until it went out of sight," I reported proudly.

"I was in New York then," she said, "and I was there when that dirigible came back and burned in a ball of fire right there in New York."

"Boy, that must have been scary. Did you see it up close?"

"No, I was at work right in the middle of the city."

"Momma says you were a Power's model there."

"Yes, I was," she said matter-of-factly.

Then she went on to tell me all about New York: the sky-scrapers and the streets teeming with people, and the hot dog vendors on the street (I had never heard of a hot dog before, so she had to explain that), and milk delivery, and hawkers going down calling out to the houses: "Any bags? Any bones? Any bottles?" Then she talked about the "Great White Way," where she worked. And she had to explain to me what a Power's model was; my mother hadn't.

"I had to dress up in fancy new clothes, and I had to walk like this," she demonstrated, putting her feet straight out in front of each other, her arms akimbo.

We were now at her garden. I said, "Nobody from the Bay, as far as I know, ever goes to New York. They all go to Boston. So why did you come here?"

"Here at the Bay, I can walk to the grocery store and the post office. I can walk to church. We have a movie every two weeks. I have my garden. And, best of all, we have the sunset over the Bay. Nothing in the world is nicer than that."

When I got home, I said to Momma, "I think, next to you, Mrs. Partridge is the nicest lady at the Bay."

Years later, after doing a stint of work in New York myself, living in a one-room apartment, eating off a hot plate, dodging the taxis on the street, and sunburning the roof of my mouth from looking up at all the tall buildings, I couldn't wait to get back to the sunsets of the Bay myself, and I couldn't look at them without thinking of Georgie Partridge.

Emma

Living out along the North Side at Campbell's Cove had more disadvantages than advantages. There was a story that a neighbouring parish priest had put a curse on the land along the shore, as a result of a pitched battle he'd had with some rebellious parishioners. He invoked the shore sands to overtake the farmland to impoverish those who farmed it. Whatever the truth of the legend, the land was sour and yielded poor crops. Next door to Campbell's Cove was Rock Barra, a name that suggested the rugged terrain.

During the worst of times, Ky Gillis, who was estranged from his daughter and her family, met his undernourished, ragamuffin grandchildren along the North Side road and said to them, "Come out to your grandfather's, dears, where you will get lots of blueberries and buttermilk." Such was life in this northern Appalachia. Such was the world of Emma and her husband, D.A.

Their forty acres, much of it shore land, barely sustained them. Still, Emma was out on it every day, in her bib-overalls and straw hat, nursing every last seedling to maturity. D.A., on the other hand, was more content to sit in his rocking chair by the kitchen stove cradling his favourite pipe. As outspoken and gregarious as Emma was, D.A. was, in contrast, passive and resigned.

Visitors who dropped in on them unannounced in the summertime would be greeted by Emma at the car. "Woy didn't yez let us know yez were comin'? Save us, look at the look a' me. If I knowed yez were comin', I'd leastwise have put on a dress." Emma had her pride. D.A. would stay in his place in the kitchen until they came in. He and Emma were childless, as barren as the land they worked. During the conversation, visitors invariably asked D.A. about what stock he had, besides the horse in the pasture along the driveway. Removing his pipe, he'd say, "A cow, a calf, and a white pig."

D.A. — he was never called anything but D.A. — gave centre stage to Emma. When asked a question he was characteristically pithy, as in, "How're you doing, D.A.?" "Gettin' along," he'd say, maybe repeating it once but no more. Emma was more effusive and interested in telling you about the "goin's on," as she called the local gossip.

This day she had a couple of good ones: "Annabelle Ryan from up along. Y'know her — she's a cousin of your mother's — how close I couldn't say — y'know, she lives in that big gable house way back from the road in Priest Pond. She allus has lots of visitors of a Sunday, and she's never sparin' with a cup of tea. Well, she had a crowd in and had the biscuits and wild strawberry jam already on the table. Then she looked out the window and saw a woman who she couldn't stand comin' up the lane. So she swept the dishes of strawberry jam off the table and replaced them with applesauce. 'I wouldn't give that 'hore any of my good jam,' she said. She was quite the caution, herself."

Later on she told them one on herself, "It was Lent an' I was in a dither about what to fast from. So, I decided to fast from listenin' in on the party line. It gits dreadful quiet out here in the winter — with D.A. so quiet 'n all — if yez can't listen in on the party line, y'know, to get the goin's on. So I says to myself that's about as big a penance as I could ever do. An' I was doin' all right until this day a fella hung himself way over in South Lake. Well sir, the phone was ringin' off the hook, as many rings as there was people on the road. So I just had t'break my fast to find out what all the hurrah was about. But I confessed it to Fr. Ronnie 'fore I went up for communion ag'in."

Besides fasting from the party line, Emma made a daily trip to church during the Lenten season. She always got there in time to make the Stations of the Cross before Mass. Whereas others meditated in silence before each station, that wasn't the case with Emma. She saluted each station, her loudest exclamation reserved for the three times the weight of the cross overcame Jesus. "Jesus, y' fell," she'd intone reverently; then, "Jesus, y' fell ag'in." The rest of those there would be thoroughly amused, stifling their giggles in their mitts.

Emma and D.A. saw out their days at Campbell's Cove. True to form, D.A. was the first to go. He died without a word. Emma soon followed him without leaving the forty acres to anything but scrub growth. She may have been fulfilling the priest's old curse on the land.

Charlie's Story

Lord A'mighty things was some hard durin' the hungry 30s. We hadn't a cent for anythin'. Well, yes, we had a few coppers. Put one every Sunday in the collection. The clothes on our backs had to do ten years. Socks were more darning than sock. Boot soles was wore so thin we had to put cardboard insoles into them. I met Lem Russell in his jauntin' cart t'other day and asked, "How y'doin' Lem?" "Peace and poverty," said Lem. He said his brother Alfred was "a little thin but a good colour." Lem was headin' for the cheese factory for free whey to bake biscuits so his missus wouldn't have to buy cream a' tartar. "She couldn't afford to buy it anyways," he said.

Me, I ain't got a tooth in me mouth. Couldn't pay for them false teeth some people got. I dips me biscuits into me tea to soften them up. The missus, now, she's got a bad stomach. All's she can get into her all day 'til supper is a dropped egg on dipped toast. We was quite a pair, I'll tell ya.

Still'n'all, we wasn't as bad off as those city fellas who had to ride the rails. We grew our own stuff. They didn't even have that. Not even a garden, fer God's sakes.

Leastwise, we had our vegetables and a few b'iled dinners. Old Laughie MacKinnon used to come around with his meat wagon. I don't know where he got his scrub cattle for slaughter, but his beef was as tough as an old boot. All's he'd say to the wife was, "That's good bif, ma'am." It was even hard t' soften up in a b'iled dinner, but it gave flavour to the turnips, carrots, and taters. An' it was okay to the Missus's belly. Fridays' we either had pickled herrin' or mackerel b'iled in oatmeal.

I was over t' MacPhee's t'other day and his Missus had a roast in the oven. I said t'her, "the smell of a roast is as good as a meal." Somethin' we never had at home.

Most of us along the shore up at the North Side farmed and fished, if you'd call it that. We went out for lobster, but when we could sell any of them, we got next to nawtin' for them, so we spread them on the land. The land was cursed by a mad priest years back. It wasn't good to grow anythin'. Even hay was scarce; most of the stuff was flyaway. I was talkin' to Sigs Russell t'other day an' asked how his hay was holdin' out. "First hen fell through the loft this mornin'," says Sigs. He allus had somethin' funny to say, even in the hard times.

Our best time was in winter when the big snows came. We got on shovelin' snow for the railroad. Bring yer own shovel an make a dollar an' a half a day. We'd make 'nough t'get us through t'summer, fer kerosene, n'flour, n'tea, n'sugar. Kerosene was fer the lantern. That's all we used — lantern in the barn and then on the kitchen table. We didn't need much light. We had nawtin' t'read 'r anythin' the like of that. The missus would warn, "Lantern on the table, trouble in the stable." But I didn't have any truck with that. All's we had was a horse, a cow, an' a bunch of chickens.

Still 'n all the house was pretty dark. One black night we heard a noise scrapin' on the shingles outside an' I went out. It was Ky Gillis tryin' t'find the door. Ky said, "Where, in the name of God, are the holes in this house?" He came in t'visit an' there was a pot of tea on the back of the stove — it was allus there. We gave him a cup of tea an' it was so hot he had t'saucer it.

I could go on all night tellin' ya 'bout how hard the times was. But then, after the war, we both got the pension. Never had it so good.

Rome Wasn't Built in a Day

Big John Gilfoy wasn't what you'd call lazy. It was just if he hadn't to do the essentials, he'd put them off 'til the next day — or the next week for that matter. "Why not take 'er easy today and give 'er hell tomorrow?" he'd say.

The neighbours would long since have done the milking and separating, but Big John would lie in the barn at 10 o'clock at night milking his eight cows in the dim lantern light. Nobody ever criticized him. They'd say, "Well, that's Big John's way. He's the last to get the crop in in the spring and the last to harvest it in the fall."

"Big John'll be late for his funeral," Sadie Jenkins, his neighbour observed. "But he's such a kind sort. I was goin' into Kensington to church last week — walking. Big John came along in his horse and wagon and offered to drive me to my church. 'But you'll be late for Mass yourself if you drive me across town to my church,' I said. 'Well now, Sadie,' says he, 'an act of charity takes care of bein' a bit late for Mass.' He got me there on time and didn't mind in the least about whether prole would be starin' at him for comin' in halfway through his own church."

When a neighbour came down with the flu, Big John would be the first one there to help out. He would clean the stables, do the milking, and feed the stock, even if it meant he wouldn't get his own barnwork done until nearly midnight. And, when he got home, he'd say to his wife, "My that Annie MacPherson's a great cook. She had a stew that would warm the cockles of yer heart."

His wife Claudia's only fault with Big John was that he seemed better for the neighbours than he was for her and their own place. "You always leave your fiddle at the gate," she often said to him when he got home from such joyful coming-to-the-assistance of the neighbours. Still and all, she wasn't the least bit jealous of Annie MacPherson because Big John always said to her, "You're the best cook in the county." And his large body and ample stomach were testament to that.

Claudia was Big John's opposite. She was no more than five foot three and trim as a sapling. She always had her housework done before "Pepper Young's Family" came over the radio in the afternoon — a soap opera she never missed. And she was neat as a pin. She kept Big John well turned out, but she drew the line at doing the barn work no matter how late Big John was going to get around to it. In fact, it was often the evening radio programs that kept Big John from the barn. He just *had* to listen to "The Shadow," "Suspense," and "Luz Radio Theatre," and he'd spend part of the next day down at MacPhee's store discussing the previous night's shows with his cronies.

Unself-conscious, he'd tell his friends about one of his cows getting into his neighbour's vegetable garden, eating the tops of all her vegetables and his neighbour coming to complain about it. "All right," said Big John. "I'll send you over a quart of cream!"

"You gonna fix that fence, Jack?" a crony asks. "All in due time," said Big John, "It's a dry summer, sure, the cow was making 'er for the brook. That's where I found the rest of them."

"Dry summer, you said it," another crony put in. "Me oats is so short I'm gonna hafta lather it t'mow it. Matter a' fact, me own cows was down at that brook, too."

"And mine, too," admitted another, "broke right down the rail fence."

"Well," said Big John. "The situation with that garden ain't as bad as I thought. Still 'n all, I best fix the fence today. The missus wouldn't like to lose a friend in her neighbour."

"Maybe she'll help y'fix that fence," said a crony.

"Naw, tho' she grew up on a farm, she never once milked a cow. She was a house girl. Her sister, now, milked twice a day," said Big John.

"Just like me own missus," said a crony. "She was drug up in town. Sure, if I ast her to milk she'd sit down on a rock in the middle of the pasture with a pail 'twixt her legs and wait for the cow to back up t'her to get milked — just like a car."

"By the Lord Harry that's a good one," laughed Big John. Big John was not a cussing man, his usual expressions being "Cripes," "Lord A'mighty," and "By the Lord Harry."

"Well, lads, I'd best be gettin' along," he said, already thinking of getting that fence fixed. But he didn't go straight home. Rather he meandered across the fields and down to the brook where he had retrieved his cows the previous day. The grain in the low land was in full stalk despite the dry summer, and the brook was cool and inviting. He removed his boots and socks, rolled up his overalls, and waded in, enjoying the cool flow of waters and the shade of the overhanging alders. Red-winged blackbirds were there, but they scattered when he approached. "I wonder why," he mused. "They should know I wouldn't hurt a fly." He stayed over much later than he intended.

When he got home, Claudia met him in the porch. "Where were you all day?" she said. "It's almost sundown, and you haven't fixed that fence yet."

"Now, Claudia," he said, "slow and easy wins the race. Rome wasn't built in a day."

"But let's get at it," she said. "I'll come along to help you."

"By the Lord Harry, doesn't that beat all," said Big John Gilfoy.

Little Paul

In the 1930s and for some years thereafter, psychiatry was unheard of in rural PEI. There was Falconwood Hospital in Charlottetown for people suffering from severe mental illnesses, but, except for those who went totally mad, mentally ill people stayed right in the village either living with their families or by themselves. Usually they were civil enough and people looked upon them benignly.

No one was terribly concerned when Henry Andrew struck the wall during the sermon in church and shouted, "I desire to be heard." Some even thought that he was just ahead of his time. Cassie Elias was thought to be a nuisance more than anything else. She was a roader, going from door to door on her bad days. She had a mouth on her and took it out on the housewives who let her in. If they saw her coming, they locked their doors. After several unanswered hammerings, Cassie would go off mumbling invectives at the house.

Sam Anderson had his bouts of madness, too. It usually meant that people avoided him during the phase of the full moon. Most times otherwise, he was a reclusive eccentric. One late November, he borrowed my father's muskrat coat and hadn't returned it by February. My father had to make a trip to Charlottetown on a Monday, so he asked Sam to return his coat. "Okay," said Sam, "but I want it back on Tuesday."

That weekend on a cold, blustery winter's Sunday night, our parents were out for a game of auction at a neighbour's, and our older sisters were minding the house. The moon was full. We were all engaged in a game of Rings, where the players threw rubber rings on a hanging game board arranged with hooks, each hook assigned a numerical score.

In the midst of the game, Sam Anderson darkened our kitchen, carrying my father's coat. A huge man, he was dressed in a heavy mackinaw, a fur cap pulled down over his ears and face showing only his wild eyes, and he wore lumberman's rubber boots. He was an imposing, scary figure. He peeled off his coat and got into the game. The more involved he got and the more he missed the target, the hotter he got, eventually removing his plaid shirt, pants, and boots — right down to his Stanfields. Still he kept missing the board, the rubber rings bounding onto the floor. Then he ordered us to open the windows and doors to cool him off. The winds and drifts came coursing through the house. He was now frothing at the mouth, and we were all terrified. What to do?

My mother had baked a chocolate cake with heaps of boiled white icing for the weekend. My eldest sister, the most resourceful one, suggested that Sam have some cake. Anything to divert him. She placed the cake in front of him, and he ate the whole of it, great gobs of icing clinging to his mustache and chin. The ruse did the trick. Having polished off the cake, Sam donned his clothes and bolted out into the night.

On his way home, Sam ran into Glen MacLean who had himself done a stint at Falconwood. He said to Sam, "You'd better be careful or pretty soon they'll be feeding you off a big spoon." That warning kept Sam home on every full moon thereafter.

Which brings us around to Little Paul, the recognized psychologist in the village. A character right out of Grimm's Fairy Tales, Little Paul earned his reputation the hard way. An early victim of infantile paralysis, his legs failed to grow beyond his first year of life. They remained buckled under his buttocks. To compensate, his arms developed long and strong, and, to get about, he swung himself along on those arms, his hands making fists on the ground. As a youngster he made a good goaltender in pickup hockey games. His hands were so quick, few pucks got past him. Once when he came visiting, a little girl, looking out the window, said, "Mom, there's a little man half-cut-off coming here." Little Paul was, however, anything but half a man.

Little Paul made his own way through life. A shoemaker and harnessmaker by trade, he set himself up on a saddle-like seat by his workbench, all his tools within arms' reach. His house, as small as a goblin's, had two tiny rooms, a kitchen-workroom and a bedroom. He lived on biscuits and black tea, and drew on his ever-present pipe and Picobac tobacco. His face and hands were as leathery as the materials of his trade. He was also a superb fiddler and was in constant demand to play at dances.

He'd tune up his fiddle, saying to his accompanist, "Sound yer 'A,'" and then swing into a selection of jigs, reels, and strathspeys. He always named the tune after he played it, saying such as, "That's 'Nellie in the Cornfield.' Some people calls it 'Smash the Window.'" Whatever the name, he played it as sweetly as the best of the Cape Breton fiddlers. But fiddling almost spelled his doom.

"More rum for the fiddler," the common saying, became all too applicable to Little Paul. When people wanted him to play for a dance or a chivaree, and he was unwilling to go, they simply primed him with rum and carted him off. When he went over the Bay on one occasion, Albert Dan, a burley compatriot, stuffed him into a bran bag and carried him off on his back. When he got to the hall, he dumped Little Paul out on the stage and ordered him to play. And play he did, as well as if sober.

One bitterly cold night in February, they were bringing him home — in the bran bag — and, unknown to the drivers, he tumbled out of the back of the woodsleigh. He wasn't discovered until hours later, and his hands were severely frostbitten, to the extent that the doctors thought they would have to amputate. Since his hands were his livelihood and his method of conveyance, Little Paul was deathly afraid.

His hands healed, and he swore off drink from that day on. He continued his leatherwork and played his fiddle, but he avoided his rowdy friends. That's also when he became a psychologist. People suffering from melancholia called on him for counselling. He had a large, unpaying clientele. He was especially effective with bachelors like himself. On them he used the directive approach. For example, to Johnny Stephen he diagnosed: "You don't steal, Johnny, so it can't be your conscience; and you go to church, so it can't be religion; and, good God, at the look of you, it can't be women." Johnny went away somewhat reassured, but Little Paul avoided Henry Andrew, Sam Anderson, and Cassie Elias as beyond his expertise. He would just advise neighbours to avoid them during the full moon, the only time he ever latched his own door against the callers.

Sir Roderick:
Recollections of a Country Doctor

If Dr. Roddie MacDonald, who died in 1961 at the age of 103, were still living today, he would have been one of the profession's most excited and enthusiastic respondents to such advances as ultrasound, CT-scanning, and "see-through vision." As well, he would have been one of the most informed about the procedures and their potential. As informed and welcoming as he was of the penicillins and aureomycins and streptomycins in the 1940s, these miraculous bacterial-fighting drugs that saved so many lives in the latter stages of the Second World War and thereafter. In his eighties then, he had a new appreciation for the old poultices made from the scrapings of clay cellar walls where such moulds as penicillin and other mycins were cultivated naturally, and for how science gave credence and large-scale production to a drug that was really a product of folk medicine. As informed and welcoming as he was of the Ehrlich serum when it became available to his dispensary before the turn of the century to help him and other men of medicine stave off the greatest local killer disease of all, diphtheria.

Although technology had not yet blessed medicine with "see-through vision," Dr. Roddie MacDonald was considered by many in his time to be a genuine medical visionary. He was considered among his peers as a fine diagnostician, and, as his years of practice approached the seventh decade, he was frequently called into consultation on diagnoses by other doctors. Aside from the regular tongue-depressor, say-ah, ears, nose, and throat kind of examination, he had a particular sensitivity to evidence of health revealed in the eyes, to the quality of the skin, and even to such detail as the health quality of the fingernails, and what they revealed to close examination. His patients recall his thorough and pervasive tapping with his fingers on various parts of their anatomy and his listening to the messages that tapping gave him. He would rest two fingers on the ailing part of the body, tap those two fingers gently with his index and middle finger, bend down close to the tapping, listen, and then diagnose.

Dr. Roddie would be the first to tell you that when he began the practice of medicine in 1888 as a country doctor serving the area of approximately 100 square miles surrounding the village of St. Peter's Bay, a lot of maladies had no real means of treatment. People died of "inflammation of the bowels" as they called it, but it was undoubtedly colon cancer they died of. Many also had "bladder trouble." My uncle coming home from being away for years met Peter Sutherland on the train and everyone he asked about, Peter would say, "Well, you know begod, she's got bladder trouble." "Bladder trouble" could mean anything from prostatitis to the necessity of a hysterectomy. In cases of appendicitis, occasionally the doctor would feel constrained to operate, and the kitchen table made for a primitive surgical theatre; but he rarely did so. Frequently, the appendix would rupture (or "burst," as they called it), and it was then a question of whether the patient could absorb the poison into his system or not. Survival depended upon it.

I've already mentioned that instances of diphtheria were the great killers before the days of the serum. Patients were put into isolation to protect the rest of the household, even to the extent that sometimes people would fix up a room in the granary and isolate patients there until they survived or expired — usually the latter. Consumption, or what is now called tuberculosis, in a family called for similar isolation, but never to the granary. And the only treatment for the Spanish Flu after the First World War, aside from going to bed and keeping warm, was a shot of whisky given at regular intervals. History records that the whisky had little effect. So, many died. It is, in the final analysis, phenomenonal that, although almost constantly exposed to communicable diseases, these doctors themselves rarely contracted much more than a sniffle. That was certainly true of the robust Dr. Roddie MacDonald.

And robust he was — of solid Selkirk settler, Maple Hills stock. In his later years his family had a reunion there, all members still living with an average age of over ninety years. To what did he attribute such health? Composure and serenity, most assuredly, but, to be sure, not regular sleep. His calls took him out at all hours of day and night, but to his advantage he could sleep at the drop of a hat and anywhere: in a driving wagon, in a sleigh, in his office chair, or before the fire. A steady and wholesome diet was essential to him. He was especially insistent on a hearty breakfast and his own always included oatmeal porridge and a boiled egg. His advice to me when I was a small boy: to eat my porridge every day. "It'll put a poultice on your stomach," he claimed. It was the same advice that the Leahy clinic gave a university colleague of mine for his ulcers a generation later, except my advice was free, and I never did have ulcers ever after.

Exercise, interests, involvements, and hobbies also contributed to his remaining young and active in spirit. He was an avid vegetable gardener, usually taking every spare minute in the summer season to be in his garden. It was large, abundant, and weedless. After finishing with a patient in his office, he'd often say, "Do you want to take a look at my garden?" In winter he enjoyed splitting the daily supply of firewood for the range and furnace, and spent spare hours mending harness or making new harness. He was an excellent harnessmaker. He needed to be because his horses were always spirited, running out of the stuff and breaking it.

He was, as well, an avid reader of the medical journals and of literature. He stayed on top of the most recent scholarship and research in medicine, and he read the classics or at least recited the poets. But his most compelling side interests were politics and playing cards. In politics he was a Tory in a district that invariably voted Liberal. The highlight moments in politics were when the party insiders came to his house to drown their sorrows on election night. I still have vivid memories of Dr. Roddie bidding good-bye to Lou Burge after an all-night sublimination of their sorrows. It was 8:30 in the morning; it had been daylight for three hours. The doctor had a kerosene oil lamp in his hand, the lamp at a garish angle, black smoke clouding the globe, and he left his friend at the door, both of them in bitter tears, the lamp well past enlightenment.

When the urge came upon him to have a game of auction, he could fabricate the flimsiest of excuses. These were the days prior to the Dominion Observatory's Official Time Signal's 2:00 daily appearance on radio. My father worked for the CNR and had a railway watch, and presumably got the daily correct time from the telegraph at the station. The doctor would cross the yard to our place, pocket watch in hand, and say, "Tom, do you have the correct time?" What he really wanted was a game of auction, and whatever the hour of day or night, he and my parents would sit in to a rousing three-hander. Other times when they played in larger partner games, he always insisted upon my mother being his partner — she was both a good player and lucky — and he called her his "angelic spirit." They invariably won. He loved it and took full credit for the victory.

Dr. Roddie played cards with gusto. Loving to win, he hummed gleefully when he had a good hand — a dead giveaway — and got more than a little irascible when he was losing. Once while playing 45s for a goose, he had the 5 of trumps and was 35. In order to win with a grand flourish, he stuck the 5 between his lips, the more dramatically to bring it down on the table with his fist to claim the game and the goose. Everybody could see the card. The only trouble was he forgot about it himself and another player went out from 35 on tricks with the jack and ace. Dr. Roddie got up in a head of steam and said, "Where's my cap?" smacking it on his head and storming out the door. But he was back for a game the next night.

In the days of the more self-contained rural community on PEI, the most prominent and respected individuals were the clergy, doctor, and teacher or teachers, depending on the community's size. Dr. Roddie was accorded that respect in his home community. The longevity of his devotion to the sick, stretching over seventy years in the community, without ever taking a vacation, was one measure of that. His simple, yet profound philosophy of life, a simplicity reflected in Robbie Burns' "A Cotter's Saturday Night" and "A Man's a Man for A'That," and in the "short and simple annals of the poor" philosophy of Gray's "Elegy," were essential to him. His steadfast adherence to Christian principles as expressed in Roman Catholicism was also important to him. He was a man of prayer and meditation, a thoughtful Christian. Never much of a singer, while he was on his calls he used to hum hymns in his own special tuneless way. But it was his Christian dedication to duty and to physical care of persons that carried him through. It was, therefore, no surprise to anyone to see him honoured on October 25, 1952, at the age of ninety-four, with the knighthood of St. Gregory. This was the highest order that Rome could give a prominent layman of the Roman Catholic Church, and was a singular honour to Sir Roderick living in a small community of four hundred people so distant from the Holy City of Rome as to be practically invisible.

Sir Roderick's sudden prestige brought him a certain fame and international coverage. Within two years he was the subject of stories in the Toronto *Star*, *Maclean's* magazine, and *Time* magazine and was photographed by no less than Youssef Karsh himself. Yet, when I, on one occasion, brought a young journalist to interview him, he'd had enough of fame. I remember him coming down on the kitchen table with the flat of his hand and saying, "I will not permit my name to be prostituted to the vulgar mob again." There was a certain finality in that statement, finality punctuated by the fullness of his ninety-six years of life.

For all his serenity and concern, Dr. Roddie had a brush-fire temper, but it usually subsided shortly after the initial flame. On one Sunday evening he was preparing supper for a few guests, and he left the lower door of the kitchen cupboard open while he was doing something else. A mother cat and a half-dozen of her kittens seized the opportunity to attack the remains of the noonday Sunday roast stored there. The doctor saw them, caught them by the scruffs of their necks, and threw them into a corner, vowing, "I'll bag them up, By Gob! I'll bag them up," casting his fist to the heavens. A couple of weeks later, one of his Sunday guests was back for a visit and, seeing the kittens alive and well and still in the kitchen, said, "Did you bag them up, Doctor?" "Bag what up, dear?" said Roddie. "Did you bag up the cats?" "Oh the darlin's; I wouldn't touch them for the world," said Roddie. Two of his linguistic idiosyncrasies were evident in that snippet of dialogue: one, he always said "By Gob" — never "by God" — and, two, he called everyone dear, something he undoubtedly picked up from years of bedside mannering.

As well, anything that seemed to disparage his fierce Scottish pride would draw his immediate ire. I was talking with him one day about St. Dunstan's College — I was a student there at the time — and he went into a reverie about the place where he, too, had studied some twenty years before the turn of the twentieth century. He spoke of the hardships of studying with primitive tallow lamps and of the water being frozen in the basins in the morning and of the harsh rules of discipline. And then he talked with passion about the great MacDonalds and MacIntyres who built "the St. Dunstan's College," as he called it. Suddenly he went into a rage saying, "We built the St. Dunstan's College, and *damn them*, they took it away from us." By this he meant the Irish takeover expressed in a long line of Irish rectors at St. Dunstan's: the Currans, Crokens, and Murphys. After he calmed down he said, "For heaven's sake don't tell anybody I said that." His temper had been satisfied in the instant of its saying.

The peculiarity was that, although he was a rabid Scottish partisan, and a die-hard Tory, Dr. Roddie was a religious ecumenist. He was a sectarian by religious adherence, but certainly not a sectarian philosophically, which made him most suited to the religiously open-minded community of St. Peter's. He treated everyone, well-off and poor, believer and heathen, with equality and with equanimity.

Much of Dr. Roddie's medicine was practised at the bedsides of the sick in the area under his care, but as well, many came to his office for medicine and treatment over those seventy years of his practice. And the office, as you might expect, was quite different from a doctor's office we find today: it was, in fact, a combination office, drugstore, consultation room, and occasional operating room. What patients remember most was the wall-to-wall collection of large bottles and boxed drugs. The solid substances were ground and mixed to a powder with mortar and pestle, and carefully wrapped in paper envelopes in single doses, and the liquid substances were mixed in gawdawfully flavoured concoctions, the cure as distasteful as the disease, and dispensed in what are now collectors' item medicine bottles. The office smelled like an apothecary; in fact, so did the old doctor himself. He recorded his calls, the prescribed medicine, and the bill dutifully in large and tall bookkeeper's ledgers. As you might imagine, the barter system was still common then, and there was little money in the countryside. The mere fact that people were unable to pay did not exclude them, however, from medical help, even if the cost of a call may have been no more than fifty cents, or the cost of a baby's delivery (a confinement case, as it was called) $2, or of an appendectomy $15, or whatever the family could spare.

When he was getting close to retirement, Dr. Roddie requested that his ledgers containing outstanding bills be burned. They were two full ledgers containing, I would guess, about thirty entries per page and about two hundred pages per ledger, or about twelve thousand outstanding bills in all, or close to two hundred outstanding bills a year over a seventy-year period, an immolation to the man's service.

A good deal has been made about the days when PEI was emerging out of Prohibition, when people had to pay for a "script" from the doctor and present it at the liquor store in order to get a bottle of spirits. Doctors were thought of as profiteers in those transitional years. But when one considered the infrequency of bills being paid, then a case could be made for this kind of subsidization. I cannot really recall very many people complaining. About the inconvenience, yes, but about the fee to the doctor, no.

Quite aside from the esteem accorded him locally as Dr. Roddie, and more widely as Sir Roderick, Dr. Roddie was at the heart of things a family man. He was married to Josephine Mac-Donald, a little bit of a thing, for fifty-five years from 1893 to her death in 1948. Sir Roderick and Josephine had seven children, five boys and two girls. Josephine was, unfortunately, one of the first sufferers from Alzheimer's that I've ever encountered, and for several years was a constant care for the family, particularly for her daughter, Jean, who looked after her.

Christmas day and the doctor's birthday, May 16, were the two big family feasts. As many of the family as could make it were on hand for these. On such occasions the doctor saw to it that everyone, including the grandchildren, got a liberal share of Scotch whisky and, as the day progressed, conviviality was in the ascendancy. On his eightieth birthday, as the happy day devolved into evening's melancholy, the doctor was seen crying on his son-in-law's shoulder and saying, "How are you all going to survive when I am gone?" The fact was that he outlived his son-in-law by a dozen years, and a few others as well. About the Scotch whisky, which he always loved with true Scottish patriotism, he spoke to my father when he was eighty-six and said, "You know, by Gob, Tom, I think I've got control of it." But he would never agree with temperance or taking pledges against drinking, saying, "It's a bad sign of a dog if you have to muzzle him."

When he was ninety-five, one day he was coming down the back stairs and lost his balance halfway down. As quick as a billy-goat he jumped and landed on both feet, square into the middle of the kitchen and said, "I'm in the ninety-fifth year, and I'm not in me dotage yet!" He was never in his dotage, in fact; not then, or not at ninety-six when he decided against driving his car any longer, or not when he retired at ninety-seven from the practice of medicine, or not even until June 3, 1961, when he died at the age of one hundred and three years without being able to put in his beloved garden that spring.

An Ounce of Prevention

Nowadays, if you mention taking doses of sulphur and molasses as a spring tonic, or drinking water soaked with tamarack bark, or carrying around half an onion in your pocket to stave off colds, or taking kerosene oil internally to break up croup, or taking lactic acid for celiac disease, or drinking well-cured buttermilk for diarrhea, or two ounces of whisky for fever, or a spoonful of awful-tasting medicines from the country doctor's dispensary for a variety of ailments — if you mention all of these to your grandchildren or even to your children, they retch, go "ugh, ugh," and cannot believe that anyone could suffer such ignominy. If they need to medicate, they are into innocuous and easy-to-swallow pills, capsules, vitamins, and herbs, or a mildly discomforting shot in a prominent muscle. No pain; lots of gain. The penicillins, sulfas, and cortisones were unheard-of in our days.

But I knew all too well that first list of medicines when I was a youngster. As an infant I was celiac, and my life was saved by Dr. Tidmarsh of Charlottetown. He prescribed the treatment of the day: drops of lactic acid diluted in water, to "establish the chemical balance in my stomach" so that I could retain my food and grow strong. Later, I developed severe bouts of bronchitis. Sometimes it could be broken by breathing the steam from the pouring stem of a kettle containing a boiling mixture of wintergreen and water. Sometimes that wouldn't do the job, and I was forced to take a spoonful of kerosene oil mixed with brown sugar. It was extremely distasteful — not to mention what it was doing to my stomach — but it always broke the croup. I survived.

Our whole family took its daily dose of cod liver oil, straight from the bottle, with no chaser, before going off to school for the day, and, in the spring of the year, a liberal intake of sulphur and molasses to clean the blood. I remember rubbing my skin and combing my hair in the dark of my bedroom to bring out a blue phosphorescence caused by the sulphur emanating from my pores. Our treatment when we had pneumonia was an ounce of hot whisky in a hot toddy. I've never really liked whisky from that day to this.

When I was seven years old, I contracted red measles and whooping cough, which eventually developed into double pneumonia. I was bedridden from April 14 to May 24. On May 24, I stood on my bed to see the Union Jacks on passing cars and trucks to mark the Queen's birthday, the first big national holiday of the year. Sulfa drugs were not yet on the market. A few years later, my brother took pneumonia on a Tuesday, was treated with sulfa, and was up on Saturday night to listen to the hockey game on radio — a must-listen for all of us in those days. Being Montreal Canadiens fans, we listened to the French broadcast on CHNC New Carlisle. No Foster Hewitt and the Toronto Maple Leafs for us.

Next door to us when I was a boy was Dr. Roddie MacDonald, our country doctor. The medicines he prescribed he mixed himself in his own dispensary. He would grind up mysterious powders with his mortar and pestle, mix them with fluids, and they were the bitterest elixirs you'd ever have to take. They would be for everything from colds to bladder trouble. Also in his dispensary was a large bottle of small white pills, which his daughter told us were placebos. After checking out the meaning of the word in our dictionary, and when the doctor was out on sick calls, we used to pilfer handfuls of them and eat them like candy. They had a semisweet minty flavour. They were for people who had no apparent signs of illness — and for hypochondriacs — who just had to see the doctor. He would put a supply of placebos in little pill boxes with instructions to take one before each meal, and they went away happy, never knowing the difference. The pills were free of charge. The local stores carried Carter's Little Liver pills, Minard's Liniment, and Beef Iron and Wine. The last, because of its alcoholic content, in Prohibition years did a thriving business.

Both my father and I suffered each year from summer complaint: loose bowels. Accordingly, he always kept a crock of buttermilk in our clay cellar and, when the flying axehandles were upon us, he'd go down and skim the half-inch of mould from the top of the crock and bring up a glassful of well-cured buttermilk for each of us. Cure was almost instantaneous.

When I went off to boarding school as a thirteen-year-old, I got introduced to the benefits of tamarack juice. My roommate had a bucket of the soaking bark on the upper shelf of our room and took a swig of it every morning upon rising. He also carried half an onion around in his pocket to stave off colds. I soon was converted to taking a daily share of the tamarack juice, but, out of respect for my classmates, avoided carrying the onion. I never had a cold in all that year in boarding school.

To this day, I have difficulty coming around to the plethora of bottled vitamins and quick cures, opting rather for a nutritious, balanced diet. But, when the need arises, I am not averse to going back to mustard plasters for chest colds, hot rum and honey for the sniffles, and a kerosene oil rub for aches and pains, and to make one concession to the times, chicken soup for the soul.

Peter Talks about the Farm

"Where I grew up," says Peter MacIntyre, "most of the farms were forty acres runnin' back from the road. Or double that to eighty acres — the front forty and the back forty. Part of the back forty was woods, sometimes nearly all of it. The back forty was a place for retreat. When my father came home from the war, he spent a lot of time on the back forty. Straightenin' out his mind, he called it. When most of the rest of us got into trouble or wanted a quick reality fix, we struck 'er for the woods too.

"Another thing about the back forty was that's where the cows were always pasturin' and runnin' into the bogs to get the flies off their legs. The girls in the family had to fetch them home at milkin' time and had to chase them through the bogs to round them up. 'Damn cows,' they'd complain, 'I'll never marry a farmer, you can bet on that.' But the mud was good for their legs and the air for their peaches-and-cream complexion. At the dances the fellas would be looking them over, and you'd hear a fella say, 'Now there's a filly I wouldn't mind havin' in my barn.'

"On our farm, the boys and father did the milkin' and feedin' the stock — the cows, horses, and pigs — and forked and shovelled endless manure. Every now and then we'd catch a cow or horse in heat. (I could never somehow tell when a sow was in heat.) Father and a neighbour would go out and get a bull or a stud horse and come home. The ninnyin' or bawlin' would be something wicked. For modesty and privacy, the act of intercourse was done behind a high board fence in the corner between the machinery shed and the barn. We were barred from the action, but I could never understand how my father couldn't see us all — boys and girls together — watchin' the goin's-on with great curiosity from the shed roof. Even the clumsiest one of us could scale it, easy. Sex education for us happened right there.

"Despite all the education we got at home, and if the girls didn't want to marry a farmer, that meant we had to go to school to read and write and find out about the big world out there, outside our village, where some of us would end up goin'. Oh yes, and I had to learn my sums, too. 'A boy who can't do his sums will never amount to anything,' my teacher said. Or else he'd end up like Jimmy Larkin down the road who said, 'Sure now, there were four of us there. The two Crokens is one, and Muttart is two, and myself is three.' And then he'd scratch his head. Perplexed. And learning too that the Island was called 'The million acre farm' simply defied our imagination. When asked by the teacher, 'How big is Australia?' One of my class-mates said, 'Oh, just a little bigger than the Island.' And when hearing about troubles in the History books, like the Seven Years War or the Riel Rebellion, we'd say, 'Those poor fellas. Isn't it too bad that they weren't livin' on the Island?'

"As I grew older and stronger, I took on more responsi-bilities around the farm, havin' to stay home to do the ploughin' and harrowin' in the spring and the croppin' in the fall. And, because we lived close to the shore, I spread lobster shells we got from the factory and mussel mud from the river onto the land for fertilizer. My heroes were the men of the threshin' gangs, especially Joe Ford, who had the biggest appetite of anyone at the dinner table. He'd take a slice of bread, slather it with butter, fold it in four, and stuff it into his mouth, sayin', 'The goddamn bread is so thin you can inhale it.' Or the fellas who loaded the railroad reefer cars with potatoes, carrying a 75-pound bag of spuds under each arm and hefting them to the top of the pile.

"Like every other young buck, as I got to be sixteen, I be-gan to feel my blood risin' and started to go to the dances, 'To look over the stock,' as one of my friends put it. Goin' to dances meant dancin', but it also meant provin' your manhood. One time, after being out all night, I got home after sunrise and my poppa met me at the door. He had a big hardwood stock behind his back. 'Where were you?' he said. 'I was fightin',' I said. 'Did you beat him?' he said. 'Yes, I beat him,' I said. 'Well then, come on in the house and have your breakfast,' he said.

"Mostly life on the farm was pretty routine. Too routine for my aunt and uncle who came home from Boston where life was more excitin'. My aunt would say, in her best Boston accent: 'They go to bed here when it gets dark under the chairs.' And my uncle would chime in and say, 'Yes, and they get up at crow piss.'

"When we lived without electricity and indoor plumbing, there was little reason to stay up after dark, and even the strongest kidneys called for an early trip to the outhouse in the mornin'. The Truelove Taylors from out back in Strathcona came to town and stayed at the Regent Hotel. Viney, Mrs. Taylor, was in bed and asked Truelove to bring her a drink of water. 'Where'd you get it?' she said when he returned. 'I got it in that well in there,' he said. And when she asked him to blow out the light, he couldn't, 'Because it's in a little bottle.'

"And, oh yes, the routine was always broken on Sunday afternoons. There'd be a time with the fiddle and the piano and everyone around singin' 'come all ye's.' And often, especially every election time, a politician would come along to liven things up. My aunt and uncle would never think of comin' back here in the winters. Things got desperate quiet. Not even a politician came around.

"Come to think of it, the only time in winter we went to the back forty was to cut firewood, or else to get out lumber for another shed or milk house. But in winter we never seemed to have a care serious enough to make us go back there to be alone. We just sat around the kitchen tellin' stories or playin' cards, and every now and then puttin' another stick of second growth into the range."

Outhouses

Outhouses are now a rarity on this Island. But you only have to go back half a century to when indoor plumbing was equally a rarity. Driving around the countryside, you couldn't necessarily see them. They were usually built well away from the house, to the offside of an outbuilding. Schoolyards were unable to hide them, so they were there in full view.

An old classic, now long out-of-print, titled *The Specialist*, gave specific and humorous instructions on their construction, location, and accoutrements. It advised building the outhouse next to the woodpile, lest if a visitor came into the yard, the housewife going to the backhouse could divert to the woodpile to save her from embarrassment. Many homes took that advice.

Outhouses were generally boxy and small, maybe a little larger for families of six or more, requiring two or sometimes three holes. The two-holer was the most common. I often wondered about the wisdom of schools having only two-holers in the panelled-off girls' and boys' sections. At home, we had a three-holer for a household of nine. When the whole family was short-taken with what we called the "flying axehandles," even then a three-holer wasn't enough. In school, part of the teacher's job was to regulate visits to avoid overcrowding. This often resulted in crossed legs and wet bloomers for some of the girls in class. Boys seemed to be able to exercise more bladder control.

Outhouses kept a bucket of lime, a scoopful to be inserted down the hole after doing your business. Toilet paper being a thing of the future, *The Specialist* advocated the use of the mail-order catalogue as the alternative, giving specific advice to get anxious for the next edition in your mailbox when you got to the "harness section" of the present one. In our comfort station we kept an ample supply of reading material: back issues of the *Saturday Evening Post* and the *Family Herald and Weekly Star*. We were under specific instructions to use only the Eaton's catalogue, not the reading material, to do our wipe-up.

The Specialist further suggested cutting notches in some seats to discourage users from sitting and reading well beyond their allotted time.

Outhouses in those days were spared the bane of graffiti so common to present washrooms. More common then, especially in those of the schools, were initials carved into the wooden walls and such artwork as "J.R. loves T.M." enclosed in a heart. And, Islanders always being interested in the weather, such notes as, "Feb. 2/41. Heavy snow. I had to shovel my way in here today." As a matter of fact, winter was always a challenge when you had to go, especially at night when you had to bring along a kerosene lantern to find your way, not to mention the frosty seat that hastened your stay.

Outhouses, because of their size and being built on sills rather than foundations, were fair game for the annual Hallowe'en pranksters. It usually took no more than a half-dozen young bucks to capsize one. The schools' were always the first targets. And, on All Souls' Day, the sturdier students of the school were assigned to aright them. Often, they were the very ones who had participated in the turnover the night before. No accusations were made; no questions asked; it was part of the ritual.

Outhouses being inconvenient for late night calls necessitated people having chamber pots in their bedrooms. These, too, are now a rarity, coveted by antique-buyers at auction sales. But in their heyday they were a great convenience and, on occasion, a threatening missile, as in the line from the old song: "...I went to Paddy's house and Paddy was in bed, so I upped with the piss pot and hit him on the head." When my dad was a young man in Souris, he and his friends were in need of more sustenance, and, although it was late at night, they called on the MacInnis Hotel to acquire some "Half and Half," a common spirit of the time. They threw pebbles up to the MacInnis's bedroom to awaken them. Mrs. MacInnis raised the window and angrily asked, "Wha'd'yus want?" "Half and Half," they said. Whereupon she grabbed the chamber pot and hurled it at them shouting, "There's yer 'arf and 'arf. 'Arf mine and 'arf the old man's."

Despite the proliferation of outhouses in the countryside, sometimes people simply had to take to the woods. There being no catalogues to use there, the topic of conversation often centred on what to use as an alternative. Fern fronds were common, but not entirely satisfactory because of their open spaces. The consensus was for burdock leaves because of their size and their furry underside. But, what of wintertime? A resourceful friend said, "Did you ever try snow?"

In the end, when you come right down to it, indoor washrooms aren't always fail-safe either. Some years ago, I studied in a seminary in which total silence was to be observed at all times. A little Irish priest, having done his business in a stall, discovered he had no toilet paper in the dispenser. He waited until someone came and occupied the stall next to him, then he rapped gently on the divider and said, "Ah mister, could you give me some t'ilet paper?" Not recognizing the voice to be a member of faculty, the chap took a piece of toilet paper and tore off a stamp-sized corner and, reaching under the stall, handed it to him. The Irish priest took it and shouted, "What the hell do you think I am, a canary?"

The Culinary Arts

Even though no Islander is more than fifteen minutes from the ocean, Janie MacSween had never been to the shore. She grew up on a family farm in Emerald, went to a one-room school, married young, and, before she knew it, had a houseful of children. She was pregnant every second year. Her husband, James, was an industrious farmer with a sizeable herd of Ayrshire milk cows, a piggery, and a potato warehouse. Work on the farm left little time for going to the shore.

Anything of the harvest of the sea they got from the fish pedlar who came into their yard every Thursday. Not that the MacSweens were at all fond of fish, but being Catholics at a time when Fridays were "fish days," their purchase from the fish man was part of their religion. Janie stuck to choosing either cod or hake, and cooked it the only way she knew how: she boiled the bejasus out of it. For winter, she bought a full supply of salt cod and stored it in the cool clay cellar of the house. She boiled a batch of it each Friday, too — sometimes even more on the "fast days" during Lent. It didn't taste any better than if she'd boiled an old boot.

Cooking everything to a frazzle was the hallmark of Janie's culinary arts. She roasted her beef until it was charred on the outside, and she boiled all the sweetness out of turnips. But, that aside, she never made any claims about knowing how to do fish.

Fish of any kind. One day her James went to Borden to sign a bill of lading for a carload of potatoes he was shipping on the CNR, and, while there, he bought a bucket of clams from a couple of urchins along the Borden shore road, and brought them home to Janie. It was just after noon on a Friday. "You can cook them up for dinner. They're fish, y'know," he said to Janie, and left for the grading warehouse.

Never having seen a clam before, let alone having cooked them, Janie decided they had somehow to be removed from their shells. So she got out a paring knife, and, four hours later, her hands cut from sharp edges and a slipping knife, she had the job done. Then she — what else — gave them a good boiling. Nobody at the table was enthusiastic about eating them.

The next summer, her aunts came home from the Boston States and, soon after, upon returning from a day at Cavendish, came home with a bucket of clams. Having learned a painful lesson before, Janie suggested, "You ladies do the clams and I'll get the rest of the supper." To her amazement, they put the clams, fully clad in their shells, into the pot and, in ten minutes, they were steamed and ready to serve. This time, the whole family ate them with gusto.

One thing Janie was very good at was vegetable gardening. Her practical sense told her her garden was a necessity to feed her large family with hearty meals. And she had huge crops of green tomatoes, cucumbers, and cauliflower for making her chows and mustard pickles. Her single indulgence in non-practicality was in growing decorative gourds to grace her dining-room table. Having more than enough for her own household, she shared a basket of them with her neighbour, Flora.

Flora lived with her husband, Clifford, in a trailer at the corner of the road. They had no children and no garden, and Clifford was unwell, so anything to brighten their lives moved Janie to make this offering. The next day after delivering the gourds, Janie got a call from Flora about her problems with cooking them. "I been b'ilin' them for two hours and they're still 's hard as flint," said Flora.

"Well, I guess not knowing what to do with clams wasn't so bad after all," said Janie. Flora had no idea what she was talking about, but Janie took consolation in knowing that she wasn't the only one to be mystified by the unfamiliar. She would tell all around how Flora tried to boil gourds for dinner, but she never once told anyone about her culinary failure with clams.

Holding the Farm

Mary MacDonald walked to the back of the farm. The milk cattle, Ayrshires, were pastured in the field beside the stand of spruce running down a slope to the brook bordering on the MacKay farm neighbouring theirs. It was a Sunday, but she was dressed in rubber boots and wore bib-overalls and a plaid shirt. She came here to do some thinking. Her husband, Andrew, had two weeks ago been diagnosed with pancreatic cancer, and the doctors gave him only weeks to live. He was already too weak to join her for this walk. His skin was jaundiced, and he was becoming quiet and uncommunicative.

Andrew had been a traditional farmer, sticking to pure-bred Ayrshires when his neighbours stocked Holsteins for better milk production, and insisting on mixed farming when so many others were getting into monoculture. "Mixed farming may not bring in boom years," he'd say to his neighbours, "but there's a livin' in it and it's better for the land." Already some of them were growing potatoes in fields three years in a row, leeching the land of every drop of nutrients left in them. "Short-term gain but long-term pain," he'd warn. He was a stubborn Scot, strong on principle. But now he was unable even to do the chores.

What to do? The question had played on Mary's mind ever since Andrew's diagnosis. "I grew up on this farm. My mother and father gave it to us when we married and retired to that bungalow in Kensington. This is where we raised our boys. I'm not ready to give all that up. Not just yet." The Ayrshires watched her while she talked aloud. "You don't understand my problem," she said to them directly. "If you could, you'd be as concerned as me. It's your fate, too." She was especially addressing her favourite, called Silva, because she was born in the woods. Though smaller than the rest of the herd, Silva was the hardiest and seemed to be the most sensitive.

Mary had resisted getting the word of Andrew's diagnosis to their four sons. She still hadn't worked up the courage to do so. They had all got a good education and left the Island for greener pastures in Ontario and Alberta. Andrew and Mary wanted them to be educated, but they harboured the desire that one of them would eventually take over the farm. Andrew, in fact, had been more adamant about it, making it a duty for each of the boys as he came of age. The eldest son, Colin, just as stubborn as his father, had said with finality, "You won't get me to be up to my knees in pig shit for the rest of my life." "Ach, ye'll be gettin' far worse than pig shit in the oil fields of Alberta, me boy," his father came back. But to the oilfields in Alberta Colin went, and, after two years as a roughneck, he now had a cushy office job in Calgary. He and Andrew were cool with one another after several arguments about staying home on the farm. Neil, the second, was just not cut out for farming. The artistic one of the lot, he had done a music degree in college and then got on in the violin section of the Toronto Symphony. "He'd help with the hayin'," Andrew would say to Mary, "but he never liked gettin' clay under his finger nails." Angus got a business degree and was offered a job with the Royal Bank. "He's doing well, Andrew. He just got on with their inspection team," said Mary. "We could use his talent for figures right here in Indian River." Andrew was a great worker, but, having left school in Grade Six, he was not so good with figures. He left the farm management to Mary. "I often wish I had the chances our boys had," he'd sometimes complain.

Andrew put his final hopes in his youngest, Rory. Rory liked farming, stayed home to help with the crops each summer, and had a special knack with the animals. He was a natural to take over the farm. He graduated from the Atlantic Veterinary College, keeping his father's dreams of an heir to the farm alive. But he went off and opened a small animal clinic in Dundas, Ontario. "Imagine, with all that schooling and he goes off to care for cats and dogs and budgie birds, for God's sake, when he should be back here caring for the cattle and horses and pigs, and even the chickens," Andrew complained ruefully to Mary. Mary was usually cautious in her reply, knowing only too well Andrew's red hair and fiery temper. "Maybe one of them will have a change of heart and come home to take over the farm," she'd console. "I'll not live to see the day," Andrew would say.

Now, in the pasture, Mary thought of Andrew's self-fulfilling prophecy. "Maybe one will have a change of heart," she thought. She resolved then and there to call each of the boys and let them know of their father's condition. That night, after she got Andrew to bed for the night, she got on the phone to each of the boys. Colin and Nancy were expecting their second and there were complications. "She's threatening a miscarriage, Mother. Your news comes at a bad time for us. But we'll be there to support you. Does Dad still resent me for pulling up stakes and moving west?" "That's something we're not concerned about right now, Colin. You will come though when things get bad for him? I'd like to see you reconciled before he goes," Mary's voice was pleading. "Don't worry, Mother, I'll be there. I have lots of frequent flyer points." After she set down the phone Mary thought Colin's last remark insensitive. But that was Colin, always using the advantage. She had no time to mull it over; she had three more calls to make. Neil's orchestra was going on tour the following week, but he promised to call every two days to keep in touch. He, too, promised to come home. Angus just happened to be assigned to do the banks in Nova Scotia, so his weekends would be free, and, now with the bridge there, he'd have no problem getting back and forth to the Island. He had promised his wife to come back to Toronto and take her to a performance in the National Arts Centre in Ottawa next weekend, but he was sure she'd understand.

Mary left young Rory for last, and it turned out to be a good decision. "When it comes to trouble in the family, Mother, you know you can depend on all of us to come together. That's the Island way. We're not that long away to forget that," he said. "You don't know how good that makes me feel," said Mary, a wisp of grey hair getting caught up in a salty tear. "I can get someone to take over my clinic, and I'll make arrangements to be home in a few days. I'll let you know the day and flight time, so you can have someone pick me up at the Charlottetown airport." Mary was sure she could handle the chores until he came. They had a milk machine and a good separator, so there'd be lots of skim milk for the pigs and calves. And, although it was October, the stock was all out on pasture and would be for a few more weeks — until after the November snows came.

Mary had not raised the idea of one of them to come back and take over the farm. She was always subtle that way. She knew intuitively that the tone of her voice planted certain seeds of responsibility. Sure, she could have gone on a rant about corporate takeovers of land all over the Island, and especially in Indian River. Had Andrew his health and a couple snorts aboard, he'd go on for hours about it. That wasn't Mary's way. She shared Andrew's conviction, but not his bluster. "When the time comes...," she whispered to herself. "When the time comes...."

The following Thursday, Rory called to say he'd be arriving on Air Canada the next evening at five o'clock. Mary had noticed a rapid deterioration in Andrew's condition, so she was comforted by his coming. Seeing to Andrew left her little time to do the chores, and she was already having to rely on the neighbours for help getting the milkers to the barn and back to the pasture. Rory got in on schedule and was met at the airport by John Allan MacKay, the neighbour. "It's good to have you here, Rory. Your father is getting weaker every day. Your mother sure needs you," he said as they got the luggage into the back of his half-ton truck.

Rory was shocked at how tired his mother looked. She was always a strong woman, able to handle any situation, but all her care was taking its toll. "You must come upstairs right away and see your father," she said. Andrew lay in bed a mere shadow of his former self, his ruddy complexion displaced by an ashen yellow and his eyes staring. "Hello, Dad, I'm glad I came. How are you doing?" "I think I'll soon be goin' down the river," Andrew said. "But you get on now and help your mother with the chores." "I'll do them myself, Dad. I'm not that far away from doing chores. That will leave Mother in the house if you need to call for her."

Rory immediately donned his father's overalls and rubber boots and headed for the pasture to round up the milkers. He was pleased and surprised to see what good shape everything was in. The fence wire was taut and secure, the gates didn't sag, and the grasslands were lush. The evening's quietude and the fresh salt air coming off the Gulf were a definite break from

Ontario's smog and the rush-rush in his clinic. "If only there was enough business on the Island for me to move my clinic here to Indian River," he mused.

After he finished the chores and returned the Ayrshires to pasture, he returned to the house. It was already 8:30 P.M., and he was ravenously hungry. His mother had prepared pork chops, mashed potatoes, and turnips, and she sat down to eat with him. "Your father hasn't been able to eat anything for three days now. Dr. McMahon told me to give him stout, and he's been able to get a few mouthsful into him, but no more."

"I think we should call the others tonight and suggest they come as soon as possible," Rory said. "Do you want me to make the calls, Mother?"

"Would you be a dear? I'm afraid it might be too much for me." Mary got up to fetch some tea and hot ginger cake. Rory finished his meal and went into the downstairs hall to the phone. He had some difficulty tracking down Neil, eventually reaching him in Sudbury, but he reached both Colin and Angus at home. Each said they would be home in two days. "I wouldn't leave it any longer," Rory wanted to make that clear. It was Friday night. He said he'd meet them at the airport at 5:00 P.M. on Monday. He was there to greet them when they arrived. "I'm glad you came," he told them. "I don't think Dad has any more than a day or two to go."

As soon as they arrived home, Colin, Neil, and Angus each made a call on their father. The sickroom smelled of death, and the father, though quite conscious, could barely speak over a whisper. Colin said, "Dad, I'm sorry we had a disagreement about my taking over the farm. It's been ten years since then. I hope you can find it in your heart to forgive me."

Andrew struggled an answer, "One of you will have to take it over...lest it will go to the corporations." "We will see that it won't. That's a promise," said Colin. Angus and Neil nodded agreement. Acknowledging that a reconciliation between the father and son was paramount, they chose to be silent. "Well then, as long as the farm is kept in the family... and someone is here to look after Mary...I forgive..." (and his voice trailed off). "We had better leave now, Father," Colin signalled to his brothers, and they followed him from the room.

Rory, meanwhile, had brought the milkers to the barn, and with the four brothers doing the chores the work was done in a whipstitch. "You lads go back to the house and I'll take the cattle back to the pasture," Colin offered. He returned them to the back pasture adjacent to the stand of spruce and the brook running through it. He then walked along the back line of the farm towards its far corner, which ran along the Gulf shoreline. He used to come here to sit on the low cliff until his disagreements with his father subsided. It was a special place to him, even now, watching the waves ebb and flow along the strand, balls of foam rolling like tumbleweed being carried up the sand by the onshore breeze, staying on until the sun sank low in the west, casting his world in a red and purple glow. "Oh, God," he said, "it's good to be back here." Knowing dinner would be awaiting him, he jogged back to the house.

Mary had prepared a hearty boiled dinner: potatoes, carrots, turnips, parsnips, onions, and cabbage — all home-grown — and lots of stew beef from the freezer. "Just like the old days," she said, ladling a heaping bowlful for each. "It was always your father's favourite. Now he can hardly keep an ounce of stout down. Isn't it grand though to have you all here to share it, especially since everything came from our farm."

"The materials for this stew would set you back about $30.00 at Loblaws in Toronto these days," Angus said. "Maybe a little less here on the Island."

"That's probably what I'd be paying if we didn't have the farm," Mary said, not looking directly at any of the boys, but nonetheless hoping her underlying implication would sink in. She then suggested that they decide on shifts to keep an all-night vigil with their father.

"First of all, Mother, you are excluded. You really should get some rest. We'll divide the night among the four of us," Neil said. "I would be happy to take the first shift — from eight to eleven." He knew his father would still be alert enough to hear Lord MacDonald's Reel. Neil had brought his violin along, and, although he hadn't played much other than classical music lately, he was sure he could recapture the reel as his father liked it. After he settled in with his father, Neil brought out the instrument and, without asking, swung right into the reel. When he finished, his father whispered, "Thank you, Son. Could you play it again soft and low?" Neil bowed the strings so light as to render a soothing melody and played on and on that way well past his father's falling into a deep sleep.

While his father slept, Neil stood at the bedroom window. The full moon illuminated the barnyard, the hip-roofed cattle barn, the pighouse and henhouse, the pumphouse, and a neat array of farm equipment: a mower, baler, harrows, ploughs, and the John Deere tractor. "My father's and mother's heritage," he thought. "It would be a shame to see it all go to auction sale when Dad dies. We can't let that happen."

Eleven o'clock came soon, and Angus came in to break Neil's reverie. "His breathing is shallow, but he's been asleep since nine o'clock," Neil reported to Angus. Angus pulled up a chair by his father's bedside. His work with figures and with the inspection team were furthest from his mind. Rather his thoughts were on his family days here on the farm, and of what good providers his mother and father were. Looking at his prostrate father, he said, "Not having much education yourself never deterred you from seeing that each one of us got a good university education. For that we owe a lot to your calloused hands." By midnight he noticed a further shallowing of his father's breathing. And then, within moments a complete shutdown, a peaceful passing.

Angus summoned everyone to the room, and in the moments following they formed a ring of solidarity around their mother. They shared their tears and each felt the anguish of this first break in their family chain. "We should all try to get some rest now," Colin spoke as the eldest. "I'll call the funeral home first thing in the morning."

"You all go. I'll stay on a bit longer," Mary said simply. In the hour she spent alone with her dead husband, her mourning was mixed with concerns about the farm's future. Never a thought about her own.

Andrew had a typical Island wake and funeral: people from near and far came to both, the neighbours brought in loads of food. St. Mary's Church in Indian River was rarely used now for services, but because of its appealing architecture and terrific acoustics had become a venue for musical performances. The church gave him — a long-standing member and supporter of the church — a solemn and fitting funeral. He was then laid to rest in the parish graveyard. The MacDonald home then invited all to tea and lunch. Afterwards, they trailed off and the family was left to itself. John Allan MacKay's parting words were, "Now Mary, what are you going to do about the farm?" The sons overheard the question, but neither they nor Mary offered John Allan an answer.

Later that afternoon the sons each made calls to Air Canada to confirm their return flights the next day. Colin was especially anxious to get back to Calgary and to his pregnant wife. Rory had already had calls about emergencies in his clinic. Angus was concerned about overextending the generosity of his inspection team colleagues, and Neil assured his symphony orchestra that he would join it in its next performance, in Ottawa.

That left chores and then dinnertime to discuss the farm's future with Mary. "My coming home is out of the question, at least in the near future," Colin began. "Jennifer and I have to get through this pregnancy, and, besides, being a Western girl, coming here would be a big adjustment for her. The timing couldn't be worse."

Angus was next. "If you were to sell the farm, Mom, oh, I know, Dad is hardly cold in his grave and the idea of selling would make him sit right up. But we have to be practical. The farm would bring a tidy sum, enough to give you, Mom, a comfortable living in a place like Kensington for the rest of your days."

Rory could feel an increasing pressure building up within him. "Selling the farm is out of the question. It would go against anything you, Mom, and Dad stood for. It's not a question of money and Mom's security. It's blood. It's our link to the Island. It's where I want to come back to, to retire."

"So, you can't come either," Mary was downcast. "Until you retire?"

"I'm sorry, Mom. I sorta thought you might be relying on me, but I'm locked in in Dundas, I want you all to understand that. The clinic is just on its feet. I've still so many outstanding bills to pay."

Neil got up and moved to the teapot, filled his cup and shuffled toward the kitchen window. He stood there for a long while without turning around. St. Mary's Church where they went earlier in the day was in clear view to the south. Although it was almost dark, the last rays of the setting sun were still lighting its spire. He then returned to the table, ran his finger around the rim of his teacup, and, without looking up, began, "You know, during the service this morning I was thinking what a grand place this is for performance. I was thinking maybe I could make a go of it here with my music, playing solo or with a small chamber orchestra. I know, I was never much at farming, but if we could get a good hired man, someone to work with me for a while and train me, I'm sure I could handle it."

"But, what about the symphony and your commitments there?" Angus asked.

"I will have to go back and settle things and pick up my stuff in Toronto, but two weeks should do it. Do you think the MacKays would be willing to help out until then, Mom?" Neil said.

"My goodness, of course they would, and the other neighbours, too. It'll be grand to have you here with me, Neil. And performing almost next door in St. Mary's. And we'll have to start looking right away for a nice Island farm girl for you to marry." Mary's exuberance brought a hearty laugh to an otherwise sombre day. "Not exactly another Andrew MacDonald for the farm," she thought, "But he'll do."

Auction 45s

They were sitting around the kitchen table in Souris, playing auction 45s, the two older aunties home from the States
playing host. Auction 45s and straight 45s were the popular
games for whiling away an evening across the Island, before the
distractions of television replaced them. Straight 45s was a fast
game, often played for prizes of geese or ducks or mitts or socks
as fund-raisers for the church or some community need. As
many as ten could play at a table, and the first one to win three
games took the prize. Auction 45s was more complex, involving
bidding, working with partners, going up or down depending on
the outcome of the played hand, and requiring a score of 125 to
win. The best auction game had six players, three teams of two.
Because it was a longer game, and less intense than straight 45s,
it left more room for talk and sharing stories.

The elderly aunties from the States had grown up in Elmira, and they had an impressive memory of the people and events
of their generation. They were Katherine, a straight-as-an-ar-
row retired nurse, very much focused on the game, and exact
on historical dates and events; and Agnes, her witty sister, who
was less interested in the outcome of the game than she was in
telling and hearing a good story. Her memory was equally acute.
The remaining four at the table were family from the next generation, trying their best to keep the auction tradition alive, and
revelling in the stories the aunties interspersed into the game.
They were John, Adele, Ray, and Basil. Other guests in the house,
Fran and Doug, and Inez, sat on the sidelines, ready to sit in
for a hand or two and waiting to serve lunch after the auction
games, and to join in for a game of 45s after everyone ate.

"Well now, if yus are all ready I'll deal out the cards," said
John, riffing the deck.

He dealt the first hand, five cards each, four in the kitty,
and Katherine opened with a bid of twenty. Each one passed until the bidding came back to John. "I'll hold ya," he said. "Would
you hold 25?" said Katherine. "Yes." "Well I'll bid 25 then." "Hold
ya." John had the five, jack, and ace of diamonds, but the kitty

and three-card draw yielded him nothing, and his partner, Ray, was of small support. He went down to 25 in the hole, the other two teams garnering 10 points each. "Not a great way to start — in the hole," John said to Ray. "That sounds like the Daisy Dust Pan Man," said Agnes. "Oh, Aunt Agnes, can you tell us that story?" said Adele. "I love to hear it again." Agnes obliged, "Johnny Ben was pretty sick, and his wife, Cecilia, was expecting the priest to come to him. A knock came to the door, and she answered it with a lit blessed candle in her hand, but it wasn't the priest at all. 'I'm your Daisy Dust Pan Man', he said. 'Oh! your hole,' she blurted out and slammed the door in his face. She was some mad."

"Who was Johnny Ben, Ma?" John asked. "Was he George B's brother?" "Oh no, he was Old George's brother. George B had a brother Jim killed in the war, and two sisters Annie and Florence." "I thought you told me Jim was the fiddler?" "No, that was another Jim, none of that family, and he was only a half-assed fiddler, sure." "But we used to hear good fiddlin' coming from George B's house, Ma." "That was Johnny Ben. Lord, he was good on the fiddle."

"Whose deal?" "It's yours Basil, you're next to John," said Katherine. "You got the score down, Basil?" "Yes."

Basil dealt, and Adele, when it came to her, bid 25. "You shouldn't do that when the bid's going into your partner," chided Katherine. "Basil might have got it for twenty." But Adele had a strong hand of spades, except for the jack. When the hand was being played, Agnes reneged her jack off Adele's five, the best trump. "You didn't follow suit. You can't renege the jack off the five!" Katherine was sharp as a hawk. "Wish't I was thinking about Johnny Ben and the cats. I forgot to follow suit. Here, take it," she said, handing her the jack. "Johnny Ben had too many cats, so one day a stroller was on the road, and he gave him a junk of pork if he'd take them in a bag and drown them in South Lake. The stroller was going by Dan Murphy's, and Dan had a lot of mice around, so he gave the stroller a junk of pork for the bag of cats. Well, sir, in a day the cats were all back at Johnny Ben's, and there he was, stuck with them and out a roast of pork."

"Who were the strollers, Auntie?" asked Basil, who was home from Ottawa. "Well, there was no Old Age Pension or anything like that then, and these fellas would be traipsing the roads. George's Carrie would always take them in. That Carrie, she's sure to be in Heaven. She'd take in all the strollers on the road."

"*Osha Misha*," said Katherine invoking an old Gaelic saying from her youth.

It was now Ray's deal, but he was having trouble getting everyone's attention from the stories and the laughter. Everyone was jumping in with stories about the fella from up East who got his "pelvis broke," as the doctor told him, but he didn't know what a pelvis was. And about the fella who said his birthday was June 21. His parents didn't have a calendar, but they wouldn't be able to read it anyway, so when the priest was baptizing him and asked for his date of birth, they just said the twenty-first. They had no idea what date it was. Everyone was talking at once. "One at a time. One at a time." Katherine wanted to get on with the game.

When the bidding came around to John, he said, "None of this foolin' around, I bid 30 for 60." "That's not a proper bid. If Tommy Harris was here he wouldn't allow it. If you want to bid 30, you can, but can't double it," Katherine ruled. "Basil's the scorekeeper. Let him rule," said John. "It's okay with me, but if you go down, you'll go down 60 and that'll put you 85 in the hole," said Basil. "That's all right with me. You too, Ray?" John said to his partner, who nodded assent. He made the bid handily and garnered the 60 points. "It was in the hands of the gods. They told me I was goin' to get it," said John, slapping his fist down hard on the table.

"In the olden days they played with a lamp on the table and the men would come down with their fist when playing a winning card. They loved to see the lamp jump. It was dangerous. Sometimes the lamp would crash down and break. Lucky we have electricity," observed Katherine over the rim of her glasses.

"Speaking of the gods. Do you remember Nellie Roddie out in the Glen, who used to tell fortunes for a dollar, Katherine? Annie Conway had a shine for Leonard Charlie, so she went out to Nellie to get her teacup read, and Nellie said, 'Jump when you got the chance.' She's kind of eccentric, y'know," said Agnes. "Sure, she's a second cousin of our own," said Katherine. "Now it's coming out. The truth," teased Inez from the sidelines. "Yes, but her mother was a MacPhee," said Katherine. Inez was a MacPhee before she married Ray. "That puts you in your place," said Katherine.

"Nellie Roddie got it honest. Her uncle used to read heads," said Agnes. "The bumps, you know." "What do you call that?" "Phrenology," put in Doug from the kitchen. "It's an old science." "He probably didn't have a name for it, but he did it anyway," said Agnes. "Nellie's still living," said Katherine. "We'll have to get out to the Glen to see her while we're home."

The 60 points that John and Ray won became a solid basis for their going on to win the game. Besides, the tea was hot and the lunch was ready. Fran, Doug, and Inez brought the lunch to the table: fresh biscuits and cheese, egg and chicken sandwiches, and chocolate cake with boiled icing. "Who wants sugar?" Doug asked, "That's like old Sadie on the North Side. She'd say, 'Put shukers in your tea, dear, and put it 'round.'" said Agnes. "And Ky Gillis about going to a house where they were pretty stingy," said Katherine. "He told about it: 'A bar'l of sugar in the corner and not a bit of sweet'nin' in the tea.'" "I'll have a piece of that cheese," said Agnes. "As Dan Murphy would say, 'a bit of cheese will stand by me for the day.'"

Everybody dug in. "Too bad we couldn't have a song," said Adele. "If poor uncle Clum were here, he'd sing Cod Liver Oil for us. Remember he used to call it Cod Liver Ile?"

"Lord, but he had a great voice. He sang the Mass for the priest at St. Columba's every morning," said Katherine.

Ray told a story that he heard from Pete Holland. Charlie Ben was old and in his dotage, so Pete went up to visit him and to have a game of cards. After they'd played for an hour, Charlie said, "Now, Dotty, dear, you can bring us some tea and lunch." Dotty brought lunch, and Charlie, absent-minded as he was, played a biscuit and Pete put out one, too, and Charlie took it in. After a similar winning with a cookie, Charlie played another biscuit. But this time Pete covered it with a piece of cake, saying, "That's my trick, Charlie, the cake is best trump."

"I don't believe that story for a minute," said Adele. "Charlie was never in his dotage." "Well that's how Pete Holland told it," said Ray.

"The two plates of sandwiches are devoured," said Katherine. "So maybe we could clear the table and bring everyone in for a H.A." H.A. was a straight 45s game of elimination, the last one being the H.A. Doug hadn't played this form of the game before and asked, "What's the H.A.?" Fran, his wife, ever ladylike said, "It's the horse's rectum, dear." "The east end of a horse going west," chimed in John. "The horse's arse," said Agnes. "Pretend nothing." "There's one in every house," said Katherine, getting in the last word.

Words We've Outlived

Long before Trivial Pursuit, and well before TV, parlour games made for Sunday-night entertainment around the house. And, if truth be told, they weren't played in the parlour — it being reserved for the visit of the clergyman and for wakes — but in the kitchen, in close proximity to the range, especially in winter. Kitchens were large and could seat as many as twenty without crowding,

The MacPhee home in Clear Springs was a favourite place to come on Sunday nights. Mary Ellen had always a game worth the competition, and she and John Allan were the best of hosts. She had egg sandwiches and cake with boiled icing for lunch after the games, and John Allan had a supply of overproof rum in the pantry for the men. "The best the rumrunners had this year," he'd say with pride, holding up the bottle to show his friends its clarity.

This wasn't the first time they played it, but it was a favourite game for Mary Ellen, who had come to Clear Springs as a schoolteacher and only later had married John Allan and raised her family — all of whom had gone away — on the family farm. She was still a touch schoolmarmish, even after all those years. So, when everyone settled in — there were eight couples that night — Mary Ellen set the stage. "Four couples a side," she directed, "and we are going to see which team can come up with words and expressions that we've outlived.

"Whichever team comes up with the most words wins. I have a nice prize for the winning team, but you'll have to wait until the game is over to find out what it is." She got her glasses out of her apron pocket and donned them. She then took out a folded page of scribbler paper from the same pocket and unfolded it with a flourish.

"To get us started, I put together a wee verse this afternoon I'd like to read to you."

"Oh, I thought that paper was for keeping score," offered Angus MacCormack. "We halft' keep tally, y'know."

"I have a paper for that, too," said Mary Ellen, impatient to share her verse. "We'll keep score in good time. Here's my verse."

How do you qualify for an Islander
if you come here from away?
Even if you've lived here half a century,
You're still an émigré.
How do you tell the difference between an Islander
and someone from away?
It may not be as much in *what*
As in *how* we say.
They may say "owt" and "abowt" for out and about,
but we say it "oot" and "aboot."
They may put it this way:
"My wife puts ice in her whisky. Right?"
But we say it:
"Me woife puts oice in her whisky. Roight?"
They stain their wood with linseed oil,
and we use "b'iled linseed ile,"
and we're sure to eat our meat before it "spiles."
People come to our Island from far and near,
and, no matter where they come from,
whether it's the US or Korea,
when they're here with us, we say,
"We're desp'rate glad t'see ya."

Mary Ellen took a modest bow to the obligatory applause
of her neighbours.

"What's an *émigré*?" asked Sara MacCormack, who had
to leave school in Grade Four to look after the family when her
mother died in childbirth.

"That's just a fancy word for people who came from away,"
her husband, Angus, told her gently.

Mary Ellen then made up the teams: the MacCormacks
— "Angus, you'll be the captain" — Aiden and Jennie MacDonald, Kenny John Dan and Daisy MacDonald, Alex and Dorothy
MacKinnon. "That's your side. John Allan and I — John Allan,
you'll be our captain" — Peter and Ada MacPhee, D.A. and
Emma Gillis, and Willie and Mary MacInnis (a bachelor and
spinster, brother and sister, who looked after their ancient parents). "That's our side."

"Angus, your team can start first. Try for things around the farm." That was easy enough. They named *hay barracks, stukes, ciles of hay, dump rake, single tree, brace and bit, hay fork, one-horse plough,* and *"hit the hay."* "Does 'hit the hay' count?" "No, and your time's up. Your team's turn, John Allan."

They came up with *taters, blue stone, beater digger, krupper, dump cart, stripper, orkin, box sled,* and *"poor man's fertilizer"* before their time ran out.

"That's nine to eight for our team," Mary Ellen entered the score.

"What about taters?" asked Kenny John Dan. "'Member that old song about taters? 'Did y'ever see the divil with his little wooden shovel diggin' taters in the garden with his tail curled up? But the taters were so big that the divil couldn't dig, so he ran around the garden with his tail curled up.'" Kenny had a good voice and loved to sing.

"Taters qualify," ruled Mary Ellen. "Shall we move on to things around the home? John Allan, your team's turn to start." They listed *latch key, put a stick of second growth in the stove, base burner, ising glass, slop pail,* and *washstand soap.* "Remember John Andrew goin' to the store and askin', 'Gimme some of that washstand soap. I'm tired of shavin' with P and G.' Har, P and G was still pretty draggy on the razor."

"That's six. What about you, Angus?" His team came up with *gruel, bloomers, corset staves, gum rubbers, overhauls,* and *petticoats.* "That's six, too. It gives us a tie on that one," said Angus.

Kenny John Dan broke into another song: "'Leanin' on the old slop pail, in the old corral.' It was pretty uncomfortable, but it beat goin' to the backhouse on cold winter nights, I'll tell ya."

"Let's move on. The next group is open-ended. Just say the old words as they hit you. Angus, your turn to start," Mary Ellen directed.

"This oughta be easy," said Angus, inviting his team. They began with fishing: *single-stroke motor, hand linin', skiff;* then *mud digger,* and "How about *basket social, tea party,* and *scoff*?"

said Daisy. "And *flyin' axehandles* for summer complaint," she added. Aiden, who owned an old Model A Ford, entered *"crankin' the spark"* and a diagnosis the garageman gave him when the car broke down: "The nibblin' pin is off the bobblin' rod."

"Not bad," said Angus, "twelve if y'count both *flyin' axehandles* and *summer complaint*. We'll hafta go some to beat ya." His team got right down to *shank's mare, crow piss, groik, clart, pismire, scriss, the probs, a wee doc'n'doris, shake, teddy grum, drop of the craithar, a jillick*. That, too, was twelve.

"That's the works," said Mary Ellen. "Looks like our team beat you by one."

"Time for a *jillick* of rum," said John Allan, inviting the men to the pantry for a *drop of craithar.*

"And I'll set down a pot of good North Side tea to go with the lunch." Mary Ellen took the lifter and put the score sheet into the flaming second growth in the range. "It was really a tie if we accept 'hit the hay,'" she said, "I think we should." All agreed.

"But what about the prize?" said Ada. "What was it anyways? I'm awful curious."

"You'll have to wait 'til next Sunday, when I'll put it up again," said Mary Ellen.

After Leaving the Road, Clara Writes Back

Dear Olive,

I am up by the YMCA in the blue house. I was at Charlotte Residence a short time, but it was all older women and you couldn't use the phone. I was up on the third floor, so I found that hard on the wind, and you couldn't have company there. McQuaids's was a nice place, but he said my room was too expensive, and I'd have to share it, so I left. I put my name in at a seniors' home but got sick and gave that up, so I'm older now. I love this place. They do my laundry and get my meals. I've lived in so many places, I know a lot of people.

My only aunt that is living had her ninetieth birthday Sunday, so the family was all there, and we went to Smitty's, so we had our choice of eats. The cheapest was steak, so I took that. It was $8, but it sure was well-cooked. I took a lot of pictures, so I hope they turn out good. I must pick them up Friday. My cousin died about two weeks ago, then the next week her husband died, so that was a sad time. I went to the doctor. He says I'm in A-one shape, so that's good to know. I suppose your family is all grown-up now.

I went down to your brother's wake the other night, but it was full to the back and my friend was with me. She gets mad very easy and she wanted to go to the K-mart. I was very disappointed, but I went with her anyways. I went there in the afternoon, but I waited at the mall and she never showed up. She said she had a sore back, but if she would walk that far that night I don't think it was too bad. Anyways, I walked out to the funeral yesterday morning. When I was at Rochford Square, I had a boyfriend for a while. One night he said, "I'm not coming back no more." And he stole $60 from my purse. He was something, eh? He has a new woman now — my friend, but not anymore. He lives with her.

I had so many clothes I never wore, so I sent them to the Salvation Army. A girl here gives me a lot of nice tops, but her slacks are too tight. I am quite fleshy now. I got my hair washed and set Saturday. They won't put it up here like the other places did. I go to church twice on Sunday. I joined since I came to town, but I don't know if I'm any better or not. My room is small, so I'm sort of crowded, but as long as a person is happy is the main thing. I guess I have no more news this time. I know you are busy with all the family. Bye-bye.

Clara

Coasting

Coasting was a favourite winter pastime at St. Peter's Bay. Surrounded by hills on every side leading into the village, it made for choose-your-hill coasting. Since cars were stored away for the winter, roads being left unploughed, sledders had nothing to contend with other than the occasional horse and driving sleigh.

Most of the sleds were homemade, their runners shod with discarded driving-wagon rims, cut to fit, and screwed into the runners. They were best in light snow cover, but not terribly good on ice, as they slewed out of control. When the hills were icy, the best sled was the commercially made sled, built with narrow, skate-like runners, and having a steering bar on the front. They could reach upwards of thirty miles an hour on glib ice and were still controllable. Still, only the kids whose parents could afford them had them, and they were the envy of those who had to compete using homemade sleds.

In our family, we had one of each variety to share among the four of us. My older brother, naturally, had first dibs on the better sled, the rest of us getting an occasional turn. We didn't object, thinking it better to learn the art on the slower vehicle, but we took the speedster when we got the chance. That was how I met my Waterloo.

On a magnificent January day, following a silver thaw and a healthy covering of sleet, the hillsides glistened like polished silver sparkling in the brilliant sunlight. I beat my brother home from school, secured the speedster sled, and headed for the sloping farm fields beyond our home. Struggling under slippery footing, I made it to the top of the slope and prepared to take the long, fast run to the bottom. What I didn't take into account was the barbed wire fence running straight across the lower field.

Unless you've experienced it, you can hardly imagine the excitement of coming hellbent for leather down a long icy slope on a flimsy sled. The rush of air, the releasing elation, the speed of light, but then the impending doom of the barbed wire fence — too soon.

I crouched as low as possible to avoid being caught up. Steering away was out of the question. Rolling off the sled at this rate of speed didn't seem an option. If you want to know the truth, I was afraid to roll.

My crouch was not enough to limbo under the lowest strand. One of its barbs scored a direct hit on my forehead, splitting me from eyebrow to hairline. Fortunately, my next-door neighbour was Dr. Roddie MacDonald. He stitched me up so well that, years later, the scar disappeared.

After that experience, I left the speedster sled to my older brother and was quite satisfied to coast on the more cumbersome homemade one.

The National Pastime

My brother, Bill, was a hockey nut. From the time he was five years old, he couldn't get enough of skating and playing hockey. Early on, he would pad his feet with three pairs of heavy wool-knit socks to get into a pair of size six skates several sizes too big for him — the only pair we had — and strike out for the frozen Bay in front of our house. One mid-November morning, after an unseasonable freeze-up the previous night, he was on the thin skin of Bay ice at daylight. I watched him from the shore as he took feathering strides on the glassy surface, an ominous cracking accompanying his strides. The ice was gone by mid-afternoon.

By the time ice came for good, he'd be out there for an hour before school and then, after school, until dark, darting, stick-handling, feinting, and shooting into his homemade net. When the snow covered the ice, he was the first out there to clear away a rink. After he'd finish, a gaggle of other boys from the village swooped down to play on the cleared surface. Rather than complain, he welcomed the competition.

They would don their skates and stuff Eaton's catalogues into their long stockings for shin-guards, pick up their warped hockey sticks, and be ready to join in the game. Bill would already have on his homemade pads and his skates, sharpened by the local blacksmith to give him an edge. The Griffin boys were too poor to have skates, so they played in their "lumberman's rubbers." Abandoned rubber boots served as goal posts, and, because goalies had no gear, lifting the puck was against the rules. This rule appealed especially to Bill, giving him the practice of stick-handling and deking the goalie out of position and slipping the puck behind him.

The only fights that ever happened were when players like Charlie Mullin, whose old stick was so warped that he couldn't help lifting his shots, caught the goalie in the chest or the belly or, God forbid, in the groin, and had the goalie come at him wielding his stick like a tomahawk. Or, if Abbie Griffin's brother, Basie, caused a goal by the opposition and incurred his big brother's wrath. Abbie, even in his rubber boots, was as good as most of the better players. Basie was a sulker. Bill, meanwhile, dipsy-doodled like Max Bentley and always scored the most goals.

He also had a small rink in the backyard of our home, diligently flooded from the hand pump in the pantry, for playing shinny and practising his shot. For him, Saturday nights were a special time. Everyone else tuned to "Hockey Night in Canada" out of Toronto on the national radio network. But Foster Hewitt's "Hello Canada…," intoned in his nasal Ontario dialect, was not for Bill. Rather he tuned into CHNC New Carlisle, the only Maritime station to carry his beloved Montreal Canadiens on the air — in French, Réné Lecavalier's excited voice announcing over the roars of the crowd, "Johnny Gagnon lance! Brimseck bloque! Morenz lance −o−o−o un but!"

On Monday in school, Bill would enter the scoring summaries of all weekend games into the blank pages of his school texts. Going back to those old books stashed for years in the attic, one finds a neat-handed history of the original six NHL teams in the 1930s and early 40s, recording goals, assists, penalties, and shots on goal. Years later, when he was a sportswriter for the *Patriot*, he was constantly on call — frequently late at night from a local watering hole — to settle an argument about sports history. His early preoccupation had given him an encyclopedic memory for facts and statistics, and he was never wrong.

Playing hockey on the vast expanse of St. Peter's Bay had its advantages. A good skater and puck carrier could skirt the opposition as widely as he wished, drawing them well out of position, and then make a sharp turn towards the goalie, abandoned by his defenders, now a sitting duck for any deft shooter. The play was one of Bill's favourite plays.

When he got to St. Dunstan's and turned out for the hockey team, he met an entirely new challenge. Playing in a rink, within the confinement of boards, was worlds away from pond hockey. Besides, all of the other players had had years of experience in the various ice barns across the Island and elsewhere. What was he to do, confined as he was to going up and down the ice on the right wing, digging the puck out of corners, and being checked closely by his opposite number? Here his shooting practices from our backyard rink came in handy. No longer confined to not lifting the puck, he developed a patented, accurate, high shot off the right wing to the upper corner of the net. The only other player to use such a shot habitually in his repertoire was Ron Ellis of the Toronto Maple Leafs.

Bill was never a star on his college team. That term was reserved for such stellar performers as teammates Cart Mac-Donald, Bert Methot, and Joe Maher. But he was a steady performer, and he scored many key goals to contribute to the team's success. His finest hour in hockey was as a member of the storied St. Dunstan's Saints Maritime Collegiate Hockey Champions in 1947. Even making McGill University team as a graduate student, a team with several future NHLers, didn't top that accomplishment.

His uncanny ability to get his wing shot past the opposition goalies brought him the nickname "Fluke" from his classmate, Johnny Bradley. Bradley also applied it to Bill's equal ability to guess what questions were going to be on the course examinations and to study for those only. And those, he was rarely off the mark, and his predictions were in constant demand from his classmates, especially those who were more hooligan than scholar.

His playing days behind him, Bill gave over his time to coaching youngsters, heading the PEI Minor Hockey Association and the PEI Sports Hall of Fame, and writing his widely read daily sports column in the Charlottetown *Patriot*. From our youth, he and I were avid readers of Andy O'Brien and Elmer "Fergie" Ferguson's sports columns in the Montreal *Gazette*. Bill's own columns later impressed these two paragons of the art. They became close friends with him and were among those responsible for his eventually being given the National Sports Writer of the Year Award in Toronto.

Despite a long, painful siege of cancer, Bill continued to write his column until the final months of his life. Part of his daily fare was watching "Sports Desk" on The Sports Network (TSN). The morning he died, he was obviously sinking fast and, being the only one with him at the time, the solemnity of the moment moved me to shut off "Sports Desk."

"Turn that back on," he ordered. He was dead two hours later, no doubt to be greeted on the other side by Elmer Ferguson, Andy O'Brien, and a host of long-gone heroes of the NHL's original six teams.

Dance with the one who brought you.

If you lose, say little; if you win, say less.

Uncle Gus

A. A. Aylward's Furniture Exchange stood at 222 Richmond Street in Charlottetown, immediately across the street from St. Paul's stately Anglican Church, and next door to Jimmy Duffy's confectionery store — a front for his back-room speakeasy.

As a boy, I sometimes spent overnights at the home attached to the business, a guest of Uncle Gus and Aunt Jen, the latter my father's sister. A favourite memory was to awaken early in the morning to the clip-clop sounds of the horse-drawn milk delivery, followed soon afterwards by the church bells calling people to early services.

Aunt Jen was a generous, intelligent woman, who made the best apple pies you ever threw a lip over. Uncle Gus was my idol. Tall, at least to my slow growth, and spare, he had the brightest eyes and kindest face. He was an expert fly-fisher and, as I became adept at rowing a punt, he brought me with him to all his favourite fishing spots, the best being Larkin's Mill Pond in Selkirk. The waterway ran deep for about a mile beyond the head of the dam. I would row along slowly, while he stood back aft and cast hither and yon until he got several rises. We would then drop anchor and both of us would cast until we made several strikes and then move on to the next promising hole. We always bagged our limit and would return home well after dark in his half-ton Plymouth, the punt tucked firmly in the truck's box.

Our hours together gave me a chance to hear his story. Orphaned in his early youth, Gus ran errands around town to eke out his survival. He delivered groceries, ran messages, raked leaves, and did every odd job that people offered him. Being a waif about the streets, he got to know many people, especially the prominent merchants for whom he made deliveries. One generous merchant got him a job as a deck hand on a local schooner that shipped back and forth from the Island to Pictou, Nova Scotia. He loved life at sea and, in due course, captained the schooner. By then, Prohibition was in full bloom.

Two of Charlottetown's most prominent citizens, merchants whom he had served since his street days, invited him to use the schooner (which they owned) for rum-running outside the twelve-mile limit. This he did without qualms of conscience, and, for three years, business was highly profitable for the silent partners. Uncle Gus's only remuneration was a modest salary.

In due course, the long hand of the law reached out, impounded the schooner, and laid charges against Uncle Gus, whereupon with advice and funding from his mentors, he and Aunt Jen fled to Florida and awaited the protection of the statute of limitations. That done, they returned to the Island and, for being tight-lipped about his silent partners who were now the very elite of Charlottetown society, they rewarded him by setting him up in a second-hand furniture business.

The business turned out to be a bonanza. Still emerging out of the Great Depression, people were financially unable to buy new furnishings. Uncle Gus and Aunt Jen went mostly to Montreal to buy used goods and shipped them by railroad back to Charlottetown. In an adjacent warehouse, he and his two employees sanded and varnished them to make them look like new. They branched out to everything from needles to anchors — dish sets, cutlery, and knick-knacks. Uncle Gus turned out to be an astute businessman; his powers of observation and assessment of what customers were able to pay were flawless. He often spoke to them in a whisper, making them feel taken into his full confidence.

On one occasion, a young man came into the shop with a fiddle tucked under his coat wanting to sell it. As it turned out, the man had borrowed the instrument from my father with no intention of returning it. Uncle Gus recognized the fiddle as my father's, but, pitying the young man, made him an offer, bought the fiddle, and offered to return it to my dad. My dad admitted that he didn't play well and suggested that his brother-in-law sell it to get his money back — which he did, at a substantial profit.

With the end of the Second World War and the closing down of the air-training stations on the Island, Uncle Gus purchased much of the furniture from the air bases at close-out prices, and made enough profit from that to retire from the business and devote his full energies to harvesting oysters and fly-fishing for trout. By then, the second-hand furniture business was on the wane, so his decision to sell was another astute move.

After his retirement, hardly a day went by that he didn't fly-fish at all of his favourite haunts: Larkin's Pond, McAskill River, the Indian Bridge, Billy Ben's at Dingwell's Mill, and the Midgell and Morell Rivers. When free from my summer job, I accompanied him. His patience to await the movement of fish was legendary, and he was a firm believer in the effect of the sol-lunar periods on their feeding habits.

Only once did he show a disinclination to cast his line. We were at McAskill River where we had to trudge through a marsh to get to the flowing water. He had schooled me on how to do it: "Under each bullrush protruding from the water is a firm root," he'd say. "You step from root to root. Otherwise you'll go over your boots." I made my way to the river but noticed that he remained on the hillside, his head in his hands and his gear still unarranged. I came back to him and noticed that he was pretty green around the gills. He then told me that he and Aunt Jen had made several bottles of cherry wine and stored it in the cellar, that she was away on a shopping trip, and he had drunk it all the previous day. "So, how are you going to explain that to Aunt Jen when she gets home?" I asked. "Oh, I'll tell her that all the bottles popped under the pressure," he whispered. He always whispered when telling a white lie. "Let's go home," I said, "I don't think the fish are rising today anyway." We left. I drove.

I recently asked my eldest sister what were her best memories of Uncle Gus and Aunt Jen, and she answered immediately, "Bananas!" Childless themselves, they came to our house almost every Sunday. When we were children eating our ginger snaps, we'd eat them in the shape of two people riding in a half-ton truck, and make motoring sounds, "Uncle Gus and Aunt Jen are coming. Rhum-rhum-rhum, here they come." Uncle Gus always brought a bunch of bananas — still on the stock. They were something the country stores still didn't carry.

He won our hearts with them. And at Christmas he brought a crate of oranges shipped from a contact he still had from his Florida refuge days.

Uncle Gus lived to a ripe old age. I was with him when he died quietly in the Charlottetown Hospital. In his last conscious moments, a nurse came into the ward with the night lunch cart. Seeing his condition, she went to the adjoining bed where a crusty old man from Dromore — more commonly known as Little Hell — lay. "Could I give you some apple juice?" she asked him, "Naw," he said. When she left, he announced, "If it was shine she had, I'd be glad to have taken a drop." Uncle Gus's eyes twinkled, no doubt thinking that if it was still the Prohibition, he'd be willing to supply the old man. Moments later, his own time came.

The White Hope

George Leslie was no Davie Crockett. But he and his brother Harry were among the last Islanders to come across a bear in the woods on the Souris Line Road. They didn't shoot the bear; they had axes rather than rifles. Instead, they nervously played dead, and the bear nosed them and moved off. But George Leslie went on to become a legend on the Island, not as a hunter of bears but as a heavyweight boxer.

Ring people were casting about across North America to find the great "white hope" to unseat Joe Louis from the heavyweight crown, and for a while they thought Leslie might be the one. After all, the Island had produced Wild Bert Kenny, so another great find was not unreasonable. Leslie had size, strength, and stamina, and an enviable knockout record. He had stood up well against a good stable of Island boxers, such an Benny Binns, Irish Leo Kelly, and Danny MacCormack. He had, as a matter of fact, the shortest non-fight victory in boxing history. The match was held in Souris, the home ground of both him and his opponent, Lloyd MacInnis. When the bell sounded for round one, Leslie came charging like a bull across the ring, scaring MacInnis so much that he jumped through the ropes and took off for the dressing room, refusing to return.

Leslie was being handled by Big Jim Pendergast, himself a formidable challenger in the earlier Dempsey era. Big Jim had Leslie on a rigorous training regimen: five miles a day of road work and two hours in the gym, sparring, skipping, and working out on the light and heavy punching bags. My uncle, Gus Aylward, a former seaman and sports enthusiast, was in a supporting role. What that meant, essentially, was that Gus boarded and fed Leslie and Pendergast, the latter a first cousin of Aylward's wife, my Aunt Jen. I first met Leslie at their home on Richmond Street. A boy of six, I had come to Charlottetown with my mother on the daily train, and we stopped in at my aunt's for the noon meal. I noticed that my Aunt Jen had two large roast chickens in the oven, pots of vegetables, and apple pie. The dining room table was set for six.

At noon, Uncle Gus, Big Jim, and the "white hope" re-turned from Leslie's road work. Leslie was sweat-soaked, had a huge white towel over his head, and shuffled about, shadow boxing. Then everyone sat into the table. The mystery of the two roast chickens soon resolved itself. One chicken was for Leslie; and the other, for the rest of us. The way he went at that chicken was all the evidence I needed to explain the wisdom of Lloyd MacInnis's retreat from the ring before the bell in Souris.

I remember having a certain queasiness in my stomach and not being able to bring my hand to fork to mouth. I felt a mixture of fear and awe. The others at the table did not appear to share my temerity. I couldn't, however, resist Aunt Jen's apple pie; I would risk annihilation for that.

Leslie had a fight coming up the next week, and promot-ers from the States were to be there to see for themselves his promise as a world-class challenger. It was at this fight that he was discovered to have a "glass jaw." Opponents could flail away at his stomach and upper body without drawing so much as a flinch, but a sharp blow to the chin felled him like an oak. That tragic flaw in his makeup, now discovered and exploited by op-ponents, snuffed out his dream of being the great "white hope." Big Jim, another of his many ventures behind him, returned to his farm; Uncle Gus, to his second-hand furniture business; and George Leslie, his legendary days over, went off to Toronto where he was for years the uniformed doorman at the King Ed-ward Hotel.

My own interest in boxing began on that day at Richmond Street. Everyone tuned in on radio to the Friday night fights at Madison Square Garden or the old St. Nicholas Arena in New York. The blow-by-blow commentaries of Don Dunphy and Bill Corum, the flamboyant language of the ring announcer Harry Ballow: "And may the better contestant emerge triumphant"; or, when introducing the middleweight Kid Gavilan: "The classy, clever, courageous, crowd-pleasing, Cuban champion, ladies and gentlemen, Kid Gavilan," all commentaries paint-ing images of boxing heroes to shorten the distance between New York and PEI, bringing us listeners to ringside. Right from the opening announcement: "The organist and vocalist, Miss

Gladys Gooding, and now-please-our national anthem," to the rapid-fire descriptions by Dunphy of Beau Jack's famed and devastating "bolo punch," a wind-up uppercut that stopped many an antagonist.

Introduced early in my life to the Friday night fights, my first experience was the short-lived, much hullabalooed return bout between Joe Louis and Max Schmeling, where much more was at stake than the fight itself. This time was the meteoric rise of Hitler and his master race ideology, and the aftermath of Hitler's snubbing of Jesse Owens's heroics in the recent Berlin Olympics. None of this was lost on the pre-fight hype.

We still hadn't a radio at our house, so we had to adjourn to my uncle's — my father with sons in tow — to tune in. I was a mere child of eight at the time (June 20, 1938), and, because the fight did not begin until after 11 P.M., I was struggling against being overtaken by Morpheus. I went to the pantry pump to see if a drink of cold water would freshen me up, and, when I returned, the fight was over. Just like that, Louis felled Schmeling in the first round.

That victory made Joe Louis a culture hero in the western world. Still, the search for a white hope went on even to the extent of scouting our own George Leslie from the Island. Undeterred, Louis went on to defend his title twenty-five times and to take time out to enlist in the Second World War. He dispatched twenty of those opponents by knockout, and I cannot recall missing one of those fights on radio. After each fight, Bill Corum did the post-fight interview, asking, "How did you finish him off, Joe?" And Louis, in his quiet way, would mumble, "A lef' hook and a right cross." That was his trademark, always the same deadly combination undoing the likes of Two-ton Tony Galento, Arturo Godoy, and Tami Moriello, the last surviving less than a minute before the "Brown Bomber" poleaxed him.

My interest in boxing was further abetted by a neighbour, Carl Anderson. He had a boat-building shop where he built small yachts for pleasure craft. He also subscribed to *Ring Magazine* and had stacks of back issues on a shelf. While he worked, steaming boards of Nova Scotia pine for moulding the hull and crafting the knees, he schooled me on boxing history, past and present. A flyweight of a man, standing little more than five feet tall, he spoke with an animated stammer. Never a boxer himself, he did have one distinguished mark on his escutcheon. As one of the last of the Island's Provincial Police — before the RCMP came — he had singlehandedly boarded a rum-running vessel and placed the hostile and threatening crew under arrest. Too small to be transferred to the RCMP, he turned to yacht and ice-boat building. He'd tell me, " J-j-joe Gans. Now there was a fighter. The b-b-best p-p-pound for p-p-pound fighter ever, e-e-even tho' he was just a l-l-lightweight. His f-f-fight with B-b-battling Nelson was one of the g-g-greatest of all time." He added vivid descriptions of the Manassas Mauler, Jack Dempsey, and his fights with Luis Angel Firpo (whom he called "F-f-fripo") and Georges Carpentier (whom he called "C-c-carpenter," feeling a professional empathy with the name). He also followed the local scene through the daily *Patriot* and was, for a time, excited to the point of exclamation about George Leslie, our own aspirant to the heavyweight rankings.

I even went on to do some boxing myself, especially at college, and despite having a head full of dreams, I was never very good at it. I was a sucker for a feint, dropping my guard, and getting hit every time flush on the nose. With George Leslie, it was his "glass jaw"; with me it was a too-prominent nose. Still, sometimes in my dreams I hear the deep sonorous voice of Bill Corum doing his commercial on those Friday night fights from Madison Square Garden: "...brought to you by Gillette Blue Blades, with the sharpest edges ever honed."

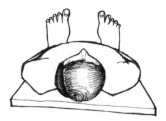

Boarding House

If your pay was only $19.20 a week in 1944, you'd better get yourself a cheap place for bed and board. That's where Ma Manglow came in handy. She had this big flat-faced house sitting next to the sidewalk on Fitzroy Street, right in the heart of Charlottetown. She had three large bedrooms for boarders — three to a room — and space for her daughter, son-in-law, their infant, and for her ne'er-do-well son, as well as for herself and her husband. The husband, John Manglow, had one glass eye and not much more vision out of the other. No such thing as permanent disability in those years, so he sat on the bench in front of the house and conversed with the passers-by, or else he kept a tally on the number of callers who came to Mrs. B. and her lovely daughter next door. Mrs. B. told him proudly that they ran an escort service for visiting dignitaries. John, who was without schooling, would have to ask the boarders at suppertime, "What's a dignitary?" And they'd say, "Those are the kinds of fellas who dig around at nighttime — mostly in cemeteries."

"I'll be damned. That's why her and her daughter goes out every night." John seemed satisfied with the answer.

Mrs. Manglow ran the whole operation. She had that stocky, strong-armed body of a girl who grew up on the farm on PEI and had to do more barnwork than housework. She moved the whole family to town after John lost an eye to a cantankerous knot in felling a tree in the woods. "I can't do all the work by meself, with John half-blind and Jake on the run half the night, and Maggie up the stump," she said over tea to her next-door neighbour. "So it's off to Charlottetown. I'm still on the near side of sixty, y'know."

That's where we came across her. She had two rules for accepting boarders: first, they had to be male, and second, they had to be labourers. That made for nine guy boarders of various shapes and sizes.

The board was $9 a week, straight up and payable on Saturdays — $8 if you went home for Sunday. For that, Ma fed everybody breakfast in the early morning, dinner in the evening, and packed a lunchpail for each. Dinner was the Island variety: lots of boiled dinners, meat, turnips, and carrots — all you could eat — with fresh-baked bread, butter, cake, and tea. And wherever she got the idea of serving pie after a breakfast of bacon, eggs, and toast, none of us ever knew; it wasn't something we experienced at home. But every morning Ma had a hot, fresh pie on the table. It was a welcome innovation.

Her family got the same fare as us boarders. They ate after the table was cleared. Maggie, her infant on her hip, helped Ma with dinner and cleaned up after meals. Maggie's husband, Joe, worked long hours as a lineman with Maritime Electric. Jake, when he wasn't in jail for being drunk and disorderly, did nothing to help.

"I don't know what we're gonna do about Jake." Ma was up to her elbows in the sinkful of dishes. Maggie was drying. "Maybe if we'd stayed on the farm out in Peakes, he wouldn't have such a wild crowd to hang around with like those Eastenders."

"Well, I wish't he'd soon grow up," said Ma.

"Ma, he's thirty. He's past growin' up," said Maggie.

That was after suppertime. The boarders were out of the house already. The MacAulay brothers, who were older and worked for the telephone company, were off to the Legion to play cribbage and drink beer, something they did every night of the week. They were from Cardigan but didn't have a home to go to, their parents being long dead. The Costello boys, cousins from Kelly's Cross, were off to dancing lancers at the Benevolent Irish Society dancehall downtown. My brother, Bill, and I joined our friends in front of the Roxy restaurant to watch the parade of girls going by, hoping to be picked up or at least to be seen. The street was called Dizzy Block because the girls (and sometimes boys, too) went round and round the block all night. When we tired of girl-watching, we'd enter the restaurant and have a BLT and milk before going home to Ma's boarding house. Except for this night.

Billy McNeely came running from his place in the East End to say there was a big fight going on back there. So we all rushed to the scene. Lo and behold, there was Jake and three of his scoundrels trying to take on Irish Leo Kelly and his brother Crazy George. It was no contest: Irish Leo was a ferocious professional boxer, and George was a terror to evildoers, recently committed by Magistrate Martin to "keep the peace" for his propensity for lying in wait and waylaying young RAF trainees on their way back to the air base from a night out in Charlottetown.

Jake, the instigator, took the severest beating and was left bleeding and unconscious on the sidewalk by his retreating comrades. Leo and George simply walked away. My brother, two friends, and I struggled home to Fitzroy Street with Jake.

Ma met us at the door and ordered us to carry him to the kitchen couch. Next, she set a pot of water to boil and went to her sideboard and brought out several soft towels. Jake was still out cold when she began to swab him with hot towels. His nose was askew and Ma observed that he was missing more teeth to complement an already toothless foremouth. Both eyebrows were split, and from the moans and groans he made while we transported him, we suspected his ribs were either badly bruised or broken.

Jake's eyes flicked open and he slurred, "What're you doin' here, Ma?"

"I don't know about me, but you're lucky these lads got you here is all. You could as easy as bled to death out there in the street."

Ma got an old bedsheet and tore it in long strips. She had us sit Jake up and remove his shirt — torn as it was, it made an easy job. She then wound the sheet around the ribcage, tight as a burial shroud, and laid him back on the couch.

"The pain is sumptin' awful," Jake moaned. "I need a drink. Y'got any shine around here?"

"You're home now, not at some dive on Dorchester Street. Y'know we don't keep shine around here," Ma was curt.

"Help me to me feet," Jake said to us, "I gotta go fer a drink." We got him upright.

"Will you go follow him to see if he's all right?" Ma pleaded with us. We declined, "He's on his own now, Ma."

Jake shuffled on down Fitzroy Street, rounded the corner,

and that's the last we or anybody else ever saw of him. The MacAulay boys suggested that he took the 7 A.M. train to the other side and was "probably working in the lumber woods in the Miramichi." That was as much to console Ma as anything else. My brother and I were just as sure that he was done in on Dorchester Street and is now well-anchored on the floor of Charlottetown Harbour. But we didn't share our theory with Ma or the rest of her family.

From that day onward, Ma went about her work in a daze. She did the basics, but we no longer had fresh bread and cake for dinner, nor pie for breakfast. Her husband, John, took up his daily place on the bench in front of the house as if nothing had happened.

The Man Who Was a Racehorse

A few summers ago, Ben Johnson, the disgraced Canadian Olympic sprinter, came to Charlottetown Driving Park to pit himself against a trotter and an auto. He placed third, but raised some money for charity. People generally thought of this race as bizarre as the movie *They Shoot Horses, Don't They?* But they also thought of the event as unique and historic.

Johnson, however, was not the first man to break from the starting gate at the CDP. That honour belonged to one Joe O'Brien. Whoa now, a note of explanation is necessary to distinguish between two Joe O'Briens: the first, the legendary racehorse breeder and driver who got his start on the Island and then went on to be at the top of the sport in North America. A small, compact man with horsemanship in his gene pool, this Joe O'Brien parlayed racing into fame and fortune and is memorialized in the Halls of Fame of the industry and of PEI.

Then there was the other Joe O'Brien. This Joe was a chap around town, the earlier counterpart of what we now call "street persons." I doubt if Joe ever left the Island, let alone Charlottetown. He was also, as they say, "a few pickles short of a barrel." That admitted, Joe was a permanent and prominent fixture at the annual Old Home Week race card at the CDP.

Those were the days before the automotive starting gate, when the horses had to "score" in such a way that they had to come abreast to the starting line. If one or more of the horses bolted to the front at the point, they would incur the ire of the official starter, Dr. Dougan. Sometimes it would take as many as three false starts and recalls before they would get it right — making for a long afternoon's racing card, taking as long as hours to complete.

As the racers thundered abreast to the starting line, the warning voice of Dr. Dougan would ring over the loudspeaker, "Don't be down, Mr. Larabee! Don't be down! Pull up! Pull up!" And if Larabee repeated his bolt at the wire on the restart, Dougan would holler, "Mr. Larabee, that'll cost you ten!" Ten dollars was a hefty fine, when the purse for the winner was rarely more than a hundred dollars.

The stellar presentation of the week was the "Free For All Trot and Pace," a three-heat event giving bragging rights for the year to the winner, whether it be Tip Abbe, or Anti-aircraft, or Vella la Vella, or one of the Budlongs. If Joe O'Brien was home to drive in the race, you could be assured that he would be the favourite at the parimutuel windows whatever horse he reined. And he rarely let his betters down.

But before the feature presentation, horses were paraded to the stand, and on the track would emerge the other Joe O'Brien — to the cheers of the crowd. Dressed in an ankle-length, heavy open overcoat, baggy pants, and outsized work boots, Joe would go to the starting line and run like a leprechaun past the grandstand to the quarter pole, looking for all the world like the classical clown Jimmy Kelly — without the painted face and bulbous nose.

This Joe O'Brien, unlike Johnson, didn't attempt to outrace any horse. He simply put on a show and added to the excitement of the event.

After Old Home Week, Joe went back to his usual obscurity, until Christmastime when he made his next annual appearance. On Christmas Eve, CFCY, "The Friendly Voice of the Maritimes," brought Joe in to wish everyone a Happy Christmas. He began with the Lieutenant-Governor, then the Premier and the Mayor, and finally brought greetings to everyone across the Island.

Whereas Ben Johnson was never a part of Island heritage, both Joe O'Brien, the racing driver, and Joe O'Brien, the wannabe racehorse, were etched in Islanders' memories and it's hard to say which Joe brought them more joy.

Dies Irae

Fr. D. P. Croken wasn't cut out for higher education. Oh, he was bright enough, but he had Jansenistic tendencies, and too rigid a conscience. And he looked the part of a Jansenist, too. He had a long angular face, thin unsmiling lips, and a permanent frown. As the college rector in 1924, he cracked the whip too hard for minor misdemeanours on a group of graduating students from St. Dunstan's, denying them graduation, and that was his undoing. He got farmed out to the parishes.

In the parishes he was especially good for funerals, having that constant funereal look about him. In the confessional box he reverted to his scrupulous ways about sin, issuing immense penances.

His fellow priests tried to lighten him up a bit. Fr. Willie Monoghan, a wiry little man addicted to horse racing, thought bringing D. P. to the free-for-all final at the Provincial Exhibition one way of bringing him out of himself. The horses were thundering along at the five-eighths pole, and the crowd was already on its feet cheering them along. D. P., still seated, nudged Fr. Willie and said, "Father, did you ever say Mass in Mt. Ryan?" Willie decided then and there that horse-racing wouldn't do the trick, even though he had driven all the way from Alberton to take D. P. along.

Fr. Willie Monaghan was himself anything but rigid. He'd bet anything down to his Roman collar on the horses, and he drove his car as if he were in the Indy 500, without even bothering to think of any moral implications. He was so short that people would say, "If you see a car speeding down the western road without a driver, that's Fr. Monoghan." But when it came to reciting his obligatory daily office, even he was conscientious. On one occasion while driving home from the races nearing midnight, he had to stop by the roadside and go out to the front of his car to finish off his office in the headlights. An RCMP officer came along and stopped to ask what was his trouble. "I have to read this book," said Fr. Willie. "It must be an awful good book," said the officer, muttering. "Now I've heard everything."

Meanwhile, Fr. D. P. returned to his parish in Souris and resumed his sombre ways. He said his daily Mass for the dead in the cavernous St. Mary's Church there, always at seven in the morning. Only two other people would be there: Peter MacPhee singing the "Dies Irae" in his high nasal voice from away up in the choir loft, and Andrew Meurant praying aloud in the front pew. One morning, unable to take the distraction any longer, D. P. turned around and said, "How can I pray to God when you Peter MacPhee are singing off-key, and you Andrew Meurant are going nya-nya-nya in the front row?"

Being distracted by sounds was not a problem for Fr. Walker in the next parish in Rollo Bay. He was almost stone deaf. He got on reasonably well with his disability, except at Saturday evening confessions. They were held in the vestry at the back end of the church, a small room with kneeling benches and an Enterprise potbellied stove. The vestry was usually crowded with penitents who were embarrassed about having to speak loud enough for Fr. Walker to hear. At the time, making moonshine was considered a serious sin, a matter for confession. Roddie MacInnis was having his turn in the box and Fr. Walker was having his usual difficulty hearing him. "Father," he confessed, "I'm making a drop." "What dear? What dear?" "I'm making a drop." "What's that? What's that?" "I'm making some moonshine," Roddie said, now loud enough for all to hear. "Ah, that's a very serious sin," shouted Fr. Walker. "But, Father, Angus is at it, too," said Roddie, about his neighbour Angus Mac-Cormack. The vestry was in a laughing uproar.

Fr. Walker was a long-winded preacher, sometimes going on for well over an hour. The men parishioners, most of whom stayed at the rear of the church, would go out to have a smoke and a chat during those sermons, much to the pastor's annoyance. One Sunday morning he had a visiting celebrant, so this was his chance to read out the delinquents. During the visitor's sermon, he sneaked around to the front of the church, but the men saw him coming and ran for cover in a nearby bush, Fr. Walker in hot pursuit. As he passed by where the horses and wagons were hitched, an old fellow was sitting on the tail of his jaunting cart smoking his pipe. He said, just as nonchalant as anything, "Are you havin' trouble with your flock, Fahther?" Fr. Walker turned around and went back to his church. The old man continued puffing on his pipe.

The neighbouring parish to the north had another old timer in Fr. Ronnie MacDonald. A bushy-eyebrowed, good-humoured man, he was much loved by his flock. The entire neighbourhood was on party-line telephone service, including the pastor, and a general pastime was listening in on all calls. Fr. Ronnie had a cure for that — directing asides to the eavesdroppers. "I can hear Nancy's rooster crowing," he'd say. The comment was followed by the embarrassed click of Nancy hanging up. She got the message.

Money was scarce in the parishes along the North Shore those days. The fishery brought bottom prices and farming was at a subsistence level. Another peculiarity was that the pastor read out the "dues" from the pulpit in his annual report, often with a commentary on each one. The neighbouring pastor in St. Margaret's was the most direct in his comments: "John Mac-Cormack, two dollars, pity he drinks.... Ky Gillis, one dollar, slack for Ky."

Fr. Ronnie, on the other hand, chose lotteries as a way of supplementing the parish revenues. He had a fiddle in the house, so he put it up for lottery. There being lots of fiddlers in the parish, sales were brisk. But the winner was not a fiddler, so Fr. Ronnie took it from him and offered it up again the next year.

Fr. Ronnie's health failed, and he was replaced by un uncommonly shy younger man, Fr. Willie MacDonald. On his first Sunday, he read the gospel and preached. But he was afraid to look at the congregation, preferring rather to lower his head and run his fingers along the Gospel book in his hand. After Mass, a parishioner asked another, "Well, what do you think of the new priest?" The other said, "He'd be all right if he wouldn't be rubbing the Christly book all the time." ✝

The Remains

If there's one thing Islanders love, it's a good funeral. And when it came to anyone within a car's reach of Charlottetown, Maggie McGowan didn't miss a single chance to be there.

It started with the announcement on CFCY's 12:30 news that so-and-so of such-and-such place died, giving all the details of wake and funeral times and locations. Maggie and her husband, Fred, now retired from the Department of Highways, never missed the daily death announcements on CFCY. It may be time to go shopping or out to visit at the hospital, "But we'll have to hear the deaths," Maggie would say. "Of course," Fred would agree. In fact, soon after the death announcements, Fred would get out the phone book and pencil out the names of the deceased.

After supper, and while Fred was getting the weather forecast (the second-biggest preoccupation of Islanders was getting the weather), Maggie would go upstairs and get into one of her line of black dresses, then come down and announce, "I'm going to that wake." Fred never asked which wake because it could be any one of three or four announced on the deaths, and which could be in one or other of the several funeral parlours in Charlottetown.

Fred would be dozing in and out on his La-Z-Boy while the evening news was on but, by now, he'd be alert for the weather report. "Shush," he'd say. "I want to get the probs." Years of working on the highways made the "probs" an essential part of his life. Some things you don't let go of.

If Maggie could hold off leaving until after the weather, more often than not Fred accompanied Maggie to the wakes. He was as fond of them as she was. He was always fond of talking about the deceased to the bereaved. Most people went through the line-up of mourners with an awkward, whispered, "Sorry for your trouble." Not Fred. He'd have a story about the deceased for each one. "Sure, I knew him well. He was one of my best friends for thirty years. We played crib at the Knights' hall every week. He was a good crib player. Never made a bad discard." Or, if it was a woman, he'd tell about the time she gave him an extra big serving of dinner at the church supper. "Ah, but she had a big heart," he'd say. Fred loved to eat as well as to watch TV, to play cards, and to reminisce.

Maggie, in the meantime, had a soft heart. She shed a tear for each of the mourners in the line-up, and promised to have a plate of sandwiches and squares for those who came to their house after the funeral. And, after she went through the line-up, she'd sit with the ladies on the sidelines until the funeral home closed for the night. Fred, if he wanted to get home to watch "Front Page Challenge" (which he never missed), would have to take a taxi. Maggie's ritual was to stay right through from 7:00 to 9:00 no matter what, and then to drive home with or without Fred.

Making food for the post-funeral reception was no problem for Maggie. Large, gregarious, and with a sweet tooth, she was up every day before six and had a pan of biscuits and squares out of the oven by seven. She'd been doing that throughout raising their five children and, now that they'd gone, she saw no reason to change her routine. Besides, with a funeral almost every day of the week, she always had a place for the food. She had a basket especially for the purpose.

Both Fred and Maggie, now living in Charlottetown, had grown up on the Fortune Road in King's County. Their way with funerals came out of the up-East tradition. Questions were always asked. Were there any forerunners to the death? People saw a rough box being hauled into the lane the night before Joe Duncan's death. The dogs barked all night long before Ralph MacKinnon drowned in Morrison's Pond. A light burned after midnight at Cassie Elias's gate; she was dead in the morning. Surely, someone heard or saw a sign?

Then came the preparation of the remains, all done by experienced neighbours, never by an undertaker, followed by the wake in the home of the deceased. And, if they had to wait beyond two days for family to come home from away, it was necessary to spread around a liberal supply of baking soda to compensate for the non-embalming of the body. Another set of questions about that went on. How was the family taking it? Was there enough food brought to feed everybody who came? Who do you suppose didn't bring food? Did anyone bring along a teddy or two of rum? And who went outside to have some? I hope nothing happened like at Greeley Lewis's wake, where there were so many people standing in the kitchen that the floor gave way under their weight, and they all landed in the cellar. Whatever the case, Maggie's mother, Monica MacInnis, always brought the most food and was flushed and hot from fussing over the stove, waiting on tables, and pouring good strong North Side tea. And, who offered to stay up all night to invigilate the remains?

In the earlier days, whether the funeral was in the United Church or the Catholic Church in the village, the preoccupation was with how many horses and wagons — and later how many cars — accompanied the hearse from the home to the church. A person's prominence and popularity was measured by the number of carriages. And if it was in the United Church, what nice things did Mr. Aitken, the minister, have to say, and if it was in the Catholic Church, was Fr. MacAulay impatient because the funeral carriage came late. And who were the pall-bearers? And did anybody faint in the heat of the church?

Both Maggie and Fred knew all those questions all too well, and they often spent evenings together competing with each other about which of them remembered more details of those past events in their home community. Sometimes they would visit Maggie's ancient aunt, Melvina. And even though she suffered severely from dementia, she would try to get into the rhythm of the conversation. Sitting in her rocking chair in the corner of the parlour, she would break in every so often with a repeated refrain: "Do you remember the time that poor Mrs. Hoynes died? Well, dear God, wasn't Hoynes drunk?"

Yes, although they were both youngsters at the time, Maggie and Fred remembered Hoynes being drunk, or at least stories about him. How he and his drinking partner, Alton Anderson, would visit the graveyard in the dark of the night, and how he would throw himself on her grave and wail in sorrow. And how some people walking past the graveyard swore up and down that what they heard was God and the devil dividing up the souls, saying in eerie tones, "This one is yours, and this one is mine. This one is yours, and this one is mine...."

"And when Fr. MacAulay died after being thirty-five years in the parish," Maggie said, "He had the biggest funeral of all. Sure the church was packed, and they had a 'pontifitical' for him."

"Him being a monsignor and all, Lorsh Almighty, it was deservin' of him," agreed Fred.

So here they were in Charlottetown, getting up in years themselves. Well, they were just past sixty-five and felt they still had lots of miles on them. Still and all, they were pretty careful to prepare for their own time. When a relative, John Mac-Cormack, died at about their age and was being buried in the large cemetery in Charlottetown, at the most solemn moment in the ceremony when his casket was being lowered to its final resting place, Fred nudged his neighbour and said, "We have two plots right over there a ways." And Maggie chimed in, "We bought them years ago when the price was low. We got them for $25 each." And Fred said, "They cost ten times that now." After recovering from a sudden state of shock of such an intrusion on the solemnity of the moment, their neighbour said, "Oh, real estate is up all over the Island nowadays."

"Ain't it the truth," said Fred.

Maggie was already making her way over to shed a final tear with the family.

When You Haven't Got a Gun

The ordination oils were hardly dry on young Fr. Cairns Campbell when he got a call from his Bishop, Long Malcolm, to go to Tignish to replace the curate there for the summer months. The curate, Fr. Aubin Pitre, was to go away to study liturgical music, and the elderly Pastor, Red John Archie Mac-Donald, needed help.

Tignish was a large parish with an architecturally beautiful church, St. Simon and St. Jude, an impressive three-storey school in red Island brick called the Dalton school, a rambling glebe house, and a convent for the Sisters of Notre Dame who taught at the school.

The facts of the matter were that Fr. Red John Archie and Fr. Aubin were severely at odds with one another and hadn't spoken in more than a year. Red John Archie was of the old school, insisting on his authority as Pastor, especially when it came to dealing with curates. And in Aubin's defense, he was not the first curate to run afoul of Red John Archie's intransigence. At least five previous curates had beseeched the Bishop for a change of appointment — and got it. Fr. Aubin was authoritarian in his own right, showing little respect for the old man. And, because the parish was a mix of Irish and Acadians, the suspicion was that he showed a distinct bias for the latter, the source of his own blood and ethnicity. Besides, he was too proud to request a change. To him it would be an admission of defeat.

When young Cairns Campbell arrived in Tignish by bus from Charlottetown with his spare luggage of one suitcase, Aubin was long gone. In fact, Cairns noticed that there wasn't a trace of his belongings. Cairns's first meeting with the Pastor was an hour later at the dinner table. The housekeeper, Lucille, told him out of Red John Archie's earshot that she was glad to see him. "The two of them haven't sat down for a meal together since their blow-up a year ago," she said, "and I had to set the table for two different meals three times a day." She was a short, roly-poly kind of person with a quick laugh. She seemed to have taken their petulance in stride, without choosing sides. Even though Red John Archie was old and curmudgeonly, he had been their Pastor for decades, and was loved and admired by everyone from Seacow Pond to Tignish Shore.

On the other hand, people were more divided in their loyalties to the younger Fr. Aubin. He had a tendency to run roughshod over them, and it got worse after he and the Pastor locked horns. The morning after his arrival at Tignish, Cairns Campbell decided to take a walk around the town. It was a balmy, sunny June day, and he was in the best of spirits. He passed the post office and said good morning to people he met along the way. They seemed to have no idea who he was — it became apparent that his coming here had not been announced from the pulpit — but they deferred to a man of the cloth in a Roman collar. He soon approached the Co-operative store. A cute little girl in pigtails, a flowered blouse, and blue jeans sat on the steps to the store's entry. As soon as she saw him, she began to scream and retreated into the store. Shocked by her reaction, young Cairns followed her in, where she had taken refuge behind her mother's skirt, hanging on for dear life. Her mother was a clerk and stood behind the cash register. Her face was flushed with embarrassment.

"How in the world did I frighten the little girl?" asked Cairns, perplexed by her reaction. "Oh," said the clerk, "I'm her mother and Fr. Aubin has been preaching from the altar against girls and women wearing pants. He says it's a sin and has to be confessed." Young Cairns could hardly believe his ears in hearing that. "Well, young lady," he said, "as long as I'm here you can wear all the blue jeans and shorts you want."

"But Fr. Aubin said it was a sin...." The mother seemed unsure. After all, Fr. Aubin had exerted his authority in some matters of merit. "It's 1955, not the Victorian age," said Cairns, "and girls and women have been in slacks and jeans everywhere since the Second World War, so your daughter is farther ahead of the times than Fr. Aubin. I'll bet he wears them himself when he goes on vacation."

Young Cairns kept the incident to himself, wisely deciding not to report it to Red John Archie. Red John Archie himself had stern ideas about the old morality. The parish showed movies in order to bolster its finances. Each evening of the movies in the Parish hall, he would position himself beside the projector, and when the scene came to bubble-bathing, swimsuits, or love-making (in 1955, such scenes were much more modest than they are today), Red John Archie would hold a cardboard over the lens, blacking them out. People thought his action peculiar, but they didn't dare protest.

Young Cairns was anxious to please the old man and careful not to incur his anger. In his first week, he cast about for ways to please him. He discovered that Red John Archie enjoyed cribbage, so after dinner in the evenings he suggested a game of crib. Cairns had played the game since he was six years old, and he was used to playing fast and with good players. A game with Red John Archie could last as long as an hour. The old man would look at every combination before discarding his two cards into the kitty. He'd remove two cards from the six in his hand, then replace them and take two more. Then he'd say, "What would you do when you haven't got a gun?" and try a couple more. Cairns thought this a peculiar exclamation, but put it out of his mind. Meanwhile, Red John Archie would light his pipe and place the still-lighted match on the top of his roll-top desk. They always played at the corner of the roll-top desk, Red Archie claiming his position at the centre of the desk and Cairns scrunching up his long legs at the corner.

The desk was a beautiful piece of furniture, but the desktop was seriously scarred by Red John Archie's habit of dropping lit matches on its surface. Before a week was out, Cairns asked Red John Archie if he could restore the desk. The old man thought that a good idea. "You can carry it over to the basement of the Dalton school and work on it there," he directed. So, school being over for the year, young Cairns borrowed a teacher's desk from the school for the pastor and wrestled the roll-top desk to the school's basement. Fortunately for the teacher's desk, it had a glass protection over the surface. "Red John Archie's matches won't harm it for the while it's in his office," Cairns promised the Sister Superior in charge of the school.

The next morning, Cairns went down to the Co-op store to buy several grades of sandpaper and to seek the advice of the manager, Gerald Handrahan, about how to proceed. "You might begin with broken pieces of glass," he said. "It's great for getting old varnish off the surface. Then you can sandpaper a lot easier." Young Cairns was to find that was good advice. Coming away from the store he met several young girls playing together and wearing jeans and shorts. Their greeting to him passing them by made it clear to him that the word had got around and that his moral reform had overridden the departed Fr. Aubin. He felt good about that.

With youthful exuberance, he rushed back to the Parish house, went up to his room, and got dressed for his work. He donned a T-shirt, a grubby pair of blue jeans and sneakers, gathered his equipment, and bounded downstairs. When he passed Red John Archie's open office door, he heard an ungodly roar. "Come here, young man, where do you think you're going?" He had heard that when the old man was angry, a crimson trough of red emblazoned his forehead. It was now there in full colour. "I'm going over to the school to work on your desk," young Cairns said, meekly shifting from one foot to the other. "Not dressed like that, you aren't," said the old man. "Get back upstairs and put on your clericals." That day and thereafter, when he worked on the desk, Cairns left the house in his clericals and changed in the school basement before beginning his scraping and sanding. That evening he noticed that the old man was slower and more distracted in the cribbage game, so he arranged, by generous discarding to Red John Archie's kitties, for the old man to win. The red trough faded and they were back on good terms.

Stripping the desk was no problem, but sanding down the burn-scars and gouges took several days. The old man was unaware of the hours young Cairns spent on the work because he did it while the Pastor was taking his afternoon nap, which usually took more than two hours. Eventually, he finished the restoration to his satisfaction, and then he gave the desk three coats of the best varnish the Co-op store could supply. He finally transported the desk back to the Pastor's office. The old man came down from his nap to discover this roll-top desk gleaming and new in the middle of his office floor. "Well, well, well," he'd say over and over, looking at every nook and cranny of the desk, obviously proud of its transformation.

So, what do you suppose he did? He left the roll-top desk in the middle of the room where young Cairns had landed it, and he continued to use the substitute desk. He then demonstrated it as one would a prized artifact to everyone who dropped by to arrange a wedding, or a baptism, or a funeral. "Look there," he'd say, "what young Fr. Cairns did for me. Isn't it grand? What would you do when you haven't got a gun?" And he'd laugh heartily, never showing the least sign of a crimson trough.

That afternoon, Lucille told Cairns over a cup of tea, "I've never seen Fodder John in better fettle since two-t'ree years. You're pretty good to him."

"He takes a bit of handling. I walk around like I'm walking on eggshells, and I'm careful never to leave the house without my clericals, even when I go to the ballfield to play for the team," Cairns said.

Playing baseball was Cairns's single secular dalliance. And Tignish needed a good third baseman. He wore his clericals to the field and, having no car himself, changed into his uniform in one or other of his teammates' cars. A moral point with Red John Archie was that the games were always on Sunday afternoons. "When I was young we wouldn't even split wood on Sundays. So now it's baseball on Sundays?" He didn't quite work up a crimson trough, but he made it clear that he didn't approve. Young Cairns had long since made it a point not to argue, to let the old man have his say. "You'd better be back in time for prayers and benediction," the old man warned. "Yes, I'll be here, and would you like a game or two of cribbage after supper?" Cairns came back softly. "That'd be grand," the Pastor said.

The second Sunday afternoon pitted archrivals Tignish and Miminegash on Tignish's home field. A large crowd circled the field, there being no grandstands. The crowd was generally well-behaved, except for a few rowdies supporting each side, all of them with a load of beer aboard. With the home team ahead by four runs in the ninth inning, a Miminegash supporter, a rugged young fisherman by the name of Doucette, took exception to a remark made by one Harper of Tignish, a well-established brawler.

A fearful fight ensued. Harper had Doucette down in a ditch and was choking him with a length of barbed wire. "Will anyone help me get him off?" young Cairns addressed the onlookers. "He's going to kill that guy." No one volunteered to come to his assistance. They told young Cairns later that, should they get involved, they would be next in line for a thrashing from either Harper or Doucette. So, although he was much lighter and less strong than the two protagonists, young Cairns jumped into the ditch and put a tight choke-hold on Harper until he released his hold on the barbed wire around Doucette's neck. Doucette struggled free and retreated as fast as his wobbly legs could carry him. Meanwhile, Harper hurled slurred invectives at young Cairns, ending with, "I'll get you for this."

Young Cairns did not take Harper's warning lightly, and his teammates also showed their concern for him. "Harper's a rugged guy, and he can be mean when he's drinking," Joe Arsenault warned. "But he probably doesn't know you're a priest. He's Catholic, so maybe knowing that it's a mortal sin to hit a priest, that might count to save you."

"I'm not looking for any favours," Cairns said, slipping back into his clericals in the back seat of Joe's car.

Even though Harper didn't darken the door of the church very often, his family was faithful to a person, and Red John Archie was fond of each of them. On Monday evening, Harper's parents came to see the Pastor.

"Before anybody else tells it to you, we want to talk about what happened at the ballfield yesterday," James Harper began.

Red John Archie, sticking as he did to the glebe house, was never aware of the talk around town. He would be the last to hear of any goings-on. "So, what happened?" he asked.

"That young priest of yours tried to choke the life out of our son. That's what," Madelyn Harper said.

"He jumped our Harley from behind. He hadn't the guts to do it from the front," said James.

"Here's your priest getting into a fight, on a Sunday nonetheless, and before half the parish," put in Madelyn. "There's no place for a fella like that in Tignish."

"And you won't see a Harper in Church until you get rid of him," James slammed his fist down on the restored roll-top desk so hard he cracked its surface.

A deep crimson canyon had already set in in Red John Archie's forehead. He stoked his pipe and dropped the still-lighted match on the roll-top's surface. "I said nothing good would come out of playing baseball on Sundays. Leave this to me." He spoke with full pastoral authority.

The next morning he ordered Lucille to prepare two separate breakfasts. Then he phoned the Bishop, reported the incident, and insisted on Cairns's immediate removal. "The bus leaves for Charlottetown at 10 o'clock, and I'm ordering him to be on it," he said with finality.

The following Sunday, he announced from the pulpit that Fr. Aubin would be back in a week. A delegation from the parish came to the glebe house to try to straighten him out on the truth of the incident, but he refused to hear them.

Cairns went back to Charlottetown, his integrity intact, but he resolved never again to intervene in scuffles. You could never be sure if someone might pull out a gun.

That We Knew At SDU

In 1989, Dr. Ed MacDonald published a book, The History of St. Dunstan's University, 1855–1956. *It is an excellent record of that university's one hundred and one years of existence. When I first read it, I wondered why it chose to end its historical detail with 1956 rather than 1969 when the University, through amalgamation, became part of the University of Prince Edward Island. I have my suspicions, but they have nothing to do with the splendid scholarship of Dr. Ed, nor with his judgement. Whatever the case, Dr. Ed's book inspired me to put some more flesh, through reflections on some of the characters and events, on part of what he calls the University's Golden Age (1945–1955), a large part of which time I was a student there, having done the final two years of high school and four of university as a resident student. In 1955, I returned to the University as a member of the teaching faculty.*

Unbending Academic Standards

High school graduates of the millennium would be astounded by the course load carried by the St. Dunstan's Grade Twelve student of the 1940s and 50s. Classes went six days a week, with Thursday afternoons off, and without free periods during the day. The regimen was eleven courses without electives: English Literature, English Composition, French, Latin, History, Chemistry, Physics, Algebra, Geometry, Trigonometry, and Religion. To advance to university, students had to pass each course and to carry an overall average of 60 per cent. If they should happen to be advanced with a failure in a subject, they would have to clear that subject before being admitted into Sophomore year of university.

That caveat spelt the end of their education at the end of the Freshman year for many. Kane, a hard-working student with plenty of college potential but with no talent for Latin, was called into the Director of Studies', Fr. Roche's, office and told, "Mr. Kane, your problem is not getting into Sophomore; it's getting out of high school." This after Kane had done a solid

Freshman year. His fatal flaw, ending his career, was his failure in Grade Twelve Latin.

Mathematics was an even greater hurdle. To add to that, math was a required course for all first-year university students. In this case, if students flunked Freshman math they had to clear it before moving into Senior year. Sigsworth, an otherwise brilliant scholar, had an Achilles heel in math. He wrote supplementals, repeated the course, and failed every time. Finally, because of either Divine or human intervention, he achieved a pass. The event called for University-wide celebration which involved a solemn and high burial ceremony for his textbook. Sigsworth himself was the chief celebrant, clothed in surplice, stole, and chasuble, followed by similarly garbed deacon and subdeacon, an array of candle-bearing acolytes, censor-bearers, and led by a cross-bearer, all followed by a concourse of mourners and an assembled choir intoning the "Dies Irae."

The red-covered math text was wrapped in a white shroud and carefully deposited in a deep grave just off the southeast corner of Memorial Hall, the senior residence of the time. No cremation for this book, cremation being forbidden by Canon Law. If you were to do an archaeological dig of that small plot of soil, you would no doubt uncover the last remains of a book buried with the full ceremonials in vogue in the Catholic liturgy of the time. The text was so rigid, it could never turn to dust.

The passing grade in any given course was 50 per cent, not a great accomplishment, you may think. Grading, however, was much harsher than today. Top grades in a course were usually capped at 80 per cent, with few exceptions. True to the prevalent theological thinking of the time, a professor supervising an exam would say: "Gentlemen, nobody is perfect, so I begin marking at 90 per cent."

Then, as students got into their final year, yet another hurdle confronted them when they had to take metaphysics, the most abstract of all the philosophies. One Senior class took a particularly cavalier attitude toward the subject all year long, and when it came time for their final grades, about half the class were failed by their professor. The failure meant they would not graduate with their class in a week's time. The professor had given almost all of them a grade of 49 per cent. Amidst the consternation, a young professor, a friend of the philosopher, was asked to intervene with him to have him reconsider his grading. They met in mid-campus on a cheerful, sunny day, perfectly congenial for mediation. After exchanging pleasantries, the young professor said: "What really is the difference between 49 per cent and 50 per cent?" "One," came the answer from the righteous professor, and he stomped off.

The Rules

When my brothers and I left home for our six years of study in residence at St. Dunstan's, the main admonition our father gave us was this: "You may be expelled from St. Dunstan's for any number of reasons. If you get thrown out for drinking or rowdyism, you will be welcome home. If it's for stealing, I don't want any part of you!" Stealing was the cardinal sin in Father's set of standards. It had a lot to do with respect for other people, and stealing as the ultimate act of disrespect. It was good to be forewarned both about stealing and the prospect of being thrown out.

The shadow of suspension and expulsion still hung over the St. Dunstan's of the postwar years, an inheritance from the 1920s. In the early 1920s, the Administration established "a code of rules, suitable not only for the present time, but for future years as well." The enforcer of the code was a super-conscientious and inflexible new rector, Fr. D. P. Croken. His enforcements began with an incident wherein college men were compelled to an evening of "study as usual" the evening after their final exams were completed, rather than being able to release their tensions with an evening in town; this was followed by a general "campusing" of the students after the Christmas break and ended with the expulsion of some graduating Seniors for breaking curfew in their final semester. In this series of events, the code of rules found its most outrageous application. The public notoriety of these incidents, particularly that of the abrupt ending of the educational careers of graduating Seniors, made Islanders apprehensive about the fate of their own sons. Croken's successor as rector, Fr. James Murphy, did much to soften the code's rigidity, but the scars remained. My father's admonition in the mid-1940s grew out of that continuing apprehension.

Harsh discipline has had a long history in education. Yeats writes about Aristotle teaching Alexander the Great; he "played the taws / upon the bottom of the king of kings." Nor can we forget Dr. Johnston's recollections of lessons in Latin being driven into him at the point of the rod. St. Dunstan's, for good or ill, grew out of that "classical heritage." As one professor put it: "Gentlemen, this is the Roman system: I talk, you listen." Going back to another part of that code of rules from the 1920s, we read: "To the Prefect of Discipline alone belongs the right to inflict physical punishment on any student, and this must never under any circumstances take the form of blows about the head and ears, unseemly throwing to the floor or kicking...." As horror-stricken as a turn-of-the-century reader may be by these practices, they were still a reality into the mid-1940s at St. Dunstan's.

Two open dormitories, one of thirty-eight beds, the other of twenty-two, were housed on the top floor of the Main Building. They served many of the residential high school students. Each had a senior student prefect who was subject to the Prefect of Discipline for the entire building. The student prefects had little power over the boys, other than frightening them with inflated rhetoric. One such prefect, "Bomby" (for bombastic, a richly deserved characterization) O'Keefe, would hold forth to the students about his pugilistic prowess. Describing a fight he had downtown, he said, "God, how that second man could hit." He reminded me of stories about my Granduncle Andrew who emigrated from Souris to Boston before the First World War. Among a crowd at a zoo one day, as fascinated faces watched a pair of brown bears in their cage, Uncle Andrew held forth: "I faced thousands of them in the open." Come to think of it, "Bomby" O'Keefe grew up on the same road as Uncle Andrew, where there were more wild imaginations than there were bears.

Despite "Bomby's" rhetoric, sometimes after lights-out the boys would be restless and noisy, tossing shoes or pillows at each other. No one would hear the dark presence of the Prefect of Discipline, Fr. McGuigan. He would come unnoticed into the dorm and pound the one he thought to be the ring-leader, whose howls of pain would bring instant silence to the room, and he would leave just as quietly as he came. True to the rule, he never beat anyone on the head, inflicting pain rather on their feet. One such visit from Fr. McGuigan, more commonly known to the students as "Bulligar," a name he himself detested, would take care of disciplinary problems for a month, until he'd have to come again like a thief in the night.

Several of the dorm residents were young men from Quebec, enrolled at St. Dunstan's to learn "d' Hinglish." Most of them began that process from square one. This gave the dormers a chance for high jinks. Each dormer had a locker, for which a key was obtained from the Prefect of Discipline. Dormers would manage to have a French-speaking boy lose his key and then prepare him to go to the Prefect with his problem. The routine was: "Fodder Bulligar, I lose my fuckin' key." That would put the prefect into a double-barrelled rage, but he couldn't take it out on the innocent French-speaking dormer. However, a couple of other dormers would be sure to have their feet pounded that night.

The enrolment of a modest number of co-eds by the mid-1940s, along with the influx of a large number of returning veterans after the Second World War, resulted in a gradual reassessment of the rules. On one occasion, Fr. "Red John" Sullivan, a Rector in the 1950s, called a special faculty meeting to deal with incidents he found contravening. It was in early May when both the sap and the hormones began to rise. Red John noticed, with alarm, that young men and co-eds were walking the campus hand-in-hand, and some — God forbid — were locked in embrace. The meeting was short-lived when "Doc" Ellsworth, the much-respected professor of biology, offered as to how such behaviour was perfectly in accord with nature. "I see something wholesome and healthy in it," he said. Case closed.

On another occasion in the early 1950s, a prefect overheard roomers in his building planning a big bash when they finished their final exam that afternoon. They bragged of having a stash of liquor in their rooms. While they were away writing, their Prefect made the rounds of each room, confiscating the liquor — but leaving a note in place of each which read: "I assume this bottle is a Christmas gift for your parents when you go home tomorrow. I am, therefore, keeping it in safe-keeping for you. You may pick it up in my office on your way home." The young men came back to residence in high spirits, soon turned to amazed silence, then followed by cursing and finally by laughter. They went off to town to celebrate and picked up their bottles from the Prefect next morning on their departure for home. The only victim of the episode was the generation-old rule about possession and its penalty: expulsion. The rule was still there, but it had lost its punch.

That was equally true about the rule against skipping to town outside permitted times. Such infractions drew suspensions from the University. The following incident demonstrates how, although the rule was still there, it lost its severity in practical jokes. A student living on the top floor of Main Building was very much in love with a girl downtown and was known to sneak out at night, after lights-out, and return well after midnight. He went and returned by an enclosed fire-well at the end of the building. The Prefect and his classmates conspired to teach him a lesson. Just inside the entry to the residence hallway, they stood twenty pop bottles, arranged such that when he hit them he would then take a big step. Next they had laid twenty more bottles on their sides, such that when he took that large step he would land on them, and they would roll under him and give him an unceremonious landing. The ploy worked. The lights came up and the residents and Prefect had a great laugh at the embarrassed fellow's expense. The embarrassment was penalty enough; the effect was that he didn't sneak out again. Or didn't get caught, anyway.

Shortly thereafter came experiments in self-discipline and having student-proctors in all residences. To no one's surprise, the transition was smooth, and the older, more rigid order was put to rest.

In Uniform

The end of the Second World War brought a large influx of veterans to St. Dunstan's, as it did to every institution of higher learning in Canada. Their days of service in defence of their country were rewarded by a generous veterans' allowance paying for their education. The vast majority of them were serious about finishing their education. Some few of them, however, saw coming to college as an extended period of R and R after the hectic years in the service. Rod MacDonald, for example, literally slept for two years of college. Older and very bald, he was clearly distinguishable from his younger Freshmen. When he made it to class, he invariably fell asleep before the class began and would be snoring vigorously by mid-class. The one sitting behind him would give his chair a kick; that would stop his snoring but would not awaken him. "I can't get enough sleep. I'm sleepy all the time," he'd say in his defence. We called him Roarin' Rod.

Most veterans put the war behind them and talked about it rarely, and only then when they were among themselves downtown sharing a few drinks. Not so with Bun Callaghan. Bun had joined the army upon finishing Grade Twelve in the spring of 1945. He was posted to Quebec City and was mustered out of the service in time to be back in college by that fall, the war being over. That didn't deter him from creating an exciting series of war experiences. To the wide-eyed new Freshmen on campus he would say, "God it was awful. The planes were so fucking thick the birds had to come down and walk." After graduation, Bun went off to work in Canada's foreign service, where I am sure he expanded on his stories to the admiration of the unsuspecting.

During the war, and for a few years afterwards, many St. Dunstan's boys were enlisted in the Army Reserve. Doing so provided them with two advantages: everyday clothing, especially pants and army boots, and a bit of pocket money. Both were in short supply after paying for tuition, board, and books. Being in the reserve also entitled them to go to the mess at the Armouries downtown on nights out. During the war, many students, for one reason or another, did not join up. Those who were not particularly interested in their studies, and who hung around in groups doing not much of anything, came in for chiding from Fr. Francis McQuaid, who was the Bursar and a farmer at the time. He would herd them up, saying, "Get out of here, ye bunch of stud horses. Jine the army, ye bunch of draft-dodgers." They got moving, but they didn't join up.

After the war, Canada continued to recruit young men from college ranks to go into officers' training in the army (COTC — Canadian Officers Training Corps) and the navy (UNTD — University Naval Training Division). The young men trained once a week and went off for the summer to centres across Canada. The pay was good and the training rigorous. They, too, had uniforms to supplement their meagre wardrobes during the school year.

Part of the recruitment process was what was called the "M-Test," a check on the prospect's general knowledge. It was considered to be the toughest rite of passage. Barkis Smith, a bright but gullible recruit for the UNTD, was coming up for his test the next day, and his classmates used the occasion to play a trick on him. He was summoned to the phone, and the voice on the other end said, "Mr. Smith, this is Commander O'Keefe. I'm sorry to say that we are called back to Halifax for tomorrow, so we will have to give you your 'M-Test' by phone. Are you ready?"

"Y-y-yes, sir," said Smith.

"Just a few questions then: If you dove to the bottom of the Atlantic Ocean, how long would it take you to come to the surface?"

"I—I don't know, Sir, I can't swim."

"Second question, which would you rather be boiled in: oil or water? And why?"

"I—I can't rightly say, Sir."

"OK then, if the Leaning Tower of Pisa was on fire, which side would you get off?"

Sputter — sputter — sputter.

"I'm sorry, Mr. Smith, but you have failed the 'M-Test,' so you won't be on our list of approved recruits."

When Barkis got back to his room, everyone was waiting

for him. He was in a rage, asking, "How the Christ was I supposed to answer those questions?" And he went on to recount the interview, much to the delight of his classmates. Later that night, a kindly classmate told him it was all a joke. He took the real "M-Test" the next day and passed it with flying colours.

Women Make the Scene

Until the early 1940s, St. Dunstan's was strictly a men's school. It had been originally established in 1855 as an institution to prepare young men for the priesthood. As it happened, most graduates went on to seminaries and to postings across Canada and to the northwestern US. Rare ones went on to medical schools or to read law.

There was a strong masculinity in the student body, reflected in prowess on the athletic fields and roughhousing in the residences. The pride was reflected in their college song:

Come ye Red and White men
Sing with all your might men
For the name of SDU.
In the years hereafter
Sing with all your laughter
That you knew at SDU.

Young women of the time, if they went on to be educated beyond their communities at all, went to Prince of Wales College to get a teacher's licence. A first-class teacher's licence was the equivalent of Grade Twelve in the modern system. St. Dunstan's remained adamantly male.

Canadian women didn't get the vote until the 1920s. That first step towards equality began the move for equal rights for an education. The pressure was on to allow women to earn degrees at St. Dunstan's, but resistance held out until the early 1940s. Finally, in 1942, the first lay women (previously a minute number of Sisters of St. Martha had attended) were admitted into the proudly chauvinistic hall of learning on the hill.

The first laywomen enrollees were four in number. It was like the first black student to break the colour-barrier in Montgomery, Alabama. The four young women, all from Charlottetown, walked the two miles from Charlottetown to the campus. The rector of the time, Msgr. James Murphy, met them at the driveway, escorted them to their classroom, and then at the end of the day met them at the classroom door and escorted them to the roadway back to the city.

As their numbers gradually increased, the co-eds generally challenged the male students to greater academic performances. A select group, they were hard to keep up with, frequently walking away with the top standings. Some young men found the more attractive women a welcome distraction in their more pedestrian classes. A second-hand textbook turned up filled with marginal fantasies about the campus queen of the time. An endnote on the final page reported that, whereas she led the class, the scribbler had to repeat the course.

The first laywoman graduate, Gertrude Butler, received her BA degree in spring 1944. By 1946–47, the number of co-eds rose to sixteen. Still, by 1957, fewer than 20 per cent of the grads were women. Peculiar as this may seem to the new century when the majority of students in the local university are women, they owe much to the courageous movement by these four young women in 1942 to insist on their right to the fullness of higher education then available on Prince Edward Island.

The Nuns

No students ever called them the Sisters of St. Martha, their proper name just "The Nuns." But that was a term of endearment rather than one of disrespect. To every resident they were the greatest.

They ran the kitchen and provided nothing fancy, but rather good substantial food for active bodies. Boiled dinners, Irish stews, and roast beef were the regular fare, with fish on Fridays. The beef was invariably overdone and many found the fish unpalatable, but, if that didn't satisfy, every table had a big jar of molasses, and you could have all the bread and butter you wanted. Thursday dinner was the favourite: each table got a steamed plum pudding with caramel sauce. Arnie Hickey, a large country boy, would wolf down his meal, and, as the waiter passed his table, he'd growl, "White bread and more tea!" without raising his head. Sometimes the one nun who put out the food got impatient with the demands for more and would incur the ire of a table. She was the daughter of "Feathery Mick" Power of New Perth, so the head of the table would shout, "C'mon Feathery Mick," which only served to intensify her fiery nature. As generous as she was fiery, she always gave in when she cooled down.

On Mondays, the Nuns ran the laundry, which was located in the basement of Dalton Hall. The equipment was so ancient and rattly that the residence building would threaten to rock off its foundation. One piece of equipment was called a mangle. Judging from the condition that some clothes came back, it was appropriately named. On the other hand, the Nuns were excellent patchers and sewers, and rips and tears were carefully repaired — and the clothes were clean. The laundry nuns were also into modesty. Athletes at the time usually washed their own protective jock straps. One of them put his into the laundry by mistake, and, when he got it back, a conscientious nun had sown sides into it. Fortunately, she predated thongs and Calvin Klein.

They ran the infirmary, caring for flus and injuries with care and professionalism. The infirmary nun was always a trained nurse, and she could handle most of the maladies that came her way. Sister Camillus was there when the boys came back from overseas, carrying with them residual maladies from the war zones. She was a godsend for them. My own personal favourite was Sister John the Baptist, more affectionately called by us Sister Johnny B. She gave me my first-ever injection of penicillin. I was to leave on a hockey trip to New Brunswick and had a fever the afternoon we were to go. So I called on her infirmary and described my malady. "Lower your pants and lean over the counter," she said. Lower my pants in front of a nun, I thought! "Come on now, this won't take a minute," she said. I lowered, and she plunged a vial of penicillin into my buttocks, and I was off to New Brunswick.

They also looked after the priests' apartments. The nun who performed those duties was a big woman, a Lannigan from

Sturgeon, whose name was Sister St. John. She was always accompanied by one of the maids who were hired out of the Tignish Shore. This one was a wee girl. Because she always trailed behind the big nun, the residents called them "The Horse and Cart." She was always friendly to the students as she passed through their corridors to her destinations, being careful to shield her little maid from visions of young men getting back to their rooms in their briefs.

Fr. Adrien Arsenault, a young artistic priest, had just moved in to his apartment in Dalton Hall, and one of his first acts was to paint a mural of Picasso's *Three Musicians* filling an entire wall. When the Horse and Cart arrived at his door, Sister St. John fell back, and said in a loud nasal voice, "Look at that, will yuh? You'd think he'd have a picture of the Sacred Heart with the nine promises to touch the hearts of the students when they come to his room." The *Three Musicians* stayed.

Some of the nuns were among the first women to graduate from St. Dunstan's. Sister Bernice Cullen (Sr. Mary Peter) was the first ever, graduating *summa cum laude* in 1941. She went on to establish the first rural high school in the province, in Kinkora, and later to do a stint in running St. Vincent's Orphanage. Later, she resumed graduate studies and had a distinguished teaching career at the University and at UPEI. The second nun to graduate was Sister Mary Ida Coady in 1943. She became the college's librarian after R.V. MacKenzie took on the rectorship. As well, she taught high school courses and, later, taught in the Department of Education. All this while – and until well after her retirement – she tutored as many needy students as her hours could afford. Dozens of students owed their progress towards their degrees to her persistent help. If there was such a being as a female leprechaun, it would be Sister Mary Ida. Irish to the core, she was out of the heart of Kelly's Cross. She had an impish laugh and dancing eyes, and she loved Irish stories.

Many other nuns fulfilled their motto "Love and Service" (*Amor et Labor*) with few amenities or material rewards, caring for the University joyfully and with dedication all those years.

The Socials

St. Dunstan's boys got Thursday afternoons off to go to Charlottetown. The time span was from dinner at noon until 6:00 at suppertime. The prefects took a head count at supper (seats at table were assigned) to ensure everyone returned. When it came to nights out, college men got Saturdays until 11:00 P.M. And high school — because the school also accommodated the final three years of high school — got seven nights a year.

When I was in the eleventh grade of high school, our usual pattern was to go to the movies at the Prince Edward or the Capital Theatre. The Capital generally showed Westerns; we called them dusters. And the Prince Edward showed everything else: light and heavy drama, musicals and romance. I most often went to the Prince Edward with my classmate, Big Jim Mooney. The afternoon show's price of a ticket for people under sixteen years of age was thirteen cents; for those over sixteen it was twenty-five. I was fourteen; Big Jim was seventeen, six-foot-three, and had been shaving for three years. The trick was for me to buy the two tickets at the underage price, which I had no trouble doing because I was five-foot-four and was three years away from shaving. The ticket-taker, an irascible old bugger, would say to Big Jim, "You're more than sixteen." Jim, who talked through his nose, would deny it indignantly: "Oh no, I'm not." As often as the ticket-taker threatened not to admit us, we always got in. The difference between thirteen and twenty-five cents sounds paltry, but when you had five dollars in spending money for a whole semester, its value increased immeasurably.

For boys in from a countryside still without electricity and movies, the Prince Edward was a Shangri-La. Our sense of adventure was piqued by Edward G. Robinson, Sydney Greenstreet, and Peter Lorre, and our emerging manhood was bolstered by Rita Hayworth and Betty Grable. Not everyone's imagination was as liberated in the darkness of the theatre as was ours. In one scene on a slushy March afternoon, Deanna Durbin — a very modest actress out of Winnipeg — was taking a bubble bath. A husband and wife, in town for the day, sat in front of us. When the camera shot Durbin in the bath, the lady in the seat in front of us held her purse in front of her husband's eyes and averted her own eyes to the dark wall on her right hand. Mooney and I found this action particularly funny, and laughed out loud and struck each other on the arm, much to the displeasure of the woman in front of us. They got up and moved, she dragging her husband behind her. By the end of Grade Eleven, our first year in boarding school, we were pretty well saturated with movies, having seen one a week, so we were ready to move on to our next experience.

In the fall of our twelfth grade, Mooney and I joined the majority of the Saints (the name identifying students at St. Dunstan's) at the Thursday afternoon socials. The social, a two-hour, closely monitored dance, took place at the Holy Name Hall on Richmond Street. This ritual event gave the Saints, the vast majority of whom were male and Roman Catholic, the opportunity to meet and socialize with girls, the majority of whom were also Catholic, who attended Prince of Wales College, Notre Dame Academy, or the Charlottetown Hospital School of Nursing, as well as the few who were co-eds at the college. The eventual goal of the ritual, I assume, was same-religion marriages, marriages of mixed religion being severely frowned upon at that time. Despite that rather narrow idealism, however, girls coming to the socials, where they were treated to a wide assortment of young men and to good music for dancing, did not find their religious difference a cause for exclusion. The girls, some of them flashy and aggressive and others tense and nervous, flocked to the Hall.

The ancient dancehall was on the second floor of the building. It had a solid, if undulating, hardwood floor, two recessed ceiling lights, a small bandstand with its own separate lighting, and a table and chairs for the required chaperones — ladies of the Catholic Women's League. The boys and girls were clumped in two groups on either side of the dance floor. For the meek of heart, a vast no-man's-land separated them. Actually it was no more than thirty feet. Both boys and girls tried to appear not to be looking at each other, except for furtive glances. Mooney, standing over my group like a periscope, made a mean remark about a girl's buck teeth. "Shush your mouth, you big galoot," I said, not wanting to get us in trouble on our very first outing.

The music began shortly after 3:00. The Downtowners, or at least four of them, were engaged to play the traditional waltzes and foxtrots: Les Alexander and Elmer Gallant on the horns, Raymond Soy on piano, and Jimmy Coady on drums. The upperclassmen led off the movement across the hall to the island of girls, just a few at first, a straggle of brave souls, and then more and more. No wild party this. The couples held each other loosely — very, very loosely — to the approving eyes of the chaperones, moving stiffly around the floor, marking off the waltz steps as if they were mathematical measurements. Then Les Alexander, the bandleader, called for a Paul Jones and insisted that everyone take the floor. When the music stopped, you had yourself a partner. Big Mooney got a girl from Notre Dame who was about four-and-a-half-feet tall and could pass for twelve. I got a student nurse so tall I came up to just above her belly button. So was launched our waltzing career. Later on in the afternoon, when the Sadie Hawkins dance was called for, the tall girl came across the floor, and I tried to recede into the crowd of boys. No need, she came for Mooney. A good match. And the girl from Notre Dame chose me which, given my own height and age, was a fair exchange, too.

Except for those two dances, neither Mooney nor I ventured across the floor for the rest of the afternoon. Instead, we were part of a large proportion of boys who came to watch, who were either too bashful or too inexperienced to take the leap. As the afternoon wore on, more and more boys crossed the floor and the intensity of relationships heated up. They were no longer dancing loosely but as close as slices of bread in a sandwich, cheek to cheek, the boys' hands splayed over the girls' back, the girls' arms about the boys' necks, both looking dreamy as they moved slowly and rhythmically along the floor. Every now and then, a chaperone would cross the floor to break up a clinch that she judged to be getting out of hand. We watched and admired, but were still stuck in the voyeuristic stage of our development. Not to worry; we had four years of college ahead of us and, by the end of it, we would be as courageous and resolute in our pursuit of girls as the upperclassmen were.

High Jinks

"Punchboard" Gavin's intentions were honourable enough. He had worked for several years to pay his way through college, so was older than everyone except the Veterans. But he couldn't leave well enough alone, and, besides, he was a notorious tightwad. To supplement his savings he engaged in selling chances on punchboards (the predecessors of today's scratch-and-win lottery tickets). He seemed to be doing well with it in his own residence, Memorial Hall. Then what he thought fair game were the unsuspecting Freshmen on the stairwell between the first and second floors of Dalton Hall. The treatment for undesirables was scroofing, involving a hard rubbing on the scalp with the second knuckles of the closed fist. It burned and pained. Scroofing was followed by blackballing with a liberal application of black shoe polish to the privates. Scroofing was liberally administered as peer punishment, but "Punchboard" Gavin was one of only three to be blackballed in ten years. Gavin's punchboard was relegated to the garbage. He himself never again returned to Dalton Hall.

Many of the high jinks were of the boys-will-be-boys variety. "Dom" Donnelly was very bright academically, but was otherwise pretty stunned. He came in for a share of the practical jokes, the most exciting tying a mouse down the leg of his pajamas hanging in his closet. When he donned his pyjamas, everyone discovered how literally scared he was of mice, and all were amazed at the mess he made of his underwear in trying to escape.

Hallowe'en was a special time for creative endeavour. The corridors in Memorial Hall were hard, slippery tile, and when watered down were like ice. Not a congenial range for a steer. A steer, nonetheless, was led in on a halter and let loose on the wet floor. That poor steer was like Mr. Winkle on skates. But as Pius Callaghan used to report on hockey dust-ups in his sports column in the *Guardian:* "Cooler heads prevailed." The more conscientious residents, sensitive to cruelty to animals, subdued the steer and led him back to his barn.

In the 1890s, St. Dunstan's erected a large outdoor handball alley. It had three courts, and the open building stood about twenty-five feet tall and was sixty feet long, with a court floor of approximately thirty-five feet. It was an impressive structure and was built relatively adjacent to the college's barns, the central housing for its large farm. A young man from Quebec City who came to study philosophy asked me what this structure was. I said, "Oh, they're our elephant stalls. We use elephants to do our heavy farm work," never expecting him to believe me. He did. A couple of days later, he inquired how we got the elephants here. "We load them at the railway siding." St. Dunstan's had a train stop and a siding at the time. The story had a happy ending when Paget (for that was his name) wrote home to his father, a professor at Laval, to tell him of this wondrous sight, and his father wrote back to tell him he had been taken.

Big Bill Pendergast, a gentle giant of a man, was a heavy sleeper. He spent most afternoons in the sack in his room at the far end of third floor Dalton Hall. The room at the opposite end of the corridor was vacant. Several able-bodied colleagues transported him, bed and all, from his room to the other while Bill slept peacefully throughout the cartage. Hours later, when he awakened, he simply took bed, mattress and all, under one arm and went back to his room, where he crawled back in and resumed his siesta.

Meanwhile, St. Dunstan's High School, offering Grades Ten, Eleven, and Twelve to students at a time when only three other institutions offered those final years, had a gentlemanly, but quite naive, teacher. He was an SDU grad named Joe MacIsaac, better known to his students as "Wooden Joe." At the beginning of each year, in establishing the class enrollment, he would invariably come to his principal with this problem. He would present the list as his students had signed it and complain, "The list has 27 names and there are only 25 in the class." He would be genuinely perplexed. A cursory glance by the principal identified two names of notorious characters in downtown Charlottetown, Nick Reid and Rupe MacKay. It took Wooden Joe three years to catch on that his students were getting the upper hand on him in the very first class.

The college had a night-watchman, Jerome Blacquiere, who was thought to be quite ancient. His job called for Jerome to walk through each of the buildings in the middle of the night, presumably to check for fires. If you weren't awakened by his slow shuffling down the corridors, the smell of his kerosene lantern was enough to awaken you. The buildings themselves were in total darkness, the switchbox being shut off at the 11 o'clock curfew. Old Jerome met his nemesis on the first floor of Memorial Hall. About once a month as he entered the corridor he was greeted by two white-sheeted ghosts in the persons of Hoot Driscoll and Pete Sullivan. Jerome's shuffle would turn into a run as he retreated from the building. Hoot and Pete never, as I recall, identified themselves to him.

These were the days before central heating in the buildings. The Main Building and Dalton Hall had huge, old-style coal-fired furnaces in their basements. The Main Building had a dirt cellar, supporting walls of brick; Dalton Hall was finished in concrete. But those facts are incidental to the story. The fireman in the Main Building was the obscure Lou Monaghan. Like Boo Radley in *To Kill a Mockingbird*, he was never seen in the daylight and only rarely at night. Students watched from their windows at night to see his shadow leave his basement lair. They would then holler from their windows, "Dirty Old Lou," and could see him shake his dark fist at them in the air. They were grateful, however, next morning when the heating pipes awakened them, knocking and banging after a cold heatless night. Assurance that Dirty Lou was stoking up his furnace, sending steam coursing through the ancient heating system.

The Movie-Goer

Isn't it amazing how an insignificant event will trigger a host of related memories? This week the A&E program on cable television, "Biography," did a retrospective on the actress, Susan Hayward, the four-time Oscar nominee of the fifties and sixties.

My friend, Fr. Big Frank Aylward, and I drove to Summerside to see her perform in the lead role of *I'll Cry Tomorrow*, a film rendition of the tempestuous alcoholic life of Martha Graham. Hayward gave an award-winning performance, and was devastated in losing the Oscar that year to Anna Magnanni for her role in *The Rose Tattoo*. But that's another story. This story is about Big Aylward.

Aylward, after running his own oil-delivery business with Imperial Oil, went late to university, and then studied for the Catholic priesthood. Because of his business acumen, he was thereupon appointed to the position of Bursar at St. Dunstan's University, a position he filled with the assistance of one other person, from early in the 1950s until St. Dunstan's amalgamated with Prince of Wales College to become the University of Prince Edward Island in 1969. Being big, rough, and gruff, he earned the accolade from some students as BIF, short for Big Ignorant Frank. To those who knew him best, and who could answer his fire with fire, he was anything but BIF. He was tough, but oh so gentle. And he loved the movies.

In those days, almost all students lived in residence: men's residences and women's residences, no mixed residences. Everyone also sat down together to eat in the sizeable refectory. Four priests were assigned to eat at a table in the middle of the refectory. Their presence was to serve a number of purposes: to lead the grace before meals, to quash any rowdyism, to ensure that the women residents were treated respectfully, and to receive the various complaints students invariably lodged about the food. Because the students at adjacent tables could hear their conversation, the four priests had to be cautious in what they said. Big Aylward presided over this group.

So, in order to camouflage their conversation, they developed an elaborate code. One such code had to do with their admiration for the physical proportions of the women students. Being celibates, they felt the need to be especially guarded in this regard. However, as the old saying goes, "You may not be able to eat the meal, but there's nothing wrong with looking at the menu." At the time, arguably the most endowed sexual siren was Marilyn Monroe, married to the Yankee Clipper, Joe Dimaggio. Accordingly, beautiful young women passing their table in the refectory were categorized and coded in baseball jargon — the most comely being pitchers, the most important players on the team; followed by catchers, shortstops, centre-fielders, and on down the roster. A special category was reserved for pinch-hitters. "Hey, y'gotta see that pitcher's curves and sliders." "That catcher could handle the best pitcher's wild pitches." "Talk about playin' the hot corner." "That fielder would go to the wall to catch any hit."

The subterfuge worked. Not a student at adjacent tables had any idea what the four were talking about. That memory resurfaced — after forty years — upon watching the biography of Susan Hayward on A&E, herself hearty enough to fill any one of the positions on the baseball diamond. The night we drove to Summerside to see her in *I'll Cry Tomorrow*, the movie drew a large line-up of people. In the crowded lobby I was separated from Big Aylward by several people. Towering over the crowd, his prominent Roman nose curled down, he said in a loud voice to me, "Not too many ballplayers here tonight, eh?" Then he laughed as loud as Walter Huston in *The Treasure of Sierra Madre*. The code remained unbroken, save for plenty of inquisitive stares, but, after getting through the film, Susan Hayward restored his belief in the code's validity. On the way home he said, "She could pitch for my team any day."

The Angelic Doctor

The century had just turned the corner to the second half. It was a time of change for colleges based on the Roman and French models. St. Dunstan's in PEI was one such. Although college discipline had loosened up quite a lot after the war, with the veterans enrolling and having little stomach for it, some of the rigid ways were still holding on. One rule was that if students were caught with alcohol in their rooms, it called for immediate expulsion. No questions asked.

Murphy's class had just come off a heavy dose of final examinations, compulsory courses in metaphysics, ethics, the philosophy of nature, literature, history, and religion, and was three days away from graduation. Having a whole world ahead of them to celebrate, and four years of residence rules behind them, was too heady a speculation to go without celebration. No one could argue with that. Least of all Murphy and his pals:

Ronney, MacPhee, MacDonald, Keefe, and, well, just about everybody except McGuigan. At the alumni graduation party, the University supplied ginger ale and orange pop, and McGuigan, who had grown up with a silver spoon in his mouth, couldn't drink from a bottle. Someone had to go and get him a glass, for godssake. With the exception of the goody-goodies, everyone was invited to hoist a few in Murphy's room on the top floor of Memorial Hall. Three cases of Black Horse Ale were produced from under Murphy's bed from behind the footlocker.

Because of the risks involved, everyone spoke in hushed tones — for a time, until the spirits began to take hold. Then, the din of twenty loud voices seeped out to the corridors. Next came the inevitable rap on the door ensued by much scurrying to camouflage the evidence. Little did the boys realize, with the air reeking of cigarette smoke and beer fumes, how impossible that was to accomplish. Murphy, with a bottle of ale in his right hand, tucked the hand and bottle into his left armpit under his open jacket. Rooney, closest to the door, opened it. There stood Fr. O'Hanley, the Prefect of Discipline for the building. "Well now, boys," he said, "I was wondering if any of you could tell me how far it is from Toronto to Sudbury?" The apprehension melted, but just a bit. Murphy, who had worked summers in Ontario, said, "It's quite a piece, Father. I figure it's the best of three hundred miles." And to show the measurement, he spread his arms wide, thereby exposing the bottle of beer in his right hand. Caught red-handed. "Thanks for the information. You'll be sure to hear from me later," said Fr. O'Hanley, calm as you please, closing the door behind him.

"Holy shit," said Keefe, the worrywart of the group, "We're in for it now. There goes our four years down the urinal. Just like that."

"How can he do that?" argued MacPhee, himself a Vet. "Remember when he caught Maloney at 3 o'clock in the morning coming in with nothing on but his shoes — his clothes over his arm — pissed, to the gills? And what did he say, 'You better get to bed, Joe,' and what did he do about it? Absolutely nothin'. The Vets have changed things."

"And then there was the bunch that came back from the

North Novies reunion at the Armouries. Bombed. Holy God, you'd think O'Hanley was takin' the march-past salute as they staggered into the buildings," said Rooney. "I don't think he'll do a damn thing to us. But he'll make us stew. That's for sure."

As it turned out, the boys had little to worry about from their Prefect of Discipline. Despite being scholarly and brilliant of mind, he had not the heart for discipline. At a time when professors were to keep a distance from their students, O'Hanley actually showed a liking for them and was at the ready to help them organize and find jobs, and even to play the occasional game of hockey with them. He was thrust into the role of disciplinarian. He did not relish it.

Fr. O'Hanley had gone off to Rome in the 1930s to study philosophy at the Angelicum. He returned to St. Dunstan's not to teach philosophy, in which he had a doctoral degree, but to occupy the chairs of Latin and Greek. Every priest-professor soon picked up a nickname. O'Hanley's was "the Angelic Doctor." For him, the difference between a good man and a bad one was in the choice of causes to defend. So, although he was not a good teacher of languages — obedience forced him to do it — he devoted time to translating philosophy texts from Latin to English. He was good at that. And although obedience forced him to prefecting, he spent his time supporting students and their causes rather than being a corrections officer.

"God, he was an awful teacher," Murphy said. "I slept through every one of his classes for three years. Only a good set of crib notes saved me in exams. Do you think he'll hold that against me in the end? I'm damn sure he knew I was cribbing." Everyone looked glum. They had no answer for that one. They all knew O'Hanley knew Murphy cheated. They heard him tell a colleague, and that colleague was a blathermouth.

Whatever else he was, the Angelic Doctor was always a gentleman. He cut quite a figure crossing campus in his long soutane and Roman toga, which flew behind him in the wind like Batman's cape. He entered the classroom with a flourish, but the charisma ended there, unless we could get him off the point, which was the easiest of things to do. He could spend classes on end talking about his experiences in Europe. And if we couldn't sidetrack him on that topic, we would play to his physical strength, which was formidable. He could take a round-backed, heavy birch classroom chair in each hand, raise each to a level parallel to his chin and draw them to his chin several times. No one, not even the biggest stud in the class, could hoist one, let alone two. Then O'Hanley would observe: "M-m-m, I have phenomenal strength in my wrists." He always said that after each accomplishment. It was an expected part of the ritual, and it always drew applause from the class, some of it mocking, all of it loud. He did have phenomenal strength in his wrists. When he played hockey with us, he'd wind up at centre ice and everyone would get out of the way to let him shoot. His shot was so strong it would drive the smaller goalies right into the net.

Apart from his clothing finery brought back from Rome, the Angelic Doctor's only other modest luxury was his car. For years he drove a Model A Ford, generally called a Tin Lizzie, but which he called Elizabeth. Again he spent many classes extolling her virtues, and, like a favourite smoking pipe, she was hard to part with. Thereafter, one of his ritualistic sayings was, "M-m-m, a great man deserves a great car." He had a shiny Buick during the days of Murphy's class at the college. It was true, he probably planned to drive from the Island to Toronto and then on to Sudbury. Elizabeth could never have done it, but it was an easy run for the big flashy black Buick. So his question to the lads in the third floor room was genuinely motivated.

To be on the safe side, the boys were on their very best behaviour for the next two days, going out of their way to hold doors for O'Hanley and keeping a meek serious demeanour, answering only with an "M-m-m," when spoken to. But they were not hauled in on the mat before the Disciplinary Committee. So there Murphy and the lads were on graduation day, dressed in their gowns and mortar boards like everyone else, the faculty and dignitaries on the stage, everyone as proud as punch.

When it came time for the graduation address, the guest speaker adopted Newman's definition of the educated person as the main theme of his address. Early on he defined a gentleman as one who never inflicts pain. He was only slightly distracted by twenty voices among the graduates murmuring, "M-m-m." And he ended his speech, saying, "A great thing can only be done by a great man." As he sat to the applause of the convocation hall, the twenty voices mumbled in chorus, "M-m-m, a great man deserves a great car. M-m-m, I've got phenomenal strength in my wrists."

Bulligar

By the mid-1940s, nobody knew where his nickname originated, but it was entrenched in student lore. It was a name he detested, so no one dared mention it in his presence lest they wanted a chilling, freezing stare. Yet the first set of words Francophones — many of whom came to the Island to study — learned upon their opening days at St. Dunstan's was "Fodder Bulligar," otherwise known as Fr. Walter McGuigan, the senior prefect of discipline.

His ever-alert piercing eyes were Bulligar's most remarkable characteristic. His eyes went everywhere. Nothing escaped their notice. He knew everything that happened on campus; he made it a point to do so and took enormous pride in that kind of knowing. He also did everything fast and by the clock. He had a small wiry body. He ate sparingly and moved quickly and, sometimes, especially when pursuing misbehaviour, stealthily. When he was at his best, he displayed an impish, wily smile. And because he talked rapidly, à la Walter Winchell, he sometimes stammered.

Aside from being head prefect, Bulligar coached the college basketball team for more than a decade, and he taught all four years of college history. He brought the same kind of speed and punctuality to the classroom, beginning at the stroke of the bell and ending with its class-over ring, even if he was in mid-sentence. For the fifty-minute class he most frequently read from the text in a high-pitched, rapid-fire voice, stopping only when he wanted to redirect a wool-gathering student. Or to let them know he was on to their shenanigans. He would read a line from the text "...drinking great quantities of wine," then he would stop and look up to Slugger McCarthy and say, "Drinking great quantities of wine, Mr. McCarthy, Loyola?" McCarthy had been on the wine the previous weekend. Or MacInnis, who was playing one girlfriend, Elizabeth, off another, Mary; to him he'd say, "Lizzie had no love for Mary, Queen of Scots, Mr. MacInnis," to a blushing MacInnis. Or else he would break from the narrative to dramatize a situation, as when the Emperor Henry IV of Germany was excommunicated by Pope Gregory the Great for interfering in Church affairs. Henry repented and came to the castle at Canossa in mid-winter to seek reinstatement from the Pope, who was within the castle. The Emperor, barefoot, was outside the gates doing public penance. As Bulligar told it, the Emperor would plead, "Let me in, my feet are cold." And the Pope would reply, "O-o-oh no, your feet are not cold. Go around again." Eventually Gregory let him in, and they were reconciled.

Bulligar also took great delight in horrifying his cultured nephew who was in his class. Each chapter of the text had a section on art, music, and culture. Dealing with 19th-century music, he'd refer to the Polish composer, Frederick Chopin, calling him "choppin" and then casting a sly glance at his wincing nephew, Mark. That appeared to give Bulligar immense satisfaction. Of even greater satisfaction to him was to finish the final sentence of the final chapter in the text in the final seconds of the final class of the year, close the book, and say, "Chapter finished, are you with us, Mr. Murphy?" and then he'd leave in a flourish.

His final examinations were always one word on a carefully clipped quarter-inch of paper. "Nap I" called for eight foolscap pages on Napoleon; "Bismark," on another exam calling for similar depth of treatment. Or if it were a short quiz, the name might be "Hamlica Barca," or some such obscure figure. He returned papers without commentary, just a single grade in pencil, the grade underlined. Because of this and because a student's grades did not change beyond a few percentage points over four years of history — a required course — he was thought to show favouritism for those who did consistently well.

That suspected favouritism was bolstered by his assistance to selected students in securing summer jobs. His cousin was the Personnel Manager for the Canadian National Hotel system. That connection enabled him annually to place several

St. Dunstan's students on the staff of Jasper Park Lodge, and, because they had a solid reputation for being conscientious workers, their number increased over the years. Working at Jasper meant being able to pay for the entire next year of study, so it was quite a plum for those selected to go.

Bulligar himself rarely travelled outside the province. Once, however, he made the train trip across the country, stopping naturally, at Jasper, Alberta. The train left Charlottetown at seven o'clock in the morning and arrived at Jasper five days later in mid-afternoon. Bulligar's luggage — if you could call it that — was one manila envelope containing an extra nylon shirt, underwear, and a pair of socks, as well as a prayer book and a deck of cards. He was a sparse eater and an economical dresser. The cards were for playing bridge on the train. He was an avid bridge player, playing out a hand fast and talking all the time to distract the opposition. He bragged that he never lost a game the entire trip, "Of course, I could see every hand." The mirrors between the windows on the passenger cars made that an easy task for his quick, roving eyes. Otherwise, his travelling was restricted to Island roads. Again he prided himself in knowing precise distances between communities. Another person who equally prided himself was Fr. Ed Roche. Once they disagreed by one mile on the distance between Kinkora and Charlottetown, and Bulligar proved him wrong. "Yes, but I drove on the inside of every curve," said Roche, not giving in one inch to the expert.

One of Bulligar's jobs as senior prefect was to dole out the rare night permissions to town. Before the scheduled departure, the students assembled and those whose names weren't called were confined to campus. Confinement mostly resulted from skipping Chapel. Everyone had an assigned seat there, and Bulligar could tell who was missing in one sweeping glance from his vantage point at the rear. The expletives of those denied permission would make a sailor blush; the adjectives attributed to Bulligar were creative and amazing. What they realized years later was that he was just doing his duty. And duty was something that Fr. McGuigan always did. Without question and with dispatch.

The Goon

In the late 1940s, E. C. Segar introduced a group of long-faced, long-nosed mythic characters, called the Goons, into his *Popeye* comic strip. The prototype character was Alice the Goon. Besides, the goons wore ankle-length, single-fabric gowns. It took little imagination for the St. Dunstan's boys to see remarkable physical similarities between the goons and Fr. Fred Cass, the Chemistry professor. Tall, of ample girth, dressed in an ankle-length soutane, and having facial similarities to the goons, he picked up "The Goon" soon after the introduction of Segar's characters. The name had nothing to do with Cass's being a sap or a dope, neither of which he was, by any means; nor did it have any suggestion of his being a hired hit-man.

Despite the negative possibilities of his nickname, the Goon was clearly the most colourful and popular professor in the place. In the first place, he was an excellent teacher, making chemistry come alive to his students. Explaining molecular structure he would gesticulate with his meaty hands, describing how they "glom onto" each other. The non-scientific slang phrase made the concept unforgettable. Then he never failed anybody in exams. And, yes, he had his favourites, and unabashedly gave them top grades — some deserved, some undeserved. He was in awe of his Chinese students, a small group of elite graduates of a Hong Kong Jesuit high school, whose knowledge of and talent for chemistry outreached the general student. He had a soft spot for all co-eds, especially the pretty ones, and he was partial to the minority of Protestant students in his class. So much so that on one occasion, when marks were returned, Doley Murphy remarked after class, "The only way you can get a mark here is if you're a co-ed, a Protestant, or a goddamn Chinaman." The racial, religious, and sexual slurs aside, there was truth in Murphy's words. And, although they rarely led his class, he was equally biassed toward athletes. His higher motivation here, however, was that the Saints would be able to have strong teams. The Goon loved to win, and he would take almost any measure to ensure winning. The College had an especially good hockey team, bolstered by a number of recruits from Shawinigan, Quebec, all of them good players, but at a major linguistic disadvantage. To pass a year and remain eligible to play intercollegiate hockey, one had to maintain a 60 per cent overall average. Denis Decarie, the best of the Quebecers and the linguistically weakest, had grades in the low 50s in his classes, except in Chemistry where he garnered a grade of 92 per cent to carry his general average over 60 per cent — a general pass guaranteeing continued eligibility to play for the University.

Aside from teaching and sports, Fr. Cass's greatest preoccupation and accomplishment was in intercollegiate debating. From the time classical debating was established in 1945 as an intercollegiate competition, and over the next ten years, Cass was the team coach *par excellence.* Like Conn Smythe and Vince Lombardi, there was no place in his world for losing. Thus he brought together a team of assistants: Brendan O'Grady, the rhetorical strategist; Doc Ellsworth, the master of phrasing; and himself, the inspirer and chess master. He put together an enviable record of winning teams selected from about fifty tryout hopefuls each year. Visiting debaters sometimes accused him of rigging the judges — this was especially true when a team of Richie Cashin and Brian Mulroney from St. F. X. lost on St. Dunstan's home turf and complained bitterly, but to no avail. The crowning glory of the Cass career was when his 1952 debating team of Wally Reid and Allan MacDonald won the National Championship in Ottawa. The Cass method was to anticipate the arguments of the opposition and to have a pre-cooked, but adaptable, rebuttal. One of the more important parts of the contest, the rebuttals often determined victory or defeat. The debate was extremely close until the chief and final rebuttalist for the opposition came to the floor. He no sooner got into his speech when Allan MacDonald, feigning nervousness, stuck his fingers into the inkwell at his desk and began ever so slowly rubbing his hand down his face, creating dark blue warpaint, thus distracting the audience and the judges, and horrifying the opposition. Victory was assured, but everyone suspected that that dramatic act affected the outcome.

MacDonald probably got the idea, at least that of rubbing his face, from his mentor. Whenever Fr. Cass was bored or nervous, or when he wanted to make some kind of pronouncement, he would rub his face with his open hand, from his receded hairline down his face to his chin. When he spoke of a colleague for whom he had a long-standing dislike, he'd say: "My God, laddie, he's been tryin' to make a joke for years, and he hasn't got one off yet," while rubbing his face in disgust. When he was a young priest at the Basilica, he sometimes would sneak out at night and hoist a few with his friends. Another young curate felt obliged to squeal on him to the Bishop. Thereafter, he not only hated that curate, but his whole family and their progeny besides. His colleagues were well aware of this and would bait him, especially at breakfast before his fifth cigarette. A colleague would say, "My, but so-and-so" (of the hated family) "is a refined-looking woman." Quick as a flash he'd come down his face and say, "My God, laddie, I wonder how much she'd take to haunt a house."

In the 1940s and 50s and, in fact, until well on into the 60s, clerical teachers at St. Dunstan's were paid the paltry sum of $225 a year. In the 1960s it went up to $275 per year. It goes without saying that room and board were free. But to keep the wolf from the door, most clerics did something on the side to keep them in spending money. They'd get $10 a Sunday for going to a parish, for example. Many of them, however, chose a more lucrative route. Some spent summers chaplaining in the Air Force or the Navy, while others did year-round chaplaining with the militia, the RECCE regiment, and the Signals Corps operating out of the Charlottetown Armouries and going off to camp with them, or otherwise chaplained the army cadets at their summer-long camp at Aldershot, Nova Scotia. Fr. Cass spent his summers as a military chaplain for Camp Aldershot.

The comic strip goons were robed in white, whereas Fr. Cass' soutane was black. Well, supposedly black. In his enthusiasm in the classroom he would erase the chalkboard with the palms of his hands and then brush off his hands on his soutane. He could have passed for a worker in a flour mill. And his carelessness with his garb was equalled by his lack of care in keeping his apartment on the third floor of Dalton Hall locked, and carbon copies of his exams unshredded in his wastebasket.

As a matter of fact, his doorlock was jimmied so often it could be opened with a piece of plastic. Invariably his students would find a copy of his exam, but he got wise to that and planted several copies, sometimes hiding the real one under his mattress. The greater loss for him was his collection of mystery novels, to which he was addicted. Things got so bad that he stored his collection under lock and key in his car. "By God, laddie," he said, "they can steal my soap and shaving cream, but they are not going to get my novels."

Mystery novels and whisky were loves of his life. He couldn't wait each summer to get back to Camp Aldershot where he could spend his nights in the officers' mess drinking with his friends and telling stories. His favourite stories were out of the Island Irish tradition common to Kelly's Cross and Lot 65, one of which was about attending a funeral in a Protestant church for a man who had dropped dead in the woods. The Minister was eloquent in describing the death: "As he walked through the woods communing with his Creator, suddenly the Lord called him, and he heard that call and obeyed." Old Trainor, an Irish Mick, was at the back of the church, and said, quite loud, "That be damned fer a story. Sure, it was an owl he heard." Come to think of it, that kind of realism characterized Cass best, and, as he guffawed in its telling, it was mirrored in his face.

The Dark Angel

As the junior member of faculty at St. Dunstan's College in 1955, I was assigned with neither notice nor preparation to the job of manager and single staff-person of the students' bookstore. I was to do this along with my 34 hours a week of teaching and several other unmentionable assignments, such as serving as prefect of the Freshman residence. My mentor and auditor for the bookstore was one Fr. Michael Francis, a priest of Lebanese extraction, affectionately nicknamed by the students the Dark Angel — or, in full, Michael the Dark Angel.

At year's end, when I wrapped up the books for the bookstore, my balance was off by seven cents. The Dark Angel insisted that I go back and find those seven cents, but try as I might I could not find the imbalance. I offered to pay the seven cents. I was not paid for my bookstore work, but such a paltry sum would not drive me deeply into debt. "No, oh no, you can't do that," warned the Dark Angel. "Go back over the books until you find it." Many days later I did find it. I had failed to enter the sale price for a lead pencil sold in February, despite entering its cost price in the debit column. Then and there I was convinced of the Dark Angel's business acumen.

Michael the Dark Angel spent his best years as head of the University's Extension Department. An early disciple of the Moses Coady Co-operative Movement, he went out night after night proselytizing the Island's farming and fishing communities, ringing out in his most intense oratory: "Everyone working to-get-her." Gesticulating wildly, he either convinced or coerced those communities to join the movement. In these moments he was more Archangel Gabriel, whose final blast will signal doomsday, than the more regal Archangel Michael, the inspirer of his nickname.

Priests at St. Dunstan's took turns having Mass for the students. And when it came his turn to preach to the student body, Michael was very much the Dark Angel. His preoccupation at the time — 1950 and onward — was the drive-in theatres. Full of hellfire and brimstone, he'd declare about those of us going to the drive-ins, which included just about every student in the pews: "What are they doo-ing? They are not talking about the wea-ther! They're sin-ning! Committing black sins against God!" The pews would break into a wave of snickers. Fortunately, the Dark Angel was too caught up in the emotional force of his rhetoric—and too deaf—to notice the reaction.

Speaking of his being deaf, part of his assignment was to teach introductory Latin. He was not a natural teacher; he had no control over the boys in his all-male classes. But one fellow he really took to was Scouts Coyle, the star flying wing on the school's rugby team. The Dark Angel would pull a word out of a Latin sentence, such as *puellam*, and ask, "What case is that?" The boys would be too busy shooting spitballs, so he'd ask, "What case is that, Mr. Coyle?" Scouts Coyle would say, "Suitcase, Father, suitcase," much to the glee of his classmates, and deaf Michael would say, "That's right, Mr. Coyle, that's right."

Michael was a dyed-in-the-wool backer of the Saints rugby squad. Waddling up and down the sidelines, telling his beads for victory, he'd shout his support until he got hoarse. He was from a sports-loving family. One brother, Shana, was for years the home-plate umpire in the senior baseball league, and his brother, Joe, was the most rabid fan in the stands. On one occasion, before the major leagues were racially integrated, an all-black baseball team came on tour and played in the Charlottetown ballpark. Joe took his usual seat in the stands along the first base line. Throughout the first two innings he kept heckling the rangy first baseman, shouting, "C'mon midnight! C'mon midnight!" Finally, the first baseman loped over to the screen and pointed at Joe. "Boy," he said, "I'd say that you wuz 'bout half-past eleven you'self." Joe remained silent for the rest of the game.

Among other things, the Dark Angel was also the hypochondriac of the group. He was especially a breakfast-time complainer. As they used to say on the Island, "If it wasn't an arse it was an elbow." He would enter the staff dining room with his usual ducklike waddle, belch loudly, and complain of his stomach. One morning when his face showed particularly wretched symptoms, Ursula, the young woman waiting on tables, blurted out, "Virgin! What's the matter with you now?"

Eventually, one of his many maladies did him in. We only hope that he is now with his namesake and the choir of angels — not singing, for he had a horrible voice; nor teaching Latin, but up there trading stories of successes in the Co-operative Movement with Moses Coady and Jimmy Tompkins. Scouts Coyle would have been there to greet him, too.

The Bear

"The movement towards less discipline is unwise, for where there is no discipline there is no will-power, and where there is no will-power there is no character." The speaker is the St. Dunstan's Rector, R. V. MacKenzie. The occasion, one of his Sunday night lectures. The place, the chapel. The year, 1947. The audience, all resident students under obligation to be there. The mix, an effort to preserve as much as possible of the old in the new St. Dunstan's of the postwar period — that, along with a generous smattering of Newman's *Idea of the University*, an educational philosophy accepted without question.

These admonitions were preparations for St. Dunstan's boys to go out into the secular world. Occasionally, they had the tone of the saying of Confucius, such as, "The whole of education is bound up in reading, for the greatest thought of mankind is in books." He was quoting Frank Sheed here, whereas many of the lads in the pews thought with Stephen Leacock that the real education in universities happened in bull sessions. But MacKenzie spoke with great intensity about the "cultivation of the intellect" and about the precision of words and of ideas. Sometimes, when he suspected that his message wasn't getting across, he would get down to warnings of "spineless jellyfish" and "ships without a rudder." If you didn't get the message in public, you'd get it in private when he called you in on the mat in his office to read you out for indifference.

On one occasion, he overheard a water fight in the residence and stepped out in the corridor to find Bush Reid with a water pitcher in his hand. "Ah, Reid what are you up to? Water fighting?" "But, but, Father," pleaded Reid, "I didn't chuck no water!" MacKenzie dropped the water issue but gave Reid an unmerciful verbal flailing for his misuse of proper grammar.

The Sunday night lectures covered a wide variety of other topics. He believed it incumbent upon himself to give full commentary on Emily Post's rules of etiquette, and was especially detailed about table manners. He condemned the use of toothpicks at the table, but everyone in the dining hall watched with glee as he picked his own teeth after a roast beef dinner. Granted, the beef was often pretty stringy and had, as one of his colleagues called it, "a lot of connective tissue." We used to say, "No matter how tough the meat is, you can always cut the gravy." True to his character, however, MacKenzie never addressed personal relationships or sexual issues, both of which in the emerging new age might have drawn his listeners to the edge of their pews.

MacKenzie was tall and austere, with close-cropped hair, and a temper to match. When he got angry, he bared his teeth and scratched his head. His severe demeanour merited him the nickname, "The Bear." When he taught English Literature, however, he treated it with deep appreciation. Rather than spending time on textual analysis, he read the works aloud and with much appreciation. His favourite poem was Poe's "The Raven," which he read with an ear for its ominous drama. He'd finish with, "Ah, a great poem." No other commentary. He saved his severity for grading essays, where he exacted the same precision of language he exacted of himself. And he had a practice of reading his students' essays to the class and giving stern admonitions to writing he considered substandard.

On one occasion he gave his students a free choice of topics for an essay. Rossiter had the temerity to write an essay entitled "The Bear."

The Bear selected Rossiter's essay to read aloud in class. His tone was sarcastic and outraged. "Did anyone ever hear of a bear grinding his teeth and scratching his head? Ah, Rossiter, you know nothing about bears. They were gone from King's County before your unfortunate birth." The boys in the class could barely contain themselves, but dared not laugh until they got back to the dorm afterwards. "And to think he didn't know it was about him I was writing," said Rossiter to the backslaps of his mates.

When students came back from Christmas holidays, after receiving their first-term grades while at home, the first day was registration for the second term. The final desk in the line-up was occupied by the Rector, The Bear, and he had each person's grades in front of him. This was a fearful moment for anyone whose grades were not up to expectation. "Ah, MacDonald, you're drifting like an ice cake. You're going out to sea," he'd warn MacDonald. "Ah, Gotell, you never got out of Georgetown, and by the looks of it you never will," he'd say to another. "You may as well go home where you can do some good." The remarks were direct and cutting, and they usually had the desired effect. MacDonald and Gotell would have a better second term.

They would be running scared of their meeting with him at next registration.

The Bear took his rectorship and teaching seriously, and the times were challenging to him. The student enrollment at St. Dunstan's had swollen to 278 students at the end of the war in 1945, and continued to increase to 306 by the end of his rectorship in 1956. The mix of students — some of them returning veterans, many of whom were at least six years older than students going straight through the system — called for careful monitoring. He was rigid with the younger students, but more benign with the veterans — as long as they toed the line. On one occasion he presided over a two-week suspension of a half-dozen students, most of them vets, for breaking curfew. He was a firm believer in the literal interpretation of the biblical injunction, "The beginning of wisdom is the fear of the Lord." He was a paragon of righteousness and high dudgeon.

MacKenzie's devotion to duty and to his vow of obedience were unquestionable. He aspired to a graduate degree in literature and studied at Harvard and the University of Toronto, but necessity called him back to St. Dunstan's before he could finish. If this frustrated him, he showed no signs of it. Instead, he read voraciously and became a fine recollective scholar. And, in this respect, he was an exemplar to his students. He established a rudimentary library for the college and served as its first librarian, encouraging his students to be readers.

Among the courses he reserved for himself was Senior Religion. Toward the end of his career, he was conducting a class of Seniors coming up for graduation. The class had some thirty-five students. He began by asking, "How many of you have read the four Gospels?" Some fifteen hands went up. "The rest of you GET OUT!" he ordered. Next, "How many of you have read all of Paul's Epistles?" Six hands went up. "The rest of you GET OUT!" he ordered. Next, "How many of you have read the entire New Testament?" Two hands showed. "The rest of you GET OUT!" Then he said, "Now we'll conduct our class." And he taught the full class hour to two students.

Fr. Dick

"He is tall and slender, his bearing erect. A modest scholar, whose shyness is often mistaken for austerity, he is handsome, articulate, discerning, possessed of a gifted intellect, but without the goal of ambition or vanity.... No one is more admired; no one is less conscious of it.... Students are hard put to having a nickname on Ellsworth. In the end they must settle for 'Father Dick.'"

Ed MacDonald's entry on Doc Ellsworth, however brief, is a true characterization. He was, at once, the most admired and most feared of all the faculty in what some call the "Golden Age" of St. Dunstan's. He was alternatively called "Father Dick" and "Doc." He had a doctorate in divinity from his theological studies, and an MSc in biology. He was admired for his brilliance and feared for the rigour of his standards.

When asked about his studies in biology, he would say forthrightly, "I give a better course than I got." No one would argue with that. He stayed on top of his field, and treated his subject matter in depth and with intensity. He did everything with the utmost care, from building and treating the lab tables with several layers of protection against the inevitable formaldehyde spills and other abrasives, to keeping his microscopes in top condition. And woe to the student who maltreated those sensitive instruments.

He saw biological studies as an integral part of the liberal education the University espoused, but with his own particular twist. He thought a major contributor to our knowledge involved the part played by natural knowledge. He often told his classes, with great pride, stories about the natural, intuitive abilities of people from Western Prince County where he grew up; their ingenuity in building machinery out of discarded parts, and about a young man who built a revolver from scratch. He was equally fond of their eccentric behaviour, telling often about the fellow suffering from an infected foot who said, "By God, after three weeks I thought maybe I'd better take off the sock and have a look at it."

He was equally indignant in discovering his students' lack in the powers of observation. He asked one class how many birch trees were in the small quadrangle outside Dalton Hall.

No one could tell him. "Well, go and count them, and don't come back until you do," he ordered testily. The whole class, some forty of them, were summarily dismissed to count the birches of which there were only twelve. Similarly, in botany class when dealing with mosses, he would talk about the small mosses growing in the damper depressions on the campus lawn. When his students confessed not having seen them, he'd again order them out to find them.

These were the years when the "back to the land movement" was at the height of its idealism. Doc Ellsworth, not surprisingly, was a strong advocate. He would say to his students with great urgency, "If I were not a priest, I would be a farmer. I would be a good farmer. I would be a scientific farmer. I would be a leader in my community." Sadly, his inspiration fell on too few ears. Most of his brighter students had aspirations for medicine or for advanced study in the sciences. For them he was their source of reference. Medical schools accepted only those he recommended. Taking the role of unbiased referee too conscientiously, he would say, with a certain amount of self-pity, "I have no friends. I cannot afford to have any friends."

At this time, Catholic colleagues were forbidden to teach the theory of evolution and anything that smacked of it. This was a difficult obedience for a scholar such as the Doc. Whether the *homo sapiens* is descended from less highly organized forms such as monkeys remained debatable, but the progressive development of various bodily structures and of certain mental qualities was incontestable. Ellsworth was careful not to speak of the origin of the species issue, but he frequently implied adherence to natural selection. How could one so attuned to natural knowledge do otherwise? For example, he would smile slyly and speculate that the ten-foot-high basketball standard was a principal reason for increasing growth in height of the current generation. "A question of adaption," he'd say. How else explain the increasing average height of basketball players?

When questions about students' behaviour came up at faculty meetings, especially if they referred to natural inclinations, one word from him was usually enough to end the discussion. Otherwise, he had little tolerance for the smart aleck remark. Late in his career, he was coming out of his residence in Memorial Hall, carrying an overnight bag. A student known for his pomposity met him and said, "So I see you are going on vacation, Father?" To which he answered curtly, "I am going to bury my brother, if you call that a vacation." The squelch was perfect. The Doc went quietly to the train station to go home to West Prince where he was always most comfortable.

Sam

No one was ever quite sure where he got the name, Sam, but that was the moniker given Fr. Wilfred Pineau, Professor of French. Once he went away to finish his studies and was replaced by Fr. Charles Gallant. Gallant was asked what the students call him and he said: "Sometime dey call me Charlie; sometime dey call me Chuck; and udder time dey call me Please Note." "Please Note" actually stuck with him, but he was gone in two years. Sam came back from graduate studies.

Everybody had a soft time of it while "Please Note" was there, but Sam returned to terrorize the classroom. Early in the semester Lannon forgot about who was running the French class and made a smart-assed remark. Sam charged his desk, picked him up bodily, and hurled him out the door with the force of a bouncer at a downtown bar. When he got that angry, Sam snorted, and so he kept snorting and snorting and was unable to say anything for the rest of the period. He put a translation exercise on the board, and we worked at it in ominous silence, broken only by his incessant snorting.

Still and all, we students owed a great deal to Sam. How else could we, years afterwards, know a three-letter word for Spanish hero in crosswords, unless we translated *El Cid* in Sam's classes? Or how Russian residence students hated the meals in their dining rooms — a daily fare of lentils — as we did our own routine menu, and how they reacted by throwing their food around the refectory walls, ceilings, and floors in *Tartaran de Tarascon*.

In those days, morning attendance at Mass to begin the day was mandatory. No exceptions were allowed. During those masses, Sam heard confessions in the darkened confessional at the back of the chapel. He was a popular confessor for the students. Here he did not snort and get angry. Not like the confessor who came from the Basilica for evening confessions. He would refuse them absolution if they couldn't promise not to break their pledge, taken at confirmation, not to drink until they were 21, or if they couldn't resolve not to repeat other sins, such as masturbation. Sam, on the other hand, was heavy on the penance but otherwise an easy mark to confess to. He'd simply say, "Say d'beads t'ree times and make an act of contrition." And since many of the perceived sins were the result of raging hormones, he'd advise: "Take cold bat's" or "Run around d'track before going to bed." The latter advice, however good, didn't seem to bring a rush of daily runners that its frequency of advice seemed to warrant. You rarely saw anyone run the track except in preparation for race events.

Back in the classroom he sometimes broke the tedium by having contests on vocabulary and translation. He'd instruct the class, "Divide yourself in t'ree!" to the repressed giggles of all, until we saw the dark cloud descending on his eyes and obeyed the non-literal instruction. He also tried dictation exercises on contemporary topics. One such was about "La Banque Royale du Canada," for which one student wrote "la bonne croyals." That earned another class of snorting.

Toward the end of our studies, Sam had the Sunday Mass, and he chose to edify the students with a story about a young man who had to live out his existence in an iron lung. Great topic, but it was the way he put it that caught our fancy. He started: "Many of you have not heard of Fred Snipe, d'Boiler Kid." Wow! The image was an instant winner. From then on, Sam was known to our class as d'Boiler Kid. And, because of his volatile nature, the new nickname was more appropriate than Sam, and it stuck.

Red John

A man who frequented the streets of Charlottetown in the 1940s and 50s suffered from a peculiar malady. If a passerby suggested to him to roar, it triggered some interior mechanism that made him roar so loudly you could hear him blocks away. He was called Roarin' Neddy. An otherwise gentle giant of a man, his only significant mark on life was his roar.

Two other roarers of the time were in much more prominent positions. Their roars were the outcroppings of their formidable tempers. As well, they shared a similarity of name but not of blood relationship. They were Bishop J. A. O'Sullivan and Fr. "Red John" Sullivan. One small story puts to rest the case on O'Sullivan. A spritely little cherub, Fr. Louie Dougan was among those who sat for meals with the Bishop, and Dougan was desperately fond of milk. Unable to contain his impatience with Dougan's overimbibing any longer, O'Sullivan shouted across the table, "Dougan, if you keep drinking so much milk around here, we're going to have to buy a cow." Dougan, uncowed, came right back at him, "Ah, y'r Excellency, I think we have enough bawling around here already without having to buy a cow."

"Red John" Sullivan, in the beginning fairly low in the pecking order, was first introduced to us as the prefect of the study hall for the high school residents. There, the least misdemeanour would find him growing red in the face and showing a tic in each jaw, followed by a shattering roar, and fear in the faces of the sixty or so high school boarders who sat each night for two-and-a-half hours of invigilated study. If you were caught breaking out a novel or, God forbid, a comic book, you could expect to be thrashed over the head with it and charged in the loudest of voices to get back to your books.

By the time we got into the four years of college, we knew that Red John was to teach the three years of philosophy courses we were required to take. Because we were presumably more mature and because we had a smattering of co-eds in those courses, Red John seemed less tempestuous. That is, until you'd have the temerity to voice a disagreement with any of those ideas advanced in the texts. Red John was a textual literalist and, in exams, if you were to get a good grade, you had to parrot back exactly the text of the thesis. My friends and I were not his favourite students. We considered philosophy a topic for discussion and dialogue, and we spent hours so doing in our residence hall. We learned a good deal, but not always the pure St. Thomas Aquinas of our text books. But it didn't translate into top grades for us. Only those who carried the party line made it to the top. We were the targets for his occasional roars in class but, by now, immune to them.

After graduating from the University and having spent four years of study in Ontario, I was surprised and delighted to be invited by the Rector, R. V. MacKenzie, to come and teach at St. Dunstan's, a career that would go on for forty-one years. However, I felt considerable discomfort when, after my first year of teaching, MacKenzie retired and was replaced by Red John Sullivan.

To my equal surprise, I found Red John to be a most congenial and supportive Rector. He left his roaring behind him and embarked on a shared and delegated administration. The only apparent residue of his past was his sensitivity to external criticism of loosening discipline on the hill. Red John and several others of St. Dunstan's patronized Albert Wilson's barbershop downtown. Typically, he picked up all the gossip and scuttlebutt on the go about the University. Unfortunately, he gave priority to these items over more substantial issues at faculty meetings, leading one wiser member to muse, "Are we running our own house, or are we being run by a barbershop?"

Fr. George

Fr. George MacDonald, long-time professor of physics and mathematics, was the direct antithesis of what my father often counselled me against: "the loud voice that bespeaks the vacant mind." He had a sharp, incisive mind, and he never raised his voice. When faced with a puzzling question, or when resisting giving an opinion on a matter he didn't necessarily agree with, he would make a sound like "emh," accompanied by raising his eyebrows and looking over the rims of his glasses. After deliberating within himself, he would resolve the question and, when pushed, would give a discerning opinion.

As prefect of discipline in the senior residence after the war, he was popular with the more free-spirited veterans for being broad-minded enough to turn a blind eye to breaches of conduct that would otherwise call for suspensions. In order to supplement the meagre pay St. Dunstan's doled out to its clergymen teachers, Fr. George spent his summers teaching at the Royal Military College in Kingston, Ontario. Besides adding to his purse, the experience broadened his perspective on education and human relations. And that's where he got his leather-covered swagger stick.

The swagger stick he used as a pointer in the classroom and to rap the shins of those students in the front row. "Emh, Mr. Murphy, what's the solution to this formula?" His rap was gentle and restrained and good-humoured, not in the least rousing the fear we experienced in some other classes.

The students also admired his athletic ability. He was the assistant coach of the Maritime University Hockey Champion hockey team in 1947, a legendary team. He was also the best golfer on campus and a top marksman. He was a member of the Canadian Bisley Rifle Team, and, because of his keen eye and quick hands, he was a champion badminton player well in to his late fifties.

Because of there being several George MacDonalds about, many of his colleagues called him Cornwall George, marking his place of origin. After his Bisley experience, one colleague dubbed him "Two Gun George," but he objected to the moniker so strongly that it was soon dropped.

When Red John retired from the Rectorship in 1963, Fr. George replaced him. As it turned out, he was the last Rector of St. Dunstan's, stepping down with the amalgamation into the University of Prince Edward Island in 1969. His conciliatory and non-interfering characteristics made him the ideal negotiator for this next phase in the evolution of education on Prince Edward Island.

FRANK LEDWELL is the author of a volume of prose and poetry, *The North Shore of Home* (Acorn Press, 2002), and two collections of poetry, *Crowbush* (Ragweed, 1990) and *Dip & Veer: Reflections on the Art of Alex Colville* (Acorn Press, 1996). He has performed as a popular storyteller with the trio "Crowbush" and with "Frank Ledwell and Friends" in venues across Prince Edward Island. Frank Ledwell is a Professor Emeritus of the English Department of the University of Prince Edward Island, where he taught English and creative writing for many years. He was the first recipient of the PEI Council of the Arts' Award for Distinguished Contribution to the Literary Arts.